# WITCHY WAY TO MURDER

## ADRIENNE BLAKE

City Owl
Press

This book is a work of fiction. Names, characters, places, and incidents either are products of the author's imagination or are used fictitiously. Any resemblance to actual events or locales or persons, living or dead, is entirely coincidental and not intended by the author.

WITCHY WAY TO MURDER
Dark Encounters, Book 1

CITY OWL PRESS
www.cityowlpress.com

All Rights reserved. Except as permitted under the U.S. Copyright Act of 1976, no part of this publication may be reproduced, distributed, or transmitted in any form or by any means, or stored in a database or retrieval system, without the prior consent and permission of the publisher.

Copyright © 2023 by Adrienne Blake.

Cover Design by MiblArt. All stock photos licensed appropriately.

Edited by Tee Tate.

For information on subsidiary rights, please contact the publisher at info@cityowlpress.com.

Print Edition ISBN: 978-1-64898-311-5

Digital Edition ISBN: 978-1-64898-312-2

Printed in the United States of America

*To my dear friend, Denise. I cannot share your last journey, so take this story with you to remember me by. I will miss you, friend.*

# PRAISE FOR ADRIENNE BLAKE

"*Necromancer Abbey* features a mysterious family secret and an intriguing magical world... Kat is easy to relate to despite her unusual powers, and Henry comes off as charming in a refreshingly gentle way. Readers who enjoy their magic with equal parts romance and mystery will find plenty to hold their attention." – *Publisher's Weekly*

"*Pride and Paranormal* is a delightful twist on Pride and Prejudice with all the drama of Jane Austen's original story, and the added fun of a paranormal cast! Adrienne Blake has invented a world rich with supernatural features and interesting aspects of coven society. Many pieces of the original tale are preserved for the loyal Austen readers, but Ms. Blake seeds her retelling with scintillating plot peregrinations... A fresh, fun world and characters that deliver on drama, romance, and paranormal intrigue." – *InD'tale*

"Fans of Jane Austen along with readers of paranormal romance will adore *Pride and Paranormal*. Blake does a fantastic job of blending the classic tale along with this modern world with magic, while making it all feel timeless and classic. It's always so much fun to see people take these such well known characters and put them in a new environment with a new spin. So grab your broomstick and fly off to get this magical book!" – *E. E. Hornburg, author of* The Night's Chosen

"*Sense and Succubus* has a lighthearted and tongue-in-cheek air to it. Characters are matched with magical personalities that emphasize their roles. The Dashwood sisters are down to earth, authentic, and organic, as befits their dryad heritage. The more fiscally minded members of the Ferrars family are true to their goblin ancestry. The satyrs are ridiculous. And, the romantic rivals from the original are now portrayed by a pair of seductive, but notoriously unreliable, incubus and succubus. This modern and paranormal retelling deserves full credit for cleverness and smooth prose." – *InD'tale*

"Adrienne Blake charms in this absolutely delightful paranormal twist on the classic P&P tale! *Pride and Paranormal* brings it all-banter, suspense, humor, family antics, romance, and a strong female lead with panache. A light, whimsical tone paired with compelling and well-rounded characters suits the story perfectly, and the writing is deftly finessed with nary a wasted word. A unique, effervescent take on paranormal elements makes for a refreshing read as well." – *Kat Turner, author of Hex, Love, and Rock and Roll*

## Chapter One
# A BROKEN KETTLE

WE TUMBLED DOWN THE COLD STONE STEPS, A TANGLED MASS OF HUMAN and muscular animal limbs, locked together in a deadly embrace. The werewolf smelled of fire and stale pine, like an old magic tree that someone had torched. Adrenaline protected me from the worst of the pain, but it still hurt like hell. I heard the *clink, clink* as my wand trickled down the steps along with us, resting tantalizingly just out of reach in the wet night grass of the park.

My arms still held tight onto the werewolf's neck, desperate to keep those rancid, dripping wolf fangs from me. Not to mention the foul breath of the thing, as its snapping jaws tried to rip my throat out.

I wanted to scream, but the words stuck in my throat. If only I could reach that wand, but I dare not let go or I'd be dead in an instant. I closed my eyes; if my fingers couldn't get it perhaps if I concentrated....

The werewolf let go and howled. I thought I was free and turned my head to summon my wand properly—but too late, I realized my mistake. The beast still had me pinned to the ground. I was still trapped.

As the wand flew through the air to my fingers, the werewolf's red, fiery eyes narrowed. I lay terrified as his claws tore into my chest, seeking my heart which was beating as if it would explode. Wand or no wand, it was too late. Pain worse than anything I had ever experienced before enveloped me. The world became stained with my lifeblood, and then all went dark, as the moonlight faded, and I was dead.

---

I woke with a gasp, my hand instinctively flying to my chest, feeling for blood but finding only a scar. I wiped the sweat from my soaking forehead with my pajama sleeve, then reached for my phone. It was only five in the morning, dammit.

With a groan, I crashed back hard into my pillows. No decent witch should be awake at this ungodly hour. Especially since our days typically didn't start before midday. Goblins even later. I closed my eyes, desperate to sleep but afraid to fall back into that dream. How many nights had I had this same nightmare now? Was it a dozen? More?

After fluffing up my pillow more times than I cared to remember, I finally punched it and hauled my rear-end out of bed. Scratchpoop dropped down off the bed with a gentle *thud* and followed me out into the kitchen. Yawning, I flipped on the light, just as the cat jumped silently up onto the kitchen counter, his tail up high, showing me his butt and expecting food.

"Yeah, yeah. Gimme a minute." I said and reached for the kettle. In the mornings I typically liked coffee, but right now I didn't want a pick me up. I wanted something to put me back to sleep, and that meant tea. A nice, soothing, relaxing, sleep-inducing pot of herbal tea.

I definitely didn't feel like myself right now. Part-goblin, part witch, I had an acute sense of smell, razor-sharp hearing, greater than human strength, and was stirred when tribal skin drums played at funerals. I was the first to get swept up with hot-blooded goblin anger when surrounded by crowds of my own people—but not today. Today, all I could think of was my pillow, and how much I wanted to hug it.

After filling the kettle with fresh water and flipping the switch down, I dragged my feet to the fridge and opened the door. I reached inside and pulled out a half-eaten tin of Kitty-Kin food. I peeled off the lid and scraped the contents onto a saucer on the counter then dropped it to the floor. "There ya go, you bottomless pit of fur." Scratchpoop hunkered down and didn't seem to mind at all as I rubbed his black and white coat up and down. His fur was lovely, thick, and shiny. He was a good cat, really.

Still yawning, I slouched back to the kettle which should be whistling by now, but it wasn't. I cautiously rested the back of my hand against the shiny metal, only to find it stone cold. Was the darn thing plugged into the wall socket? I checked and it looked fine. I flipped the switch again. Nothing. It was dead. Great.

I sighed and poured some cold water into my mug and picked up my wand from the counter. I touched the surface of the water with the tip, and whispered, "*Calida Aqua!*" I watched as a goblin-green glow illuminated the cup, and the water began to boil. My grandmother would have tut-tutted at such gratuitous use of magic, but I needed my tea. I knew in my bones already that this was going to be a bad day. And it hadn't even started yet.

---

Harrison, my partner and co-founder of the unfortunately named Goblin Dicks Paranormal Detective Agency—*You lose 'em, we'll find 'em!* —was already sitting behind his desk when I arrived. He had just returned from a cruise to Bermuda, which he'd taken on doctor's orders, and his naturally green skin looked darker than ever. And he looked fit. The dark circles he'd had under his eyes were gone, suggesting restful nights, and his trim physique proved he'd been sensible with the onboard buffets.

"Good time, was it?" I asked.

He barely looked up from his computer. "You're early." Only Harrison could make that sound like a fault. Like me, he wasn't a morning person.

"Meet anyone nice onboard?"

Harrison grunted. I took that as a no. I suspected he hadn't been looking since his last boyfriend had turned out to be a demon who almost killed him. Had almost killed us both, in fact. Instinctively my hand went to my heart. Would I ever be able to forget?

"Well, you look good. I'm guessing those spa treatments really work." I always preferred my boss green. Some mixed-up sense of vanity had him change to a more human hue from time to time, but in my eyes, that made him look shifty. The green softened his features and made him look gentler. As far as a goblin could ever be described as gentle. I turned a little green myself once in a while.

"So, what's cooking? Anything hot?"

January had been dead as a dodo and this month wasn't looking much better. It was a typically flat time in the business, so I wasn't horribly worried. And the last demon gig had brought in enough money to keep us in the black for a bit. So, we were doing okay for now, but the pot would soon be running dry. We needed cases, pronto, and we both knew it.

Just as Harrison shook his head, the phone rang. I picked up the receiver since he clearly wasn't going to.

"Hello. Goblin Dicks Paranormal Detective Agency. How can I help—?" I listened as a leering voice made rude suggestions that would have made a hooker blush. "Yeah, that's real funny, pal. Get a life." I slammed the receiver down. Another of *those* calls.

"Look, Harrison, you sure we shouldn't change our name? I'm getting tired of these perverted calls."

"Nope. We're leaving it just as it is. I just had the name etched in our door and I'm not changing it again. Ignore them."

Damn. I looked back to the recently etched, frosted window in the upper panel of our door. *Goblin Dicks Paranormal Detective Agency* was neatly stenciled on the glass, in the tradition of other private dicks throughout history. Sam Spade would have been proud. Still, sometimes it sucked being only the junior partner in our business. Harrison's word was law, and frankly, Harrison wasn't always right. At least I didn't think so.

"Oh, by the way, I got this for you," Harrison said.

"Oh, what?" I turned around. "Something fun? Or chewy? Or chocolate? I could always eat more chocolate."

He slid a .38 in a leather holster across his desk.

"Oh, sweet!" Nothing says someone cares for you more than them buying you a new gun. "Aww, you shouldn't have!" I fluttered my eyelashes playfully. It was fun to tease him.

Harrison grunted. "That toy .22 of yours, wouldn't stop an angry dog. I was looking in the gun shop and saw that. I thought you could use it."

"Aww. People will say we're in love."

I pulled it out of the holster and checked it out, testing the weight and feel in my hand. I liked the balance, and it wasn't too heavy for me. Plus, it was fully loaded. Bless him; he'd thought of everything. "Thanks, Harrison. You done good!"

I sat at my own desk and turned on my computer. I picked up the framed photo of my mom. It showed her on vacation in Miami and was the first time she'd been away on her own. She was the color of a lobster, but she looked like she was having fun. Next to that was a picture of me from my police days. With my dark hair and trim build, I looked pretty hot in my cop's uniform. I was kind of a Kelly Garrett from the original Charlie's Angels. Only greener. Except when I chose not to be.

While my computer booted up, I cleaned out the coffee maker and put in some fresh water and grounds. "Six sugars," Harrison said without looking up.

"Hey, I'm not your lackey." Harrison ignored me. I thought about spitting in his mug, but he'd only say it added flavor. Typical goblin.

I sat back down at my desk while the water boiled. There was nothing in my email except junk. And an email from my detective friend, Liam Wells with a funny about a dog trying to lick his own do-das but not reaching. I knew it was his warped way of reminding me he existed. He got one out of ten for trying and I grinned anyway. It was nice knowing someone cared.

After downing the last of my coffee, I shut down the monitor and got up, slipping into my new holster and popping my .22 into my purse. "Hold the fort for a bit, I'm heading out."

"You just got here!" he snarled.

"I know, but it's not like we're busy or anything. And my kettle conked out and you know what I'm like without a real cup of tea when I need one. I'm running down to Warlock Derek's to see what he's got. I won't be long."

Warlock Derek's Antique Shoppe was just down the end of our street, and he carried a wide range of modern and old-fashioned knick-knacks you could pick up for a song. Truth be told, it was little more than a second-hand magic store, but he carried some good stuff from time to time and I liked checking it out. Last year I'd picked up a pair of Elf-crafted leather boots, wearing them was like floating on air, until one of them developed a slow puncture and I began walking in circles without realizing it.

Harrison's eyes lit up, almost glowing, making him look like an entirely different goblin. He stood up and grabbed his coat. "Ah well then, now you mention it, I haven't been down there in a while. I'll come with you. My Fitbit says it's time I stretched my legs."

*Yeah, right.* I'd bought him the Fitbit for Christmas but since he hadn't used it for anything other than telling the time, I could only deduce he wanted to come with me to see Derek, the store's owner. The man was a hot commodity after all. If you were into long-haired warlocks with ponytails, skull rings, and prison tattoos.

"But you haven't finished the coffee you asked for?"

"Oh well, I'll finish it later."

Yeah, right. "Whatever. Well, let's get going then."

I waited while he shut down his workstation and fluffed about with his hair in the reflection off the screen.

"You look super," I said.

Harrison grinned and straightened the collar on his shirt. "Yup, you're right," he said. "You lead, I'll follow."

A few minutes later we were back down on ground level, walking through Philly's Changeling Avenue heading toward the store.

It was freezing, and just about everyone was wrapped in thick scarfs and woolly coats, including myself. The sky was a dense yellow, and I would say the chance of snow was about eighty percent. The weatherman had said otherwise. Time would tell, but my money was on Mother Nature.

"So, what's with you and Derek?" I asked, just for something to say. Harrison wasn't much taller than I was, but at five-ten he was still tall for a goblin, and had a pretty good bod to boot, albeit stocky. He walked fast and I had a job keeping up with him. "You light up like a fairy fart every time I mention I go there. Got a thing for him?"

"None of your business," Harrison growled. He never looked more goblin than when he was annoyed. Which to me was kinda sexy, being part-goblin myself.

"Oooh, have I hit a raw nerve?" God, how I loved to tease him.

"Don't you have better things to interest yourself with other than my love life?"

"Nothing comes to mind. We're not exactly being rushed off our feet with cases. Or hadn't you noticed?"

Harrison growled again.

We passed a little girl sobbing on the street. She was crying over a balloon that had just popped though her mom wasn't paying much attention. She was too busy talking to a hotdog vendor.

"*Sic faciet avolare!*" I whispered as we walked past her. Out of the corner of my eye I watched as the red balloon suddenly inflated and soared into the air. The little girl was so astonished she lost hold of the string, and the balloon was soon way out of her reach in the sky. *Dammit.*

The girl screamed even louder.

"That'll teach you," her mother scolded as she looked round to see what the fuss was about.

*Oh well, win some, lose some.* I hurried along as fast as I could.

Derek's magic shoppe had huge windows chock-full of everything you ever wanted, and a million other things you never knew you did. Its organized chaos of books, knick-knacks, and colorful effusions looked totally right on our paranormal avenue but walk around the corner to the normies cross street and it looked oddly out of place.

A little tinkling bell over the door announced our arrival. It was practically tropical on the inside compared to the sub-zero temperature outside, and there was a warm, real log fire to the side of the counter. It would magically vanish in the summer to make way for more stock, I knew. I headed straight for it, desperate to warm up my hands.

Derek was over in the corner, hanging a pixie box from a hook in the ceiling. He was a very manual warlock, preferring to do a lot of the physical things for himself rather than use magic, but I could see the swarming pixies that came with the box were busy giving him gyp. He balanced precariously on his ladder as he swatted the tiny terrors away, sending a few into a wooden sign on the wall behind him that read, *Don't Shoot, Love!* with a peace sign under it. I'd promised myself if I ever moved out of my apartment, I'd get a pixie box of my own. Pixies were awesome for tending your garden, even if they could be a pain in the butt. But right now, I only had a small balcony with a few potted plants overlooking the Schuylkill River, so there just wasn't a need. Plus, Scratchpoop would probably eat them.

The second Derek turned to face us I knew something was up. The handsome warlock looked surlier than usual, and he couldn't hide whatever was bothering him from his customers, which was odd. He kept looking over Harrison's head toward the door, clearly expecting someone else to come calling.

Harrison must have noticed it too because his usual awkwardness around men he fancied was gone and his gait had turned strictly business. He glanced over his shoulder to see if anyone else was there, but we were alone.

"What can I get for you?" Derek asked, clearly trying hard to sound normal. Too hard. He stared at me, then my partner, no doubt wondering if we were here for business or pleasure, as he knew our particular line of work.

"I'm looking for a kettle," I said. "Mine died this morning and I can't live without my morning brew."

Without coming down off his ladder, Derek looked surprised, then pointed to the far corner of the shop where he kept most of the non-magical stuff. He then returned his attention to securing the pixie box. Another red flag. Though not overly chatty, I couldn't remember a single time when he hadn't at least spent a few minutes catching up on the local gossip with me. He'd always enjoyed a good natter and between us, we had a pretty good idea of what was going down in town. Maybe having Harrison with me was putting him off? Perhaps my partner wasn't his type after all. Oh well.

Convincing myself he was probably just having a bad day, I sauntered over to the corner he'd pointed out, and left Harrison where he was to ogle the warlock's butt, or strike up a conversation, whichever pleased him most.

On the way I passed a rather pretty little glass ornament. It had a round base and a long stem and was a purplish red color that looked rather unusual. The truth was, I wasn't given to knick-knacks, but I thought it would look pretty nice on a shelf in my bathroom. I turned it around and upside down in search of the sticker. $15.99 was a bit steep, but it wasn't that bad. I put it down and decided to think about it. Maybe if I found a cheap enough kettle, I could buy them both.

I spotted the kettles right in the back, surrounded by some seriously jaded electrical items that were clearly not magical at all. Some of them looked to be thirty years old and were as likely to burn down your house as make you a cup of tea. But then maybe their age spoke to their reliability. I toyed with a few, not liking anything in particular, they just wouldn't go with my kitchen decor. Don't get me wrong, I was no Betty Crocker, but even goblins liked things to look nice.

Out of the corner of my eye, on the top shelf in the farthest corner, in the darkest place, (which appealed to my sense of magical destiny), I spotted an old-fashioned silver kettle, the kind you put on a stove and didn't have to plug in at all. It was too high for me to reach, so I pulled out my wand and said, *"Veni ad me!"* Not that I needed to say anything at all. A simple summoning spell like that I could conjure in my sleep. Bigger things, yep, I needed to say the words.

The kettle was a big fat round one, quite old, with a hint of rust around the spout. It was nothing I couldn't fix with a little magic easily enough, and I kinda liked it didn't require a lead to boil water. Just a good old-fashioned stove.

Behind me I heard the doorbell tinkle again, but since I was focused on the kettle I didn't think to turn around. I soon wished I had.

Harrison shouted, "Get down!" But he was too late. His words came just as the whoosh of an evil spell zoomed around the shop floor, coating us all in a nasty black dust as the spell bomb danced around the counters and shelves, seeking its mark. And then *BOOM!* The small, ball-shaped bomb found Derek, and there was a terrible crash as the warlock went flying, and screeching pixies cried out, saved only by the circle of glittering energy Harrison managed to conjure in time to save them all from a nasty death.

Even so, the blast was powerful enough to send me sprawling, knocking the kettle out of my hand. It flew through the air, landing with a loud crash amid some glass and shiny whatnots in the middle of the store. Glass shattered everywhere, and I stayed down, face to the floor, while the splinters and shards came tinkling down, their pretty music a mockery of the mayhem around us.

## Chapter Two
## OFFICER WELLS

I PUSHED MYSELF UP FROM THE FLOOR AND DUSTED MYSELF OFF.

Behind me I was relieved to see Harrison doing the same. He'd been outside the protective circle he'd cast over the others and I was afraid he'd been killed by the blast, but apart from a cut to his cheek he looked fairly unscathed. The gleaming red blood stood out against his green skin.

The circle around the others broke with an audible pop, and a host of tiny pixies took to the air, shaking their heads, their pointy ears probably still ringing from the blast.

My partner was the first to regain his senses, and he ran to the door and out into the street, but I expected the cowardly bastard who did this was long gone.

"What the—?" I said, hopping over to the counter as I attempted to pull a shard of glass from the heel of my boot. Mists of purple and green bathed the store, cast by the magic folk that preferred not to be seen in the daylight. All around me, corks were popping back into bottles and tiny, magical creatures were groaning, or looking for new vessels to occupy and call home. It was mayhem all right. But who would want to do this, I wondered? Was it a good old-fashioned protection bombing? Derek wasn't exactly a pushover, so maybe he'd upset the wrong gangster? The Magical

Mob was rife down here in Philly. I'd seen their work all too often, and this sure felt like one of their hits.

Derek looked incensed, but not altogether surprised. He kicked his way through broken debris and made his way to me.

"God, I'm so sorry, are you okay?" He bent down and pulled the shard from my heel.

"Thanks. But why should you be sorry?" I asked, testily, holding onto the edge of a table for support. "You didn't throw the bomb."

"No, I know but I 'um...." He paused, his thoughts dangling and unsaid.

"Look, you'd better call the police. We need to report this." Straightening up, I looked Derek over, wondering if he'd bumped his head or something.

"I suppose I have to?" Derek said.

His reluctance surprised me. "Yes. Yes of course you must. Why wouldn't you want to?"

Harrison was back inside now, and he walked over to where the spell bomb had gone off.

"Did you see who threw it?" I asked, remembering Harrison's cry to get down.

He shook his head. "I heard the bell over the door but all I saw was a cloaked arm throw the spell bomb inside. I didn't see anyone's face. It all happened so fast. Whoever it was is long gone now. What about you, Derek? You got any idea who would want you dead?"

Derek shook his head and reluctantly picked up the phone.

"Not a clue. Everyone knows violence gives me the willies."

I knew in my blood he was lying but there was nothing we could do about that right now. Maybe the cops would prize it out of him? It wasn't like it was our case, so I didn't have to.

"Police. Yeah. You'd better send someone over. Someone chucked a bomb into my store. No, no. No one was hurt but my shop's a train-wreck. Yeah, yeah. Warlock Derek's, corner of Changeling Avenue and Walnut. Fine. Whenever you can." Derek hung up the phone.

Harrison started to sniff around, peering into corners, staring at things the rest of us couldn't even see. My partner might be the saddest pushover when it came to his love life, but he had the best nose in the business, and if there was anything to be found on the scene, he'd be the goblin to find it. His eyes lit up like butane gas lanterns, scouring the carnage.

"Shocking," Harrison said, shaking his head. "I suppose we should be thankful for one thing."

"Yeah, what's that?" Derek asked.

"Spell bombs focus on their intended victim. None of the other creatures here look seriously hurt."

"If you say so," Derek said sarcastically. "Shame about my stock. It's been blasted to smithereens."

"You got insurance, don't you?" Harrison asked.

Derek grunted.

Harrison continued to sniff around, but when at last he looked my way, I could tell he'd found nothing.

"Is there something you wanna tell us?" I asked directly. "Like, do you know who did this to you?"

Derek bent over to turn a stool right side up.

"Don't touch anything," I exclaimed. "The police will want to look through all this mess."

"Like what?" Derek stomped the stool down hard, defying me. "If *his* magic can't find anything, what are a bunch of police officers with no magic at all gonna find?"

"I dunno, you tell us?" I said.

Derek sighed and looked away.

"You know as well as we do, you can't use magic to solve a case," Harrison said. "It renders all evidence found with it inadmissible in court. So yes, you need the police. The only question is, are you gonna let them help you or not?" Harrison looked as skeptical as I felt.

My gaze fell on the kettle I'd been looking at before the blast. Idly, I bent down to pick it up. It was now covered in dust and the splinters of untold things, but other than that, it looked relatively unscathed. I brushed it and settled it down on what had been the counter.

"How much for that?" I asked.

"Oh that." Derek sounded like he couldn't care less, and probably didn't. His gaze kept flitting to the door. I wondered if he was watching out for the police now, or someone else. "You can have it. Gratis."

"Thanks."

I resumed looking around me. I didn't know what I expected to find, but my instinct was to help, even if it was obvious Derek didn't want us to. If only he would talk to us. His silence was just stupid.

Relieved, I heard sirens off in the distance, and a minute later the bell over the door rang again as the police arrived.

Detective Liam Wells was the first into the store. He and I were old friends, having gone through the normie's police academy together. And he was a looker, too, with deep-set, piercing blue eyes that could undress a woman at a hundred paces. And he knew it, too. For years I'd kept him at arm's length, then recently, in a moment of weakness, I'd let him kiss me. Well, actually I'd kissed him. Big mistake. The man went through women like Kleenex. So, I'd shut that door down before it even opened and hadn't seen him since. But he kept sending me videos of dogs licking their business, so I guess he still thought of me, now and then. Loser.

Liam started as soon as he saw me, then dashed straight to my side.

"Christ, Dionne, you look like hell. What happened?"

"Spell bomb."

"You were here when it went off?"

"No, I thought I'd roll around in the debris for the fun of it."

My old friend frowned, ignoring my snark as he pulled a fragment of something grey from my hair. "I guess your phone is broken again."

"Imagine that," I said, not wanting to go there.

"Mob hit you think?" Liam asked.

"Wouldn't be surprised. He's not saying much." I motioned over to Derek who, along with Harrison, was already talking to the other officers. From a distance Derek looked decidedly shifty. Liam was studying him too, and we exchanged knowing glances.

"They never do." He paused to take a good look around the debris. "Well, guess we better get to it. I'll need your statement, of course."

"Sure. There's not much to tell. We popped in to buy a kettle." I showed him said kettle, which he took from me, and examined it carefully with his gorgeous blue detective eyes, before placing it carefully back down on the counter. "I was over in the corner." I pointed to where I'd been shopping when the bomb went off. "Then *BOOM!* End of story. Harrison might have more for you, but not a lot. He cast the spell that saved everyone and was looking over to the door when they chucked the bomb in."

Liam frowned. "Well, I'm glad you're safe. It really could have been a lot worse. Those things are nasty."

"Yeah." He wasn't wrong. Spell bomb or no spell bomb, we were all lucky to still be standing. But at least I'd found my new kettle. And when all this was over, I was gonna need a large pot of tea. And a cookie. Maybe two.

I sat down on a stool and hugged my new gift while Liam questioned Derek and then Harrison. While I waited, I glanced around me at all the carnage. Thank God Harrison had cast his circle in time, or I might have been having this conversation down at the morgue. As it was, all it had done was shake things up a bit and cause a little smoke. But why? Who would want to blow up a quiet little magic store or it's peace-loving owner? Only time would tell.

## Chapter Three
## DEAD WARLOCKS

ONE THING WAS FOR SURE. THAT KETTLE CERTAINLY NEEDED A GOOD cleaning before I could use it. It probably hadn't seen a lick of water in years. Come to think of it, I could use a good scrubbing myself. So, I dumped my new purchase on the kitchen counter and headed for the shower.

Just as the calming almond and honey shampoo was soaking into my scalp, the phone rang. I tried to ignore it, darn it, the water was just the right kind of hot and the shampoo smelled so yummy, but the second it stopped ringing, the phone started again. Someone really wanted to get ahold of me.

Spewing curses my mother would have spanked me for, I climbed out of the shower, and wrapped my foaming hair in a turban towel as I dripped water all over the bathroom tile.

My phone was where I'd left it by the sink, and I snatched it up, swiping a couple of times as my fingers were so damp. "Hello," I snapped, sounding as miffed as I felt.

"Hey Dionne." It was Derek. "Did I interrupt anything?"

"No, not at all," I lied, staring down at the pool of suds at my feet and drying my face with a rough washcloth. "What's up?"

"The police have just gone. Would you come back to the store? I want to talk to you."

"Why? Has something new happened?"

"Err, no. Not exactly."

"Then what?" I asked. I was literally freezing and getting just a little bit annoyed. Why was he being so vague? If he'd needed my help, why hadn't he said so before when I was right there with him? "Look, I'll be there in an hour. I'm just taking a shower, and well, if it's not urgent...."

There was a muffled sound on the other side, and then the line went dead.

"Derek? DEREK?!" But it was no use. Sighing, I redialed the number, just to hear the line-in-use tone. Just dandy.

I dropped the phone and then the towel and climbed back into the shower which was still running.

Shoot. I could have stood here for hours under the hot jets, but now all I could do was rinse myself off and head back out into the cold. I cursed Derek's name, his mother's, and anyone else he'd ever come into contact with over the years. At the same time, I had a horrible feeling he was in trouble, and freezing cold or no, I wanted to get back to him as soon as possible.

As soon as I was shampoo and soap-free, I jumped out of the stall, grabbed my wand and pointed it at my hair. "*Comae excoquatur!*" There was no time to just blow dry it properly or do any of the fancy styles I was famous for, I just wanted it dry so I could get back downtown as fast as I could.

Once I was in fresh jeans, several warm tops, and after sliding my trusty new Airweight .38 into its leather holster, I picked up my phone and dialed Harrison's number. It went straight into voicemail.

Heck. I suspected he'd already had his shower and was sleeping it off in a nice warm bed, just where I should be right now. Just my luck.

Hmm. I didn't want to walk into potential trouble on my own, and my gut told me that's just what I'd be doing. Ever so reluctantly, I pulled up Liam's private number. He answered it on the first ring.

"You missed me, huh?" His macho confidence annoyed me, and I half-thought about trying Harrison again.

"You wish. Look. I just had a call from Derek. He sounded worried. Can you meet me at his store in twenty minutes?"

"Sure. See you there." He hung up. One thing about Liam was he knew when to jock around, and when to shut up and play professional. I couldn't fault him on that one.

After quickly tickling Scratchpoop's chin, I snatched my purse from the counter, ruefully passing my new kettle which I had yet to use, and headed out to my Miata, parked in its allotted spot outside my apartment building. I cursed the cold and my empty stomach, which right now was growling at me. It would have to wait.

Traffic was light, and I was soon back downtown, parking at our office since public parking was murder this close to Philly central. If I legged it, I knew I could be back at Derek's in under a minute.

The shop said closed and there was police tape over the front door, so I was surprised to see the front door swinging on its hinges. Instantly suspicious, I pulled my .38 from its holster under my coat and glanced carefully in the window. With so much glass everywhere, I could hardly conceal my approach, if anyone had been looking for me.

The inside of the store looked just as it did earlier, a total train wreck. Slowly I nudged the door open and stepped inside. There was no sign of Derek, and the place was as silent as Harrison on the subject of equal partnerships in our firm.

A shuffling noise in the back office caught my attention, so I advanced as quietly as I could, keeping my gun high, trying not to trample the debris that would give me away in a heartbeat.

"Where are you, Liam?" I grumbled under my breath.

A screech of tire wheels at the front of the store answered that question. I wasn't the only one to hear it. I heard a scramble just ahead of me, and darting forward, I was just in time to see two caped and hooded figures vanish out of the back door. I ran after them, but they were too quick, and by the time I got to the rear exit they'd both jumped on a motorcycle and were shooting down the back alley at fifty miles per hour.

A second later, Liam was by my side.

"Did you get a look at them? Or get the plate?" the detective asked, following my gaze down the alley. He was just in time to see the back wheel as it careened around the corner and onto the main street.

"No, not their faces. Just their clothes. They were dressed like..."

"Like what?"

"Well, like monks. And no, I didn't get their plates. I just got here myself. Looters, ya think? Dressed like monks?"

"Maybe." Liam sounded as skeptical as I did. "But Derek told us the cash register was almost empty, so if they're looters, they wouldn't have got much. Not cash, anyhow. Are you sure Derek called you from here?"

"No. But he told me to meet him here at the store, so it seems likely." My attention was drawn to the counter where the telephone receiver was off the hook and trailing on the floor.

Liam holstered his gun, and I did the same. "So, where is he?"

I raised my hands in frustration and looked around, fearing the worst. "There's no sign of him. A second hit do you think?"

"Maybe," Liam said.

He followed me back into the store where I closed the front door as the cold was getting in.

"But then where's his body?" I asked. "I mean, someone tried to blow him up earlier. If they'd come back for him, wouldn't they have killed him here? If they wanted something from him, why would they try and blow him up in the first place? Dead warlocks don't talk. It doesn't make any sense."

Liam paused and looked over my shoulder, as if seeing something that wasn't there. "No Harrison?"

"Couldn't reach him."

"I see."

Liam stared over my shoulder again. "What is it?" I asked, irritated.

"Um, am I nuts, or do you see something moving in that pile of trash over there?"

I glanced over to the exact spot where Derek had been blasted. At first, I couldn't tell what he was referring to, but then I saw a little hand waving at us from the pixie box Derek had failed to hang.

I kicked past a pile of trash and knelt near the tiny thing. A small pixie: with baby-doll pink hair, about twice the size of my thumb, and dressed in a sunflower dress was yapping away. She was too tiny for me to catch a word, and all I could hear were pointed squeaks.

I pulled out my wand and the little pixie flinched.

"Don't be afraid," I said. "I'm sorry, but I can't hear you. Would you mind if I cast a spell to amplify your voice? It won't hurt and everything will be back to normal in just a few minutes. Is that okay?"

The tiny woman nodded and smiled.

"*Vox amplificus!*" I said, pointing my wand at a slight distance, trying not to seem rude.

"Hello," said a still small falsetto voice. It must have boomed in her own ears as the tiny pixie girl almost fell back into the pixie box. "Wow! Do I really sound like that? Cool." The pixie flew a few feet in the air and somersaulted, her gossamer wings flushing pink with excitement.

"I'm a lumberjack and I'm okay...." Her song ceased in a fit of giggles and I saw other members of her family, peering warily from the box, clearly in awe though again, I couldn't hear a word they were saying.

When she settled down, her pretty heart-shaped face became quite serious.

"My name's Semolina. I wanted to tell you, I mean, I think it's the least we could do considering the warlock Derek has always been so kind to us. Mom said to tell you at once, but we weren't sure at first if they were coming back or not and I admit, I don't like goblins at the best of times, nasty green creatures."

My back bristled, being part-goblin myself. I hated it when anyone disrespected my people. "Goblins?" I interrupted. "There were goblins here?"

"Oh yes, several of them. All cloaked but we knew them before we even came out of the box because they have such a god-awful pong. They took Derek and his friend, while two of them were left to ransack the place in search of something, I couldn't quite hear what, I was hiding."

Mouth-open, I looked aghast at Liam. "They took two people?"

"Oh yes. I must say we were confused at first, 'cos the other one had quite a different smell about him, still goblin I suppose but not so horrible, like the others."

I bit my tongue and focused on the case. "So, Harrison was still here?"

"Yes, well, he never really left. Anyway, there was a kerfuffle, and then Redcap came in, and before either of them could react, one of the goblin soldiers hit them over the head, and down they both went, and were carried off out the back. None of us know what happened to them after that. Those ruffians started poking around and we were afraid to pop back out of our box."

Semolina began to cough and splutter, and though she tried to talk again, her big voice was gone.

Surprised, I rose to my full height. "Thank you, Semolina, you've been a great help."

The little pixie happily fluttered her wings and flew back inside her box. I turned to Liam. So, it was just as I'd feared, and as magical mobs went, the goblin mob was about as bad as it could get.

Without uttering a word, I knew Liam was thinking the same. Redcap, the goblin boss, had a reputation for brutality and a taste for the luxurious. There was no gem in Philly he didn't covet, and there was no limit to what he'd do to get it.

"But what on earth do you think they were looking for here?" I asked. Warlock Derek's Antique Shoppe had some nice things to be sure, but surely nothing to tempt someone in Redcap's league.

Liam shook his head. "I haven't a clue. But if the pixie's right, I have a pretty good idea where they've taken them."

So did I. My heart sank. Redcap handled all his nasty business in the basement of a pub in the nastiest part of Philadelphia, down by the docks. Although no-one could prove it, we all knew where the bodies went. Straight into the Delaware River. I shuddered. It was the last place in the world I wanted to be, but I had to go there to find Harrison.

"Can we go in your car?" I asked. "I parked mine down at the office."

"Sure," Liam replied. "Let me call it in. We're gonna need back up."

I could tell from his face that he was just as sick about going to the goblin den as I was. But go we must, so while Liam contacted the police department, I got busy securing the shop against looters. A couple of minutes later we left the shop, and after strapping myself into Liam's passenger seat, we drove at top speed down to the notorious part of the Philadelphia docks.

## *Chapter Four*
# GOBLIN RULES

LIAM HAD CLEARED MOST OF THE RUSH-HOUR TRAFFIC AND TURNED HIS sirens off. It was getting dark now, and the lights were coming on all over the City of Love. It felt anything but lovely right now.

I gazed over the multitude of lit-up techno-marvelous gadgets and gizmos, the on-board computer, the radios, and CCTV plum in the middle of the dash. Of course, I had nothing like it in my Miata, not like it could fit or anything, but sometimes I missed all the good stuff that came with being on the force. It sure came in handy from time to time.

As we drove into the wide open, rough dock area in the seedy, goblin district of Philly, Liam slowed considerably, seeming not to want to draw attention to his unmarked police car, although the shady element would still spot him at a hundred paces.

"Just remember, when we get there, not to go all gung-ho," he said. "Back up will be with us soon enough. We really shouldn't do much before they show up."

"What do you mean?"

"Remember due process. We don't have a warrant and if we go diving in without probable cause, you and I could be the ones facing prosecution and not Redcap. The goblin has lawyers coming out of his armpits."

I squirmed at the reference then turned in my seat and gave Liam one of my best long hard stares.

"Are you kidding me? Probable cause? Is blowing up Derek's shop and the testimony of a reliable eyewitness not good enough these days?"

Liam sighed, turning the wheel to take us down the next street.

"You're ex police, Dionne, I shouldn't have to spell it out to you."

"Yeah, well, talk to me like I'm an idiot, Liam, 'cos I sure as hell don't get it. We have a solid witness for heaven's sake. Semolina was perfectly rational, and you know it. You were there."

Liam shook his head. "One. There's no concrete connection between the bomb blast and the abduction of Harrison and Derek. They could be unrelated incidents."

"Wait? What? Are you nuts? Semolina told us...!"

"Two. Semolina's testimony wouldn't hold up in court."

I was really annoyed now. "What? Of all people, I never pegged you as size-ist, Liam? You know pixies legally count as people. Of course her testimony would count."

"That's not what I'm talking about. Any lawyer worth their salt would argue her wits were in question. She'd almost been blown to smithereens, remember, and even if that didn't stick, everything she said to us earlier would be deemed worthless as she gave it under the influence of magic."

"There was no magic," I gasped. "She gave her testimony freely—you were there—you saw it."

"You used your wand, Dionne."

"To amplify her voice."

"Magic is magic in the eyes of the law. It doesn't differentiate between one kind and another. The second you cast that spell you rendered her testimony worthless."

"So why didn't you stop me?"

"Like we had a choice?"

I opened my mouth to argue but there was no point. He was right of course.

Deflated, I sank a little deeper in the passenger seat and looked out of my window. I knew where we were; not that I came down here too often, but I knew the place well enough to steer clear of it.

The Rotting Corpse pub—trust my fellow goblins to come up with an ew name like that—was on the next street over. I grimaced as I caught sight of its lights around the warehouses by the docks. An eerie mist shrouded the building, and the windows cast an ominous green glow over the black Delaware River, and I shuddered. I'd never been inside, and frankly, had never wanted to.

"Have you ever met Redcap?" I asked.

Liam shook his head. "No. We suspect his hand in a lot of stuff, but he's very careful to fly under the radar and we hardly ever get past his legal team. I know anyone who blabs against him tends to have a very short life expectancy. Like I said, tread carefully."

There was no wind, and the surface of the Delaware River was totally flat. I imagined my lifeless body sinking into its icy depths, drifting slowly down into the abyss, settling beside the corpses of Derek and Harrison. And other bodies. Ugh. Nasty. That was the goblin part of me coming out I supposed. I took a deep breath and tried to stay focused.

In spite of, or perhaps because of its notoriety, the parking lot was full. Liam parked in the only available spot next to the commercial dumpster and I tried not to imagine what partying goblins would fill *that* with. Even with the doors closed, goblin rock invaded my ears, all bass drums and brazen horns. Though I knew better than to ever eat any of the meat dishes they served in these places (obtained from dubious sources), the ale was reputed to be really good.

Liam thumbed his radio. "This is Detective Liam Wells outside The Rotting Corpse pub. I requested backup. Can you please give me an update?"

The static on the other end of the radio was bad but I managed to catch the response.

"All units are busy at this time. We'll send a couple of cars over as soon as we can. Stand by."

Liam put the radio back on its stand and turned his face to mine. Without uttering a word, I knew his instinct was to hold back and wait for the cavalry. But any further delay just might get Derek and Harrison killed. Assuming they were here, assuming Redcap was behind their kidnapping. My gut told me he was.

I shook my head. "Look, you can stay here and wait for the cavalry if you like but I'm going in."

"That's not a good idea," Liam said as my hand reached for the door handle.

"Last time I checked you weren't the boss of me Liam Wells." I pushed my door open but was pleased to hear Liam's resigned sigh as he opened his own door.

Even as we climbed out of the unmarked police car, I felt questioning eyes upon us. I scanned the exterior of the building, and though I could see no one at the windows I knew they were there. Watching.

The Rotting Corpse was a three-story building with a balcony on each level, its eighteenth-century Creole design looking oddly out of sync in its Philadelphia setting. The balconies were all empty now, the cold keeping even the hardiest criminals inside. To the untrained eye it might be considered just another pub, but the intricately curved iron railings, tables and chairs were pure goblin-craft, and notoriously expensive to make. Not that anyone would deign to steal anything from here. Not unless they had a death wish. Or worse.

Neither Liam nor I knew where to begin, so we headed straight for the main entrance, the music growing louder with each footstep.

"I have a bad feeling about this," I said.

"This is your party, Dionne. Just say the word and we can turn around and head right back to the car."

"Not gonna happen. My partner needs me. I'm going in."

We climbed the five steps to the main level, and the music blasted my ears as we went through the two sets of doors leading into the main restaurant area.

The atmosphere reminded me of a normie's sports bar in the throes of a big game, only the guests were a lot more animated, and I suspected a riot could break out at any moment. In fact, even as I thought this, there was a loud crash over near the back of the bar as something short, green, and hairy was sent crashing through a window. The barman closest to the brawl put down the glass he was drying, calmly pulled out his wand and aimed it at the melee. A shot of blue mist repaired the glass in an instant, and with a second flourish the unholy mess on the floor was swept clean away. Everyone returned to their seats, as if nothing had happened. Business as usual.

The hostess before us looked human, though the slant of her eyes suggested goblin, and I wondered if she was mixed blood, like me, or whether she worked under some kind of enchantment to fit in with the unusual clientele. It was impossible to know without using my wand, and Liam wasn't about to let me use it. She was dressed in a long, cream satin dress that went all the way down to the floor. She looked good in it. Elegant. Her name tag said Emily.

"How many? Two?" Her tone was indifferent to us as she picked up a couple of menus from the reception stand and glanced over the seating chart in front of her.

"None," I replied. "We're here to see Redcap."

I felt Liam tense up next to me, but I kept my eyes trained on Emily. Who knew who was out there watching us, weighing us up?

Emily's eyes narrowed. "Is he expecting you?"

"Let's just call it—a courtesy call," I said.

Liam said nothing but flashed her his badge.

Emily looked us both up and down, then put down the two menus and sighed. "Wait here."

Liam's eyes locked onto her retreating backside and my instinct was to elbow him, but I kept the impulse under control. My own focus was on the clientele. Most of them were busy going about their own business but a handful of faces had turned to watch us, and I assumed these were pub staff, or soldiers mingling with the crowd. Either way, none of the looks were friendly.

After a minute or so Emily returned, her indifferent expression now one of obvious contempt.

Her attention shifted to the group of four that had come in behind us. "I'll be with *you* in a moment," she said to us, and smiling, she reached for four menus. She dealt with the group efficiently, showing them to a table. Then her smile collapsed as she returned to us. "Follow me."

Emily began to walk toward the unusually long bar, but at the last minute she swerved and ducked under a black curtain I'd almost missed hanging along the wall.

Behind the curtain were stone steps that echoed loudly, prohibiting any kind of stealthy approach.

The steps led down to an enormous underground cellar, where the homemade brew was stored in huge copper kettles that went from floor to ceiling. In sharp contrast to the grungy-chic upstairs, the cellar was meticulously kept, and the kettles shone brightly, like new pennies. A solitary goblin was climbing on top of one, tinkering with a tap, and he scowled when he saw us approach.

Emily turned away from him and led us to a set of offices just beyond the kettles. She knocked cautiously on the window, her hand on the doorknob though I noticed she didn't open it without consent.

"Come in," said a raspy voice on the other side of the door.

Emily turned the knob and stepped aside so we could pass.

A green goblin wearing a ghastly red woolen cap that looked suspiciously like it was covered in blood, sat behind a large, mahogany desk, and he immediately pushed the MacBook he'd been using to one side so he could get a better look at us. He was a true goblin, a pure blood if you will, and I guessed he was about half my size, which was typical for one of his years. He looked around fifty, but what really caught my attention were his long, black, manicured nails which right now he was tapping on the table as he sized us both up.

"Would you like me to wait, sir?" Emily asked.

"No. Go tend to your customers. I can handle this."

Emily nodded and did as she was told. As the door closed, the goblin's attention went to a small pharmaceutical bottle sitting on his desk. He opened the cap and poured a little into a glass of clear, water-like liquid sitting next to it. I watched as the blood red liquid infused into the other. "You must excuse me," said the goblin. "I have a sore throat."

He downed the contents of the glass in a single swallow, then grimaced, clearly not liking the taste. "What can I do for you?"

I was about to spew venom when Liam pulled out his badge and flashed it at the sitting goblin.

"My name is Detective Liam Wells, and this is Dionne Cruz, private di—umm—investigator. She's assisting me with my investigation. We are looking for a couple of missing persons. P.I. Harrison and the Warlock, Derek."

As Liam mentioned their names, the goblin's nose crinkled, like he'd just taken a second dose of his own medicine. But then he recovered himself and stared straight into Liam's eyes.

"And I am Redcap. Now we all know each other, but I regret to tell you,

I cannot help you in this matter. I do not know who your friends are, and I certainly don't know *where* they are. Sorry, but I'm a very busy man...." He pointed to the door.

"Now wait a minute," I said, but Liam kicked my foot.

"Ow," I cried, not even trying to cover it up. Why the hell wouldn't he let me speak? We had an eyewitness, dammit, putting Redcap at the scene of the crime and time was running out. That is, if they weren't both dead already.

"I appreciate that, sir," Liam said. "But would you mind if we took a look around your premises? We have reason to believe they were brought to your pub."

Redcap's eyes narrowed and he brought his nasty fingernails together. "Really? I can't imagine who would tell you that. Do you have a warrant?"

"No, sir," Liam continued. "We were hoping to have your full cooperation, since I'm sure you would want to assist us in any way that you can."

Now, Redcap smiled, revealing rows of very pointy teeth that could inflict some serious damage. He opened his palms in a gesture of faith.

"But of course, Detective Wells. Be my guest. In fact, if you'll wait but a moment, I'll show you around the place myself."

"That would be very kind," Liam said.

Inside, I wanted to scream.

Redcap punched a few keys on his MacBook, then closed the lid and got up from behind his desk.

"After you," he said to me. I didn't want his gallantry. I wanted to kick him from here to Alaska and back again, but for once in my life I took Liam's lead and kept my mouth shut.

"This pub has been in my family for several generations," Redcap explained in his raspy voice as we stepped out of his office. "Our Drunken Goblin ale is considered to be the finest in Philadelphia, if not the United States in general, so I am very proud of it."

"Very impressive," Liam said, admiring the containers.

"As you can see, I have sunk a small fortune into our brew system, but more importantly for you, I'm sure you'll agree, there is absolutely no place you can hide a person down here."

Redcap pointed to the offices next to his own. "Miss Cruz, please feel free to look behind every door you see. I assure you; you'll find nothing."

I knew he was laughing at me, but I didn't care. I'd had that bluff played on me before so without a second thought, I opened every door and stuck my head inside each. Nothing. Just a bunch of filing rooms and broom closets. After I'd checked them all, I looked despondently at Liam and shook my head.

"Let's go upstairs, shall we?" Redcap beamed. "You should see everything after all."

The goblin took us back up the way we came and into the main pub. "We are very proud of our bar area," he said, gesturing to the long red bar packed solid with goblins, humans, and all sort of magical beings. "It's not the longest in the world, but it's certainly up there. And during the holidays our spells can almost double the size of it, so no guests need ever be turned away."

Suspicion tickled me, and I itched to pull out my wand to look for concealment charms but knew better than to try it with Liam by my side. Plus, the pub was packed. If they had dragged two prisoners through such a busy bar, someone would have noticed them, even in a den of thieves like this. Redcap seemed far too shrewd to allow that.

"How about behind the bar?" Liam asked, perhaps picking up my thoughts.

"Come!" Redcap led us through his customers and opened the flap that took us behind the bar. "There's a small space out back, and a service elevator that goes from the cellar and up to the upper dining floors. Let's go for a little ride, shall we?"

He pulled open the birdcage elevator door and we bundled inside. With experienced precision he pulled the handle, and the car made its way slowly up the building. "The top floor we mostly use for private parties, but they are both basically dining floors. As you will find, Miss Cruz, there are no dead bodies here. That would be bad for business, don't you think?"

"Who said anything about them being dead?" I stated.

Redcap shrugged.

I resisted the urge to push him back down the elevator shaft, sans elevator.

"You don't mind if I...?"

"Be my guest," he said again. His easy manner told me I wouldn't find a thing, but I still looked into every nook and cranny, every cupboard and toilet, but neither Harrison nor Derek were anywhere in sight. Frustrated, I climbed back into the elevator with the others. In the faint distance, I heard sirens. It seemed the cavalry had come at last.

"Thank you, sir," Liam said. "You've been most helpful."

Thankful was the last emotion I was feeling and helpful it most certainly hadn't been. If Derek and Harrison weren't here, then where in hell were they? If only I could use my wand.

"Not at all. I like to do what I can for the local police."

We had reached the ground floor and Redcap opened the exterior doors for us, just as the uniformed cops were arriving at the main entrance.

A twisted smile curved the goblin's lips and he looked at Liam expectantly.

"Don't worry, I'll take care of it," Liam said. And after a warning glance shot my way, he headed straight for the entrance, and began ushering his colleagues back out onto the porch.

I paused, my blood seething, hating the bitter taste of defeat. Unfettered by my friend, though, I couldn't help myself.

"I know you have them," I said, so quietly only Redcap could possibly hear me. I knew Liam would kill me if he heard this. After all, he liked playing by the rules, that was his thing, that was why he was a cop. But I'd left that gig behind me, and nowadays I played by an entirely different set of rules. Goblin rules.

Redcap moved closer, and to my surprise he took my hand and brought it to his lips. His green eyes glittered in both amusement and malice.

"Prove it," he whispered in his raspy voice. Then he kissed my hand, and a moment later, he was gone.

## Chapter Five
## THE FAIRY BARN

AFTER LEAVING THE ROTTING CORPSE, LIAM HAD SUGGESTED WE GO for a drink near my office so I could collect my car. I certainly didn't want to go home just to stew, though after the excitement of The Rotting Corpse, the half-empty Fairy Barn seemed positively lame.

I sat back in my chair, my hand taking a firm grip around my ice-cold Mojito, feeling anything but relaxed. Frustration didn't cover it—I wanted to explode.

"So, what do we do now?" I asked.

"Well, I've got to get back to the station to fill out my report." Liam glanced down at my phone. "No messages from anyone? This could be a kidnapping and there might be a ransom request. Have you checked?"

"Of course, I have!" I swiped my phone on—but there was nothing, again. I remoted into the office answering service, but there was nothing there either. I shook my head sadly. And then a thought occurred to me. "Why did you stop me in there?"

"When?"

"When you kicked me."

Liam thought for a moment, then nodded. "Oh. I thought you were about to spill the beans and I didn't think telling Redcap about our tiny eyewitnesses was a good idea."

He had a point. I forgave him. I wondered about the secret inhabitants of the shop and how many there might be, hidden in the shadows. Since the place was a total wreck maybe some of them had moved on. On the other hand, the cops were keeping a pretty close eye on things so maybe they felt safe under their protection. Who knew? The shop was a mystery in itself. I just hoped they were okay.

I guzzled the remainder of my drink and checked my watch. It had been six hours since Derek and Harrison had been abducted. If the statistics were true, and they generally were, the chances of finding either of them alive now was next to nothing. We both knew it. I felt sick.

Looking up, I noticed Liam's gaze was fixed on my scar. Suddenly conscious of it as well, I tied my scarf around the front of my neck, covering it up. "Hey, eyes off the goods, mister," I said, making light of the moment.

He cracked a smile. "If it bothers you that much you should spell it off," he said, sitting back a little in his chair.

I rested my hand gently on my chest. "Not a chance. I need to be reminded of it, always. There are demons out there, Liam, and we all need to stay vigilant. I slacked off tonight and look what happened."

Liam scoffed. "Come off it, Dionne. There's no way this is your fault—you weren't even there when it happened."

He had a point. Hell, why did my head feel like it might explode? I hated this. I hated feeling out of control.

Liam slid out from his booth seat, pulled out his wallet and dropped a twenty on the table to cover our drinks. "I gotta go."

"Thanks," I said. "I'm buying next time."

"If you want to. Are you gonna be okay?" He pulled on his jacket, glancing over to the entrance, clearly wanting to get going so he could finish for the day.

"Yeah. Sorry, I guess my head's all over the place. I'm gonna go get my car then head on home for some dinner, I suppose."

He opened his mouth to say something then thought better of it. Either he wanted to say something reassuring or he wanted to invite me back to his place for a few more drinks. Both options would be pointless, and we both knew it.

Liam gave my shoulder a little squeeze of assurance. "I'll call you if I hear anything, I promise." And with that he was gone.

I picked up my still cold empty glass and pondered a refill. But since I had to drive home that was probably a bad idea, so I shoved Liam's twenty under the glass and pulled on my jacket.

Semolina had been specific. She had eyeballed Redcap. And he'd practically thrown down the gauntlet as we were leaving The Rotting Corpse. I had to think smarter. I had to *be* smarter. Certainly, smarter than Redcap.

Outside, the night had turned bitter cold, and I hunkered my neck into my shoulders, trying to keep warm. I turned toward our office which was just half a block away. There were lights on inside the building, in spite of the hour.

But I didn't make straight for my car as I'd told Liam I'd do. I mean really, I couldn't just go home, make myself a pot of tea and sink into a hot bath. No, I had to do something, anything, to stop myself from going crazy.

In something of a daze that had nothing to do with the weather, I entered the now near-empty office building and took the elevator up to our floor. Last time I'd rode it, Harrison had been with me. Grumpy and annoying as he was, he'd been alive and well. And now he was missing, possibly dead. I felt sick just thinking about it.

The elevator reached our floor and with a distracting ping, the doors opened, and I stepped out. There were about six different businesses on this level, and at this time of night, everyone except maybe janitors had gone home. It wasn't the swankiest of buildings, but it suited our newly formed business just fine. Plus, we couldn't afford anywhere else. This had been it.

As I made my way along the quiet corridor, I remembered the day Harrison and I had first checked the place out. The horrid landlady had been half-human, half-troll, with beady eyes and an overhanging forehead, and was clearly conflicted about leasing the place at all. Her human side wanted the rental income, but her inner troll almost talked us out of the deal once or twice. I couldn't tell if she couldn't bear to lease it, or if she disliked goblins in general and us in particular. What was it with trolls and property?

I'd found her ooh-ing and aah-ing really annoying, but Harrison had just taken it all in stride and focused on striking up a good bargain. He'd come into a little money, and he knew this was our chance to set ourselves up. Without missing a beat, he'd turned on the charm, complimenting her spiky iron gray hair and her patchy leather dress. As soon as her chunky eyelashes started to flutter, I knew she'd been beaten. We'd got it for half the asking price. Harrison was a smart cookie.

*Hey! Harrison might not be dead yet, so get your butt out of memory lane*, my inner witch cried. I smiled. She was right.

There was a faint light shining through the frosted window. I hadn't turned it off, since we'd fully expected to return earlier, but we *had* locked it, so it was only when I turned the knob and found the door unlocked that I caught my breath.

Instinctively it was my wand that I reached for, not my shiny new gun. With it raised ahead of me, ready to strike, I put my ear to the door. Nothing. There was dead silence on the other side.

"*Protegas me!*" I whispered. Out from the tip of my wand spewed black smoke. It twisted and turned, then came together to form a shape, rather like a police riot shield. Unlike a riot shield, however, I didn't have to hold it, the shield just hovered a little ahead of me, ready to move as I did.

Ever so slowly, I pressed on the door, praying like crazy it wouldn't creak and give me away. I remained where I was, on full alert. Nothing.

I tentatively peered through the widened gap, but all appeared still on the other side. I risked opening it a little further, my heart pounding in my ears and drowning out my breath which was now fast and heavy.

I had to go on. I put my shoulder into the door, the shield protecting my chest, my wand just to my right so I could spell around the shield if I had to. I was in the main office now.

"What the!"

All desks and cabinets had been ransacked; there were papers strewn everywhere, lamps had been knocked aside in the burglar's haste and worst of all, the glass on Mom's Miami picture had been smashed to smithereens. *Morons! Someone was gonna pay for that!*

I glanced over my shoulder to the left rear corner of the room. If anyone had still been here, that would have been the only real spot for them to hide, but it was empty.

I let my air out slow, then muttered the counter spell, "*Finis praesidium!*" The shield expanded for a second, then vanished into nothing.

I slipped my wand back inside my pants, then crossed the office to my desk. I nudged the mouse, and it opened to a locked screen. It didn't look like anyone had touched it, but I logged in, just to be sure.

Yep. The first thing to pop up was Liam's saucy email, and sighing, I closed the window. One by one I checked my drawers, but other than being in a state of disarray, nothing was missing, everything seemed to be in order. Yup, spare undies, pantyhose, packet of breath mints, stapler—hey wait, where was my darn stapler?

I sat back in my seat, and exasperated, took in the whole room. What were the odds of all these events being unconnected? A million-to-one, that's what! It had to be Redcap, surely? But what was he looking for?

I pulled out my wand again, pointing it ahead of me but at nothing in particular. Liam wasn't here and the spell left no trace that could be picked up by any police detector. "*Aliquid defuit.*" A silvery stream of smoke covered the floor, coating every surface it touched. If anything had been taken it would change from silver to blue, but the smoke remained silver. Whoever had been here had taken nothing at all.

I sighed, and still shaking my head, I pulled out my cell phone and called Liam. The poor man had put in a full day already. He was not going to be pleased.

---

The police were all over the place, taking pictures dusting for prints, telling bad jokes. I'd have felt better if Liam had been here, but when I called it in, the desk sergeant told me I'd just missed him. Liam hadn't answered his cell, either, but I'd left him a message, just in case. To be fair, he'd looked shattered when he'd left me, so I could hardly blame him for blowing me off now.

"Damn nuisance, these break-ins," one of the uniforms said, as he examined the broken lock on one of the filing cabinets. "They're all the same. No real clues and a ton of paperwork."

"Yeah. I heard Liam was with her earlier." He cocked his head back in my general direction, unaware that I had razor-sharp goblin hearing, ten times keener than a human's.

They both chuckled as if that meant something. "Yup, the man still can't get past first base, least, that's what I heard."

I was in no mood for that and was about to go chew their ears off when I heard a familiar voice in the hall. After greeting a few colleagues, Liam came into my office and immediately joined me at my desk.

"Any news?" I asked.

Liam shook his head. "We're talking to people, but no. Nothing yet." He glanced over to where the uniforms were hard at it. He parked his butt in the chair opposite me. "You're making a day of it, I see. What do you have planned next? A little arson? How about grand theft?"

I wasn't offended. He was just trying to lighten things up, after all. "I thought you were done for the day?"

"I was, but a man's gotta eat. I was mid-way through chugging down Madame Ming's Pho Noodle when you called. I'd have called back, but Madame Ming would have poisoned my chopsticks if I'd let work ruin one of her dinners."

"So, I'm just work?"

He shook his head. "You know what I mean. Anyway, the boys had you covered." He jerked his head back, indicating the uniforms. "They find anything?"

"Nothing so far as I can tell." I shot two of them a snarly grimace. Liam noticed it, but he just raised an eyebrow.

"What about your super spidey-sense? Are your toenails tingling or something?"

"Did Madame Ming put something other than beef in your Pho Noodle, 'cos you're being a jerk!" I asked, too tired to play funny. Liam wasn't the only one who had had a long day, and had he forgotten my partner was missing?

"Err, sorry," Liam said. "I'm just trying to cheer you up."

"I know," I replied, still grouchy. "No. I've touched nothing. I didn't want to mess with the scene before the *professionals* got here."

The atmosphere in the room shifted and I knew the men were done. Liam looked over to where the uniforms were wrapping things up.

"All set?"

"Just about," said the first-base guy. "We're running this lot down to the lab now." He waved a sample kit in our faces for good measure.

I knew he couldn't say but the dull expression and slight shake of his head told me they'd got nothing. I exchanged a knowing look with Liam.

"Thanks guys. Time to hustle and leave Miss Cruz to what's left of her evening. Say goodnight, Miss Cruz."

One by one the uniforms left, until finally Liam and I were alone.

I waited for the sound of the elevator to go down before shutting the office door.

"Now for a real look around," I said.

Liam nodded. Now the official police work was done, I was at liberty to do whatever the hell I wanted. I pulled out my wand, but even before that, I strolled around the walls, breathing in deeply. The scent was faint, but I hadn't been wrong.

"Definitely Goblins," I said. "Just two, I think. Dim the lights, Liam."

Liam rose and did as I asked.

I waved my wand in a full circle, making sure I captured the full room. "*Ostende mihi viam!*" I breathed.

Small red trails, like the glow of a fire began flaring up around the office. It was almost as if I could see the burglars walking. Goblins! As I suspected, there had been two of them; true goblins in my opinion, judging by the small step radius and the narrow cross lines forming around my office. As each trail emerged, both Liam and I could see where they had walked, lingered, and performed their mischief. Most of their attention had been on the locked filing cabinets, and from the thickness of the trails just in front of them, I could guess it had taken them a while to get through the locks.

Eventually, the two trails circled back to the door, and then disappeared in a smoky puff. Liam flicked the lights back on.

"I really wish they'd let us use that kind of magic on the force," Liam said.

"No kidding," I agreed. "But all magic is bad magic in the eyes of the law. You'll just have to live without it."

"Yah." I knew Liam thought the law as futile as I did on this subject, but he knew better than to waste his breath debating it. "You look beat.

There's nothing more you can do now, Dionne. Why don't you head home?"

He was right, I was exhausted. Tired, hungry, and irritable. I glanced over to the phone. "Someone could still call?"

He nodded. "Yeah, maybe, but don't forget, you can remote in, right? Come on, hun, just call it a night. You'll feel better in the morning, and after a solid night's sleep you'll think better, too."

"What about all this mess?" I asked.

"Just leave it. Worry about it tomorrow."

"Okay." Boy did I sound feeble. Inside I felt hollow and empty, but he was talking sense and I knew it. I just wasn't thinking straight.

Liam led the way out. Before I left, I flipped off the lights. It had been one hell of a day. The best thing anyone could do was to end it.

## Chapter Six
## EARLY RISER

One o'clock in the afternoon was my preferred time to get up; the witch part of me liked a sleep in, but my goblin heritage insisted on it. So, when Mom banged on my door at ten in the morning, I turned into my pillow and groaned. "Oh, go away!"

A second later I heard her key in the lock, instantly regretting I had given her one. It was for emergency use only, and well, I supposed this was an emergency.

There followed the clink of keys on the countertop, and a meow from Scratchpoop, who always loved it when she came over and would wrap himself around her legs until she fed him.

The bedroom door creaked open. I sensed her *need to know everything* entering my room, like Pinocchio's nose.

"Oh, my word, Dee-Dee, are you still in bed?"

*What kind of an asinine question was that?* "Of course, I am. What are you doing here so early?"

"Your partner is missing. Why are you sleeping in so late?"

I felt a stab of guilt at that comment. I pushed myself out of bed, conscious I was almost naked other than a tee-shirt, so grabbed a pair of flannels and pulled them on.

"There you go, kitty darling," I heard her say, back over in the kitchen.

I could hear the fuzzy moggy purring even from here. I shot a look out of my bedroom door and yep, there he was, back arched as she rubbed him while he ate. Little traitor.

"Geez, Mom. You know he's not allowed up on the counter? Put his bowl down on the floor where it belongs!"

"Oh hush, Dee-Dee, it won't do any harm," Mom said, ignoring me. "And in any case, that's what Wet Wipes are for."

"Gross."

Yawning, I forced myself into the kitchen before she could do any more harm. Scratchpoop glanced up at me, almost daring me to say something, but then stuck his head back down in his bowl and began crunching with gusto, head cocked to one side as he bit down.

I sat down in front of him and dropped my head in my hands.

Mom had her wand out and pointed it at two cups full of water she had placed on the counter. "*Calida Aqua!*" she said. Green mist covered the surface of the cups then the water began to boil.

"I tried boiling some water in that kettle thing, but I think it's broken."

"Yes, I know." Yawning, I motioned over toward my new kettle. "That's why I bought that. Well, someone gave it to me, anyway."

"You can't make a brew in that!" Mom cried. "It's filthy!"

*Said the woman who feeds my cat on the counter.* "Yes. I know. I just haven't had a chance to clean it up yet, what with everything and all."

Mom pushed a cup my way. "There. That should clear your head. I made it strong but drink it up. All of it."

"Yes, Mom."

While I waited to let the infuser work its magic, she stared at me thoughtfully.

"You know, most of the time I see you in me. The black hair, lovely trim figure, oh, and the cleverness of course." She smiled at the last. "But this glumness is one hundred percent your father."

I removed the infuser then added some of the lemon she'd cut up on a saucer. It wasn't often Mom talked about Dad, so good or bad, I always liked to hear it.

"Well, I'm glad I got something from him, other than green skin and a sassy mouth."

"The mouth, I agree about. As for the skin, at least you can switch from one to the other. Not every half-blood can do that. And in any case, that's not all you inherited from your father."

"What then?" I asked. After blowing on the surface, I took a sip of Mom's most excellent tea.

"Do you want some toast, sweetie?" she asked.

"No."

Mom sat back in her chair and thought for a moment. "Well, he was also devious and cunning."

"Gee, thanks."

"Don't be like that. Sure, you have the same qualities, but you use them in a different way, for the good of others. It helps you excel at what you do. He only ever thought about himself."

"So why did you marry him?" I had heard it a thousand times, but I never tired of hearing it.

"Because." Mom took a careful sip from her own cup before conjuring up her usual list. "Because he was handsome. And charming. And he smelled good."

I smiled at that, imagining Mom actually sniffing him.

She saw me smile and frowned. "He was also dark, brooding, and devious. Of course, I only learned this side of him after we married, but it was too late by then. His goblin side got increasingly dominant as time went on. In the end there was little of the witch I loved left."

"Harrison's all goblin, and he's okay. He can be moody at times, but all in all he's still a good man."

"And so he is," Mom agreed. "We are all born how we are, but we get to choose what's important to us and how we want to behave. Harrison is a wonderful goblin. I remember his mom, bless her dear departed soul. She was a wonderful woman, too, and her boy takes after her in so many ways. Kind and thoughtful."

"When he's not brooding and resentful." But then I remembered the gun. He really cared about me and my safety. And other little gestures he had shown over the years. I knew his qualities. Wasn't that why I'd agreed to be his partner in the first place?

"Oh, he has a dark side, just like your father, but he fights against it to do what is right. Why else did he choose to become police? Just like you."

"But he left it."

"Yes. Just like you. Because you both found it too limiting. You love the law, Dee-Dee, but you couldn't be your best with the rules they impose. It was a waste of your skills, and you knew it. So did Harrison. I was delighted the day you told me you two were going off alone. In fact, if I'm to be totally honest, there was a time I thought maybe you and he..."

I winced. "No way! I don't feel that way about Harrison at all. With him it's strictly professional." I didn't bother mentioning that he was as gay as a yellow silk handkerchief. But if he hadn't been? I decided not to think such thoughts. What was the point?

"Quite right. If you say so. So now, drink up, and get in the shower. You have stuff to do."

My tea was finished so I pushed it away. Our little pep talk had been most invigorating, but it didn't change the facts. Harrison was gone. And Derek with him. There was little, if no chance, for either of them.

"You do know he's dead already, don't you?"

Mom's aura burned almost red. "Look here, Dee-Dee, I didn't raise a quitter, I raised a witch. And a bloody good one at that! I don't want to hear that kind of talk from my daughter. So, stop moping about in this silly, fatalistic fashion and get out there and do what you're good at. Be an investigator. I believe they taught you how to do that at police school. Or were you off playing nookie with your friends?"

"It's *hooky*, Mom," I corrected.

"Whatever." But she was right of course. I didn't know Harrison was dead for sure, and I owed it to him to believe he could beat the odds. There had to be something I could do, someone I could talk to, something I could find, that would lead me to him.

"Thank you for the tea," I said. "I guess I'd better get in the shower. Are you off, then?"

"Oh no!" Mom said. "I'm staying right here for now. My daughter needs me!"

"Um, really, Mom, I'm good. I can take care of myself."

"We can all use a little help from time to time, Dee-Dee. I'm going to stay right here and clean this place up."

My gaze flitted around my immaculate apartment. I was a neat freak, so really, there was nothing to clean. But if it made her feel better, who was I to argue? It was the least I could do for her kindness in coming to check on me. And also, Scratchpoop would like the company, they'd watch the afternoon soaps together.

"All right, Mom," I said, already en route to the shower. "I won't be long."

"Good," she said, "'Cos you have a busy day ahead of you. Detectiving."

"*Detecting*, Mom." I wondered if she was doing it on purpose.

"If you say so, dear."

Moms.

## *Chapter Seven*
# DARK DUTIES

THE OFFICE WAS JUST AS I'D LEFT IT THE NIGHT BEFORE.

God, it was depressing to see Harrison's seat empty. I still couldn't believe it. But Mom's words had worked their magic, no pun, and I wasn't going to let it get me down. I was a professional. It was time to act like one.

"*Tersus sursum!*" With a swish of my wand, all the files and paraphernalia began to float through the air and returned to their proper place. The glass on Mom's picture seemed to melt, then shimmered and became whole again. Even the dust and dirt on the floor rose up and deposited itself in the trash can over by the filing cabinet. In just a moment it was like the burglary had never happened. Not even the faintest scent of goblin tracks remained. Mary Poppins, eat your heart out.

That done, I picked up the desk phone and punched in a number. It rang for a little while, and I was just on the point of hanging up, when a breathy voice on the other end answered.

"What you want, Dionne? I is kinda busy."

Finn's voice was as cracked as his morals. Spawned in Western Pennsylvania, his high-pitched screech made me want to clean out my ears. Finn was a mine-dwelling Bucca—think banshee and you'll be close enough

—as well as my snitch, preferring the exciting streets of Philadelphia to the darkness of the Pittsburgh mines.

True to his kind, he knew of any trouble going down in the city, sometimes it seemed even before it happened. As I understood it, his earth magic was limited, and he needed to buy charms to enhance them, which in turn meant he needed a job. By night he was just one of the cooks in the Rotting Corpse kitchens, making him privy to all sorts of juicy bits of news and gossip. But by day he was mine, for a price.

I didn't care for him much, he was a slippery so and so, but there was no better snitch in town and right now I needed any help I could get.

"Info, what else? What have you got for me?"

"Now really ain't a good time," Finn barked. "I is—entertaining."

I shuddered to think. "You hang up on me now, Finn, and I'll tell everyone you're a snitch. Your life won't be worth spit and you'll be drowned in one of your own soup pots before sunup." So maybe I was bluffing, but he didn't know that.

"All right, all right," he squeaked. I could hear some kind of kerfuffle on the other end of the line. "Aw, baby, don't be like that! Chills out. I'll just be a minute!"

There were more groans and grumbles. "All right, Dionne, what ya wanna know?"

He knew what I wanted all right, or he wasn't the snitch I thought him to be. But the nasty imp never gave up anything easy, I always had to drag it from him. "What have you got on the Warlock Derek, or Harrison? I need whatever you can tell me. I don't have much time."

"*Oh*, those guys," Finn said. "I might know a thang or two. Question is, how much is it worth to ya?"

The slime. "I pay you plenty as it is."

"Yeah, but this be good stuff, at least for you it is. Anyways, s'up to you, no skin off da Finn's nose."

Considering I'd just threatened to out him to the underworld of Philadelphia, I had to say, the Bucca had some pretty big brass ones. "I'll slip you an extra C on your next paycheck, how's that?"

"Make it two Cs, Dionne, there's a good witchy-poo."

I gripped my phone a little tighter. Finn was unreal. Tick tock, tick tock. "All right, all right, so spill the juice."

"Err—not here. Can we meet downtown?"

I checked the time on my phone. "When?"

"Half an hour. At The Magic Gardens. Usual spot."

I nodded. "Sure. See you then."

I hung up the phone and dialed another number. It answered on the second ring.

"Hello, city morgue, Assistant M.E. Brightflower speaking."

"Hi, Gayle, it's Dionne Cruz, how are you?"

"Dionne, hi! Oh, you know, same old same old here. We have lots of bodies coming in today. It's like Christmas come early. I'm just waiting on a few more right now, as it happens."

The paranormal expert at the city morgue certainly had an odd sense of humor. But then sometimes she had a very odd job to do, which made her perfect for it. I swallowed before asking the question I had to ask.

"Harrison was taken yesterday afternoon—well—kidnapped."

"Oh heck, no. I'm sorry, Dionne. He was a good man."

I didn't like how she immediately jumped to thinking in the past tense, but in her line of business, there were never happy endings.

"Is he on your roster?"

"I don't think so, not yet anyway. I didn't see his name on the list. Let me go double check."

I didn't breathe while the line went quiet. She was gone for just a few seconds, but it felt like ages.

"No, nothing here, sorry. Well, not sorry—you know what I mean."

"How about the warlock, Derek? They were taken together. Do you see him on your list?"

There was a brief silence while she checked again.

"Mmm, no, I don't have either here, I'm happy to say. Just the usual handful of goblin gangsters, a few civilians, a leprechaun and, ooh, a mid-shift shifter, those are always fun, but nothing unusual or out of the ordinary. I'll call you if anything changes."

"Thanks, Gayle."

"No problem, and good luck."

Next, I called the local hospital. They had nothing for me either. That was something at least. I snatched my keys, and conscious of the time, set off to meet Finn at the Gardens.

Philadelphia's Magic Gardens was situated in the heart of the tourist district, and with its mosaic and mural artwork it was a tourist mecca for the normies. So naturally, no self-respecting magical person would be seen dead there, at least, not during the day. It was the perfect place to meet Finn and *not* be seen. Not by our people, anyway.

I parked the Miata on a meter, and since I'd spotted half a dozen Parking enforcement officers lurking about, I decided not to take a chance and slipped my card into the slot.

"Two bucks an hour!" I gasped. Maybe I should have Uber'ed. Or walked. Oh well, I could expense it. Still.

I spotted Finn sitting on a park bench, throwing crumbs to some pigeons. He was tall for a Bucca, which at just around four feet still made him short for a human. He was oddly shaped, with a broad jaw, mirrored by exceptionally wide hips, making him appear stocky by any standards. The top of his head was sort of pointed, though right now it was hidden under the navy trilby he wore. A few wisps of thin black hair poked out from underneath it.

I knew he'd seen me approach, but he kept his focus on the birds and pretended not to notice me.

I sat down on the bench beside him and watched the excited birds as they pecked about on the ground. Finn still said nothing. I wasn't in the mood for games.

"Are you gonna tell me what I came to hear or am I gonna have to shake it out of you?" I did my best ventriloquist impersonation, trying not to move my lips. I felt more like Secret Squirrel than James Bond.

Finn hunkered down a fraction, looking furtively around, making sure no one was watching us.

"Word is, Derek got himself a little something on his travels Red wants. And Derek was having none of it, pretending he don't have it."

"What was it?" I asked.

"Dunno."

I shifted, agitated.

"Really, I don't," Finn insisted. "All I heard was it was something big, but even Red himself is keeping quiet about it."

I sighed. "Anything else?"

"Red offered Derek a wad of cash, which he must have turned down 'cos *BOOM!*" He gestured an explosion with his hands, causing a couple of the birds to take to the air. "You don't need no snitch to tell ya that."

"Hmm. You could have told me this on the phone."

Finn grinned. "Yeah, like I said. I 'ad company. Better we 'ad our little chat here, if ya know what I mean. Bats got big ears. Plus, she's a squealer!"

That would certainly explain the odd noises I'd heard over his phone. "And Harrison?"

"Wrong place wrong time."

"Do you at least know where they were taken?" I asked, irritated at how little my money was getting me.

"Know? No. But I 'spect two bodies'll soon wash up some place south of da Delaware River, if ya know wot I mean. That is, unless he weighed 'em down."

Cold shivers ran down my spine.

"Yup, as the Finn sees it, there's only one reason h'ed keep either of 'em alive at all."

"Yeah, what's that?" I asked.

"To find whatever he be looking for. Kill 'em, then whatever they know dies with 'em."

"Hmm." If only I knew what Redcap wanted. Harrison and I were there at the time of the explosion, and the police had been all over Derek's shop with a fine-tooth comb and had found nothing. What on earth was it?

"Thanks, Finn," I said, guessing there was nothing more he could tell me. "There'll be another C in it for you if you turn up something new. Have a nose around. See what you can find out."

"Sure, I'll keep my ears open. Oh, and I, err, I'm sorry about Harrison. I kinda liked him." Finn stood up and scattered the last of his crumbs for the birds. "Now, if ya don't mind, me lady's still waiting on the Finn. At least, I hope she be."

"Sure."

Without a wave, Finn made a path through the birds. They barely moved out of the way, and I wondered how often he came to feed them. A lot, I imagined. Woman or no woman back home, I got the sense he was lonely, and I felt sorry for him. I vaguely recalled him mentioning a younger sister or brother, but I could be wrong.

As Finn disappeared, I took a moment to collect my thoughts. I had that awful nagging feeling, the kind you got when something obvious was staring you in the face, but you just couldn't make it out.

Whatever Redcap wanted had to still be there, back at the shop. There simply wasn't any time for anything to get out. I had no choice. I had to go back there, and just maybe, if I could find whatever it was Redcap wanted, I'd have something I could use to bargain with him for their lives.

## Chapter Eight
## BLUEBERRY MUFFINS

LIAM LOOKED CUTE BALANCING HIS TRAY OF HOT DRINKS AS HE SIDLED over to our table. A couple of young women turned to check him out as soon as he shimmied on by. They giggled, but their smiles dropped the moment they caught my eye. I don't mean to be intimidating, but it's the goblin in me. I am literally a green-eyed monster. Liam dumped a most enormous, sugar-encrusted muffin in front of me.

"Eat that," he said. "You've got to eat."

"What kind is it?"

"Blueberry."

Dang—my favorite. He remembered from our time at the academy together. Truth be told, I was kinda ravenous. I'd been so focused on what I had to do that I hadn't eaten much since the abduction, and now my gut was screaming at me. Liam had taken one look at me when we'd met five minutes ago and had marched me straight into the cafe.

Rather than be boring about it and complain, I slowly eased the muffin out of the paper cup, admiring the ridges in the base of the cake, then took a bite along the crusty, top edge. It was still warm from the oven and tasted *oh so good*.

Liam watched me intently, like he was watching something naughty on his computer, then smiled. "That amazing, huh?"

"Mmm...mmm." Why waste good muffin time talking? I washed it down with some of the frothy coffee he'd also purchased and took a moment to enjoy the caffeine rush. I really needed this, and only now realized just how much.

"Thank you for coming," I said.

Liam grinned. "I could hardly let you break into the shop without a police escort, now, could I?"

"I wouldn't have done that."

Liam cocked his head to one side and smiled. "Where is Dionne Cruz and what have you done with her body?"

I laughed through more muffin and covered my mouth politely before speaking. "Oh, all right, maybe if I'd had to, but here you are, and I didn't, so there."

We were sitting by the cafe window where I was able to sit back and watch the comings and goings on the busy Philadelphia street. The sun had just gone down, but from the strong streetlights I could easily see the door to Derek's shop from this vantage point. The pavement was packed with normies at this hour, rushing this way and that as they left their offices and headed home or wherever after a day's work. Plus, there was the usual smattering of tourists, though I could only spot a handful of magical beings, the kind that blended easily with the crowd. "It's been a while since I last people-watched," I confessed. "I used to enjoy it."

"Yah, I know." Liam wiped the froth from his top lip with the back of his hand. "Who has the time these days, right?"

"Right." My attention was drawn to the shop across the street. The lights were off on the inside, and it was weird seeing the place so dark and uninhabited. Every now and then I would see the tiniest flash, like a firefly, but it would be gone in an instant. No one else seemed to notice, but maybe they just weren't looking for it.

"What do you expect to find?" Liam asked, following my gaze. "My people were all over every square inch. Do you know something I don't?"

"I can almost guarantee that, but as regards this case, I dunno." I laughed and Liam smirked at my cheek. "My sources tell me Redcap wanted something bad, but never found it. And no, before you ask, they didn't know what it was, only that it was supposed to be inside the shop."

"And you're not gonna tell me who your source is, I suppose?" Liam asked.

I shook my head. "Ask a million times and you'll get the same answer. No."

"Well, that's not a lot to go on," Liam said. "I mean, there must be a million things over there. Most of it trash. Where do you plan to begin?"

"Oh, you know how things are," I said, thoughtfully. "Sometimes, it's the little things." I wrapped the last of my muffin in a paper napkin and drained the last of my coffee. "Thanks for the refreshment but we should probably get to it. You ready?"

Liam nodded, emptying the last of his own coffee. "Come on then."

Before we left, I snatched a handful of the free sugar packets on the table and stuffed them in my pocket.

Liam glanced at me sideways but said nothing. He was used to my odd ways, I supposed.

We left the cafe, then crossed the busy street at the light, just to be safe. Liam pulled out the store keys and opened the door, then gallantly went in ahead of me to make sure everything was safe. Bless him. I could more than take care of myself, but I appreciated the gesture.

He stood over by the counter area, looking around him as if unsure quite where to begin.

"Did your men take much out of the shop when they were here?" I asked.

Liam looked thoughtful "A couple of things, nothing of note. Why?"

I pulled out my wand, and with a gentle flourish, waved it in the air. "*Aliquid defuit!*" Once again, the silvery stream of smoke coated every surface of the room. I could see five blue shadows, two near the counter, two on the floor and one on an undisturbed shelf over in the corner near where I'd first spotted my kettle. The shapes were vague; it was impossible to tell just from looking at them what they represented.

"Can you get me an inventory of what they took?"

"Why?" he asked.

"So we can eliminate them from our search."

"Okay." Liam flicked on his radio. "Hi, yes, Detective Liam Wells—can you text me a list of the items we took from Warlock Derek's? —yes—yes that will work." He flicked it off. "Done. We'll have it in a couple of minutes."

"Great."

I headed for the back room where I had seen a water cooler. I checked the hot tap was still working, then poured some of it into a plastic cup. I took out the packets of sugar and mixed them into the water.

"What are you up to?" Liam called.

"Just watch."

I returned to the main shop area with the warm sugar water in my hand and what remained of my blueberry muffin.

"I just got the list," Liam said. He turned his phone toward me so I could read it.

A couple of decommissioned wands, an old boot, and a fragment of the spell bomb. Nothing of interest to me. "Oh well," I said. "I had to check."

"Yup, I'm sorry."

I shrugged. It wasn't Liam's fault it told me nothing. I bent over in front of the pixie box and called out. "Hi little guys. I'm guessing you must be hungry. I brought you a little something to eat."

Nothing moved at first, but then a tiny pair of hands appeared around the edge of the box, then a small head, and I recognized Semolina. She smiled at me, and with a flutter of wings, she flew to the rim of the cup. She carried a teeny glass, smaller than a thimble, and scooped some of the water into it. Then she settled on my muffin and wrenched off a chunk almost the size of her head.

Liam and I watched intently as she took a tiny, cautious sip of the drink, then her eyes lit up when she tasted the sugar. I heard a few, high-pitched squeaks, and then the whole family of pixies swarmed out of the box, like excited hummingbirds flying around my hands, taking drinks and helping themselves to the muffin. One by one they politely dipped and sipped, even though I guessed they were probably famished.

I handed the muffin to Liam, who shook his head at first. "Go on," I encouraged. "They don't bite."

Hesitant at first, he sighed but did as I asked. I could tell having tiny beings buzzing around his wrist bugged him at first, but after a few tugs at the muffin he settled. "Hey this is fun. They should open a pixie petting zoo or something for the kids."

In a flash, the pixies rose in unison, their squeaks intensified, and they waved tiny little angry fists in Liam's face. Then they bolted back to their box.

"Wait, what?" Liam said, exasperated.

"You utter plankton, you just insulted them. They might be tiny, but they are sentient beings just like us, and have feelings."

"All I said was...."

"I know what you said." I shook my head. So much for buttering them up. "You should do the decent thing and apologize."

From the look on his face, Liam must have thought I'd gone off my rocker. But I arched my eyebrows and said nothing, waiting for him to comply. I needed to talk to Semolina again, she was my best hope for answers, and I couldn't have something so trifling throw off my game.

When he saw I wasn't kidding he sighed, and though he shook his head, he knelt down by the pixie box with his back turned to me. I grinned, enjoying this.

"I'm sorry," he said.

I smirked, not only because of how daft he looked, but at how foolish he must have felt. He did look rather clumsy, hunkered down, talking to a green box. I bit my lip. Must. Not. Laugh.

"I meant nothing by it, I promise. I'm just a dumb big person with no magic who doesn't know any better. Please forgive me."

Once again it was Semolina who proved brave enough to stick her head outside the box. She flew up to Liam's face, smiled, then daintily perched on his shoulder. He stood up straight and turned, to face me.

I pulled out my wand, my expression asking the question I needed to ask, and she nodded.

Following a short flourish, I said. "*Vox amplificus!*"

Semolina shook all over, like a light current had pulsed through her body, but this time she was prepared for it.

"Oh, it's so fun when you do that," Semolina squeaked, flying a little in the air, as she shimmied all over. "Like being tickled by butterfly wings. *Oh.*"

The little pixie settled down on Liam's shoulder and cast him a shy little glance, clearly sweet on him. "Thank you for the muffin. The warlock Derek leaves a pot of marigolds for us out back, but they haven't been watered and the leaves are getting dry. And of course, we all love sugar water, though Daddy drinks a little too much for his own good, if you know what I mean."

"You're very welcome," I said. "Although I do have an ulterior motive."

"The kind witch is welcome to ask whatever her heart desires. We see she is a friend to the pixies, and so we honor her."

I would have blushed if I wasn't so focused on time. "Last time we were here you told me Redcap's goblins were looking for something. Do you happen to know what it was?"

"Know, no, I wouldn't say we know, but we've all made a pretty good guess."

"Yes?"

Semolina's pretty face darkened, and she beckoned me to step closer. "The day he bought our box to the store, a man came later with another package. I didn't like him at all, he had a funny smell about him, brimstone, or something, and I got a big noseful of it every time he shifted about."

She shuddered and I stiffened. Smelling brimstone was never a good thing. "What did he do?"

"He carried a cardboard box in his hands, about the size of a—um, what do you call those things you keep shoes in?" She cut out a large rectangle in the air, as if trying to visualize it.

"A shoebox?"

"Yes, that's it, a shoebox. It looked enormous to me, but you might not think so. Anyway, Derek looked inside and asked how much. The strange thing was, the man didn't want anything for it, he just seemed anxious to get it off his hands."

"And did you see what it was? Inside the box?"

"Well, that's the thing. It didn't seem like much at all at the time. Just an ordinary purply ornament covered in a bit of dust. Derek didn't even want it, I don't think, but he got distracted by a customer and while they were talking the other man left. So, Derek stuck a sticker on it and put it over there." Semolina pointed to a spot a few feet away and I suddenly remembered the pretty little vase-type thing I had noticed on the day of the bombing.

"I see. So why do you think that's what Redcap's after?"

Semolina leaned closer, her voice quieter still. "Because, when the bomb went off, something big and nasty came of it."

"Something nasty?"

"Yes. Something shrined in a dirty black and green aura. The fog around it was so thick I couldn't see it clearly, and it all happened so fast, but the nasty thing slithered over there, and disappeared again. I guess it found a new home."

She was pointing to the corner.

"So, you didn't see what it slipped inside? Another bottle maybe?"

Semolina shook her little head. And then she was suddenly struck by an idea. "I'm not sure, but it was over by those old kettles...." Her voice trailed off, then her hand went to her throat and she coughed and hiccupped a little. The next thing she said was just a squeak. Smiling, she shrugged and flew back to her box.

Liam and I exchanged glances. And then my phone rang. The pixies howled together, as if the sound pained them. I fumbled to thumb "accept." I looked down at the image on the screen. It was Mom.

## Chapter Nine
# GOBLIN INVADERS

"Mom? Is everything okay?"

"Umm, Dee-Dee, could you come home?" Her voice was uncharacteristically flat, which pushed my angst up even higher.

"Of course. I'm on my way now. With Liam."

"Good. Err—see you both in a bit."

"Mom have you...?" Before I could finish, she hung up, which surprised me.

Liam gazed at me quizzically. "Something wrong?"

"I need to get home at once," I said, depositing the sugar water on the counter and taking what was left of the muffin from Liam. "Do you mind driving? I want to call Mom again from the car."

"Sure."

A moment later we were driving along Changeling Avenue, swerving in and out of the traffic. I pulled Mom's cell number up on my phone and dialed it, but she didn't pick up. Exasperated, my hand slumped to my lap.

Liam noticed. "You want me to use the sirens?"

I thought about it for a second, but misuse of them could get him in trouble. "No, that's okay. Just put your foot down. I have a really bad feeling that whatever that thing Semolina was talking about, it jumped into that kettle I got from Derek."

"The kettle?"

"The kettle."

"The kettle you got from Derek the Warlock?"

"Yep."

"You got a kettle from Derek the Warlock, and you're just telling me now?"

"I didn't think it was important!" I hadn't thought about it at all, I'd had other things on my mind, namely two people going missing.

"And this kettle is in your apartment?"

"You're catching on."

"With your mom?"

"With my mom."

"Redcap blew up the warlock's shop because he wanted this thing."

"That's why I'm asking you to step on it."

Liam slammed on the gas and started zipping through the traffic at breakneck speed. We were outside my apartment in next to no time at all.

I didn't need my broomstick to fly up the stairs to the second floor. My anxiety practically gave me wings, and Liam was right behind me.

The lock on my apartment was busted open and the wood around it was all splintered, like someone had pried it open with a crowbar. Freaking out, I burst in, not knowing what to expect on the other side.

My mother was sitting at the kitchen counter, seemingly unharmed, but she was wound tight as a drum. Her eyes were darting about all over the place, troubled. Her fists were tightly clenched, the knuckles showing white, and her face was deathly pale, she looked as if she'd seen a ghost. At least she was in one piece, which was a relief!

"What's going on?" I asked, looking around. My apartment didn't look burgled at all. In fact, it looked perfectly clean, even more so than usual, and smelled of pine and lemon. And something else I couldn't quite put my finger on. Mom's cell phone was sitting in front of her. I couldn't have been more confused. "Why didn't you answer when I called?"

"I, err, well, oh dear, I'm not sure what to say. So, I thought I'd wait until you got here."

Irritated, I marched over to the counter, taking the seat opposite her. Liam went off to check the rooms.

"And the door? Someone tried to break in?"

She gulped and waved her hand in front of her face, close to tears.

"Take a deep breath," I suggested.

She did as she was told and slowly calmed down.

"Try now, Mom. Was it something to do with the kettle?"

She nodded. "Yes, yes, I suppose." I noticed her hands were white and shaking.

Liam returned from his search, and silently shook his head, indicating no one was in my apartment. I took a breath. She was in shock, that much was clear, and I needed to be gentler with her.

"Liam, would you pour me a mug of water, please?"

"Sure," Liam replied, getting straight to it.

"Whatever it is, Mom, I'm sure it's not your fault, okay? No one's blaming you."

Mom looked like she might be sick. She stared down into her hands and began rubbing her palm with her thumb. "Oh, I don't know about that. I'm not sure you're going to like what I have to tell you."

"Make that two mugs," I said to Liam as he put the first down in front of me. I pulled a teabag from the drawer under the counter and popped it into the mug then touched the surface of the water with the tip of my wand.

"*Calida Aqua!*" I said. The familiar goblin green glow illuminated the cup, and the water began to boil. I popped in the tea bag, then pushed the infusing liquid over toward Mom. "Okay. Sometimes the easiest thing to do is start from the beginning. Tell me everything that happened here after I left this morning. Try that."

Mom picked up the trailing teabag thread and dunked it a few times. "Well, okay, I'll try then. Just don't get mad at me. I didn't realize what I was doing, I really didn't."

I could scarcely wait to hear what she had to say but I knew if I said anything I might upset her more and I'd have to wait even longer to hear her story. So, I sat patiently, heating the second mug of water Liam brought over, and waited for her to begin.

Liam sat down on the corner seat, a tall glass of ice-water in front of him.

"Well," Mom said, more to her cup than to either of us, "I started cleaning your apartment, like I said I would. I must say, it didn't take me very long—everything was pretty tidy, you certainly take after me for that."

I nodded, wishing she would cut to the chase.

"Everything was going just peachy, until I got to that kettle you bought, and tried to clean it."

My attention went straight to the spot where I'd left it, over by the sink. But it wasn't there. I'd been too distracted by everything else to notice it was missing.

"Where is it?" I asked, my sense of impending doom strengthening with every passing second.

"It's um, I err—"

"MOM!"

"Okay Dee-Dee, please don't shout!"

"I'm not shouting, Mom, I'm perfectly calm." At least, I thought I was.

She shot me one of her famous Mad-Mom looks. "Well, I just *had* to clean up all those nasty rust spots on it, so I tried all my usual incantations, you know, "*Macula et abierunt....*"

"What's that?" Liam interrupted.

"Spot-be-gone, Granny's favorite, but absolutely nothing would shift it. So, I thought, I know, I'll just try a little spit and polish like the normies do. I grabbed a little baking soda from your cupboard, Dee-Dee, you know how Granny always swore by it, and a lint-free cloth from under your sink and set about giving it a good old-fashioned polish."

I was magic enough to second guess what was coming next and pulled the teabag from my mug without looking at it, transfixed by her story.

"After two or three rubs a nasty, dark green whoosh oozed out of the spout and started swarming around my head, you know how I hate swarming things, and I cried out." Her eyes drooped, and she looked suspiciously guilty.

"What did you say?" I asked.

"I um, well, I just wished it would go away, that's all. I just didn't think really, the words just popped out of my mouth. But as soon as I said them, it disappeared with a *pop!*"

I dropped my head into my hands and groaned. When I sat up again, Liam was waiting, and he looked confused. "I don't get it," he said. "What came out of the kettle?"

"A Jinn," I answered. "A genie, if you like."

"What, like in Aladdin?" Liam continued. "The three wishes kind?"

"Exactly so," I answered. "Only Mom just blew one of the wishes."

Mom groaned again and I glanced her way. "What? Was that not it?"

"No, no, you were right, sweetie. Only, I realized just as soon as I said the words what I'd done. So, I rubbed the kettle again and wished it would come back. A second later, I heard a *pop!* and then the nasty whooshy green thing came back, only this time I waited for it to settle."

I stared at her incredulously. "So, you wasted two wishes?" Mom treated me to a sheepish grin. I braced myself for more disaster. "You'd better tell me what happened next."

"Well, the Jinn grew and grew, but the green mist around it was so dense I couldn't quite make out what it was at first. So, I was surprised when the mists cleared and a beautiful twelve-foot or so genie towered over me. At least I'm guessing that's how tall she was, because she had to bend over a bit to avoid hitting the light pendant over the counter."

"The Jinn was a beautiful, twelve-foot-tall woman?" Liam asked, his eyes all lit up.

I shook my head. "Does it really matter?"

"No, I suppose it doesn't," he said.

I shot him a look and felt just like my mom. But Liam shut up.

"I suppose she was," Mom said. "But mostly she was kind of green. I couldn't make out if her skin was that color or if it was just the glow from the mists around her."

"You must have been terrified," Liam said.

"Not really," Mom continued. "I might seem a little dotty, but I flatter myself I can read people pretty well. Anyway, as soon as she was fully formed, she introduced herself. She seemed nice enough then."

"She introduced herself?" Liam asked.

"But of course, they're very civilized, you know? She said her name was Sasu-Khons-Pa-Set, but since that was a bit of a mouthful to just call her Patsy. She was very nice."

"So, where is she?" I asked, looking around and getting impatient. "And you still haven't explained where the kettle is."

Mom rubbed her forehead. "Well, Patsy and I were just getting to know each other when someone tried breaking in your front door. A minute later these nasty little goblins, you know, the wrong kind, came running in with mischief on their faces, so of course, I shouted, please, make them go away! And then before I even knew what was happening, *pop!* They were gone! Just like that." She snapped her fingers at the same time.

"So, what you're telling me, Mom, is in the space of what, just a few minutes, you wasted all three of the Jinn's wishes? For nothing."

"Well, I wouldn't call it nothing," Mom said, taking a sip of her tea. "Those goblins meant business. I could tell."

"So? The kettle? Where is it?"

"Oh." She slipped off her stool and wandered over to the sink. "I was afraid they might come back, so I hid it under here."

She pulled both the kettle and a cloth out from the cupboard under the sink. This was her idea of "hiding it" — one of the first places they'd look!

"Here, give it a rub, she might come back and give you three wishes."

With more than a little trepidation I took the kettle from Mom's outstretched hand, along with the lint-free duster. It looked innocuous enough, and I turned it about in my hands, studying it. But then I was a witch. I was used to dull things having magical value.

"Go on," Mom urged. "Don't just look at it. Rub the thing!"

Liam was sitting on the edge of his seat, and I knew he wanted me to summon the Jinn, if only for curiosity's sake. So, I crunched up the cloth in my hand and rubbed it on the body of the kettle. Not once, not twice, but three times. And then I held my breath and waited.

---

Out from the spout of the kettle came a black-green mist. The fog swirled around the three of us, then united in a dense cloud just in front of my refrigerator. The mist collapsed into itself, then exploded into a mystic green fire, from which a great dark shape quickly formed into the person of the Jinn.

'Patsy' was tall and shapely, like a 1950's pin-up girl. Her hair was black and silken, and braided into a single plait that fell to the front of her ample chest. Her jewelry looked very modern, Pandora-ish even, made from white gold, or platinum perhaps. Even her bracelets looked like something you could pick up from a mall. There were glistening emeralds studded throughout her hair, and she wore a silver circular amulet about her neck. Her clothes were classic Jinn though, with sheer harem pants and fitted bra.

I thought she looked tanned, and like Mom had remarked earlier, there was a green tint all over her skin, and I couldn't tell if that was her or just a reflection of the green fire that shrouded her like a veil, or if it was her skin itself. She looked tanned everywhere, that is, except on her upper arm. There, her skin was almost white. It looked like she'd worn some kind of winding snake band, but whatever it was, was now gone. Like Mom said, she was very beautiful. The air smelled of fire and brimstone.

Her hands came together, palm to palm, and she bowed, smiling sweetly.

"Greetings, Mistress witches and Officer Wells. I trust to find you well?"

The Jinn's voice was sweet and tingly, not exactly baby doll but very excitable cheerleader.

"Hello, nice to meet you," I said. "I am Dionne Cruz, this is Detective Liam Wells, and I believe you've met my mom already."

"Yes, yes." Patsy bowed, her smile never faltering. "I have had that pleasure."

"Hello," Liam said. His eyes reflected her green light, and I could tell he didn't need magic for him to fall under her spell. He put his hand out eagerly, wanting her to shake hands and be noticed. "Very nice to meet you, too."

"Greetings, Sir," she said, though she kept her hands clasped. Liam looked a little crestfallen but retrieved his in good grace. "I am delighted to make your acquaintance. As you know, I am Sasu-Khons-Pa-Set, but you may all call me Patsy. I am the daughter of Sasur-amen and I am a free Jinn."

"What's a free Jinn?" I asked.

"Unlike most of my brothers and sisters, I was able to free myself from the bonds of my enslavement. It means I have no master, and am free to exist in your world, instead of mine."

Liam cocked his head to one side. "But you granted Mom's wishes when she asked them?"

"I am Jinn. We give wishes, that is what we do. But an enslaved Jinn answers only to one master, and their demands can be endless. It is rare for a Jinn to free themselves, but I am one of the lucky ones. I got away."

"Who was your master?" I asked.

"That I cannot say."

"Even if we wish it?" I asked.

"I'm afraid I have no more wishes I can give to you. I may not be bound to any master, but I am bound by the laws of my kind. I can only grant three wishes to a household. And yours you have used."

"But I don't live here," Mom countered. "Surely that makes a difference?"

Patsy shook her head. "I'm very sorry. One household to me is any member of the family through ten generations. I cannot help you."

"What about Liam?" I asked. "We're not related or anything. He's just a friend."

"No, sorry," Patsy said. "He is a normie. My brother broke that rule when he helped Aladdin, and now we do not speak his name. I am not like my brother. I honor the Jinn."

My heart sank. Three wishes would have been the answer to all our problems, but as it was, Patsy was now little more than a pleasant distraction. At least now I knew why Redcap was so desperate to find her. Who wouldn't move heaven and earth to get three wishes? Or commit murder?

"Is there anything you can tell us about the kidnapping?" I asked. "I mean, not as a Jinn, but as a bystander. You were there after all."

"I cannot," Patsy said, "because you wish to know it, so that would be granting a wish through the back door."

I slumped and drained the last of my tea. "You know the goblin Redcap is trying to find you?"

"I do—as many magical beings have done before, and no doubt will do again. This is the way of things for the Jinn. I have no fear of it."

Another dead end. "Is there *anything* you can do to help us?" I asked. "Forgive me, but we're desperate. My partner and the warlock Derek were both taken by the goblin mob. For all we know they could be dead already, but we need to try and find them if we can. We'll do anything we have to."

"Hmm," Patsy said. She rested her hand under her chin as she thought about this. "I suppose I could help you somehow. I cannot give you what you desire most, but I can help you in a small way."

"How is that?" I asked, desperate for anything, no matter how big or small.

"I can teach you how to be the best witch you could possibly be, and then, when you fully understand your own power, maybe you can do what you need to yourself. That way I'm not giving you anything and won't be breaking the code of the Jinn."

Before I could even ask her what she meant by that, Patsy snapped her fingers. Once again, the spooky green mist enshrouded her completely, but a moment later she reappeared, dressed in a bright blue sports top and shorts. Her single plait and emeralds were gone, and her black tresses fell neatly over her shoulders, heavy with product. She looked every bit the cheerleader I sensed she dreamed of being. And she was just as tall as I was.

"Err, so you're gonna try to teach me?" I asked. "Teach me what?"

"Well, cheerlead would be more exact, but I'm not sure yet." Patsy danced from sneakered foot to foot, then kicked a leg high in the air. I wondered what dreadful show she'd borrowed her cheerleading concept from. "It'll be super fun, don't you think?"

"What will be?"

"Well, I'm going to hang out with you, of course silly. How else do you think I'll be able to help? I'll need to see your witchy skills in action. Especially before you go up against Redcap. You won't stand a chance if you don't, Mistress Witch. He's far too ruthless and powerful."

I stared at Liam, and he looked away. I could tell he didn't have a clue what to say. Nor did I. I had enough on my plate without some bonkers teen-genie trailing along by my side. Especially one that wouldn't grant me a wish. No, I was pretty sure she'd just get in the way.

"You're very kind," I said. "Maybe we can talk about it later? Right now, though, I have to get going." I shot Liam a meaningful glance, letting him know I thought we were done here, and pushed back from the table. "It was very nice meeting you, Patsy, but we'll be fine. Now I really do have to get going."

"To do what?" Patsy asked. "Ask a few questions? Chase a few leads? No, witchy-poo, you need to up your game. Right now, you can bet if

Redcap hasn't killed them already, he's probably torturing your friends, and if he hasn't figured out what happened to me, he soon will. And when he doesn't need them anymore, all you'll be able to do is fish them out of the river."

"Thanks, Captain Obvious, now tell me something I didn't know already," I hissed, anxious to be doing something, anything rather than just hanging out in my apartment.

"Very well, then. Start thinking like Redcap. What do you think he would do?"

"I know what he would do. He would come after me, and if he didn't hurt me, he would come after something I loved, and try to get to me that way."

"Indeed. Therefore, you must do the same. What does Redcap want more than anything?"

"You. So, what are you suggesting? I offer to hand you over to him? Like a trade or something?"

"Perhaps," Patsy said. "At least it's a start. We can talk about it some more on the way."

I didn't like the sound of that one bit. Immortal or not, I wasn't about to trade up one being, to save another, even two. But the clock was ticking, and for now, that was all we had.

"All right," I said. "We'll talk about it in the car. Mom, will you be here when I get home?"

"I dunno, Dee-Dee," Mom said, "If you want me to I will, but what if those green menaces come back?"

She had a point. "Okay, but if you do decide to stay, please make up the couch for me. You can sleep in my bed as I'll be back late. And don't worry, I'll cast some enchantments on the door as we leave. I know a spell or two that will keep those goblins out."

I pulled out my wand and was just about to conjure the impregnable spell when Patsy touched my spelling arm. "If you like, we can start your training right now?"

"Huh?" I turned back to face her, unsure of her meaning.

"Using a wand is well and good, but you don't really need it," Patsy said.

"I know, I can already do a few spells without it, but I use it when I really need to focus. You know, on the big and more powerful stuff?"

I raised my arm to cast the spell again, but Patsy was insistent.

"I see you clutch your wand as if you believe you cannot cast magic without it, but you have already surpassed its limitations, your power lies within and may be tapped at will. Go ahead, try."

I shook my head, conscious of how foolish I would look in front of Liam and Mom if I failed. "What are you, Yoda?"

Patsy put her hands on her hips and frowned. She really was absurdly pretty, even when roused. Liam covered his mouth, no doubt hiding a smirk.

"Oh, very well," I said, realizing she wasn't going to back down. I felt like a total idiot, but just to shut her up I closed my eyes and said, "*Inexpugnabilem!*"

Nothing. No gray smokey haze around my impregnable castle. Nada. Just a door. A door that opened as soon as I tried it. "See!" I exclaimed. "Didn't work. Now can we go?"

As I pulled out my wand again, Patsy sighed. "Do you always give up on the first try, Dionne Cruz?" Now she sounded just like my mother now.

"I do when time is pressing, and my friends are in danger." Turning from her again, I pointed my wand at the door. "*Inexpugnabilem!*"

This time a jet of gray smoke burst from the tip of my wand, circling the entire door frame and causing the wood of the door to swell slightly. I held the handle and opened it, and it opened just fine.

"Liam, you try."

I stepped aside to let Liam have a go at it. This time the door refused to budge, even when he gave it a good tug.

"There now," I said. "Only Mom or me will be able to open that door. Nobody else will stand a chance. Same goes for the windows. So, if you do stay, you'll be safe as houses, Mom, believe me."

"Thank you, Dee-Dee," Mom said. Liam opened the door, but before leaving, I stopped and grabbed Mom's hand. "Call me if anything happens," I said. "And answer the phone if I call you. Don't just ignore it or I'll come and hex you myself."

"Alright, sweetie, I promise,"

And then I kissed her on the cheek and followed the others out in search of Redcap.

## Chapter Ten
# THE ROTTING CORPSE

I NEVER LIKE BEING ON THE WATER, ALTHOUGH I LOVE LOOKING AT IT. Heck, my own apartment overlooked the Schuylkill River, and I'd spent many a happy hour watching life float along with the current, or studying the animals housed on its banks. But water messed with my spells—acting as a conductor when close to a magical energy vortex, shorting out the spell—and since I've never liked feeling that vulnerable, I generally stay glued to dry land. So, when Liam suggested we try approaching The Rotting Corpse by boat, naturally I wasn't too excited.

"You know how much I hate being on the water," I protested. "Especially the Delaware. At least the Schuylkill River is pretty to look at. The Delaware is just a vast expanse of murky black. That, and you know I can't swim."

"You don't have to swim," Liam said. "You're on a boat. That's the whole point."

"Did you ever see Titanic? Safest ship ever built. It sank. They drowned."

"Look," Liam said in his most irritating tone, "You're the one that thought it was a good idea to take him by surprise."

"I know," I said. "I just didn't mean on a boat!"

"Well, unless you know of a spell to make us invisible, this is the only plan we've got. Now get in and put your life jacket on."

Resigned, I stepped off the dock and into the small Genesis craft Liam had said belonged to a friend. I didn't know he had such fancy friends. But anyway, he'd made a few calls and now here we were. In a final show of defiance, I played with the cords on my lifejacket and peeped on the whistle. Patsy laughed, but Liam shot me a warning look.

It was icy cold, and though I had my life jacket on, and my leather jacket was well insulated, I still had to pull my scarf up round my face to keep from freezing to death. Patsy, on the other hand, seemed impervious to the weather. Still in her cheerleader garb, you'd think she was cruising the Caribbean rather than creeping upriver at the beginning of February. I shivered just looking at her.

"Can't you magic up a coat for yourself or something?" I asked.

"Why? The cold is magnificent! We had nothing like this in Arabia. This is marvelous."

Patsy threw her hands up in the air like some kind of deranged maniac who had never seen a river before, and I shrugged. She was a big girl. Thousands of years older than I was, in fact. She could do what she liked.

Conversely, I sat huddled inside the small cabin, trying to keep my teeth from chattering as the engine roared and Liam turned us toward the center of the river. It seemed vast and black, and I liked it even less by night than I did by day. To keep my fear in check, I focused on the running lights, red to port and green to starboard, and the searchlight on the bow illuminating the water dead ahead. It was mesmerizing and comforting to watch the similar lights on the other handful of boats as we passed them.

After a little while, Patsy came to join me.

"You don't enjoy watching all the lights on the shore?" she asked. "I find it fascinating. The world looks such a different place from the water. I like watching them go out as people go to bed. It's very relaxing."

"Knock yourself out." It was still early for me, but right now I'd much rather be going to bed myself.

Still miffed to be out on this boat, I shot Liam a dirty look. I was just in time to find him ogling Patsy, like a daft schoolboy not able to take his eyes off the new teacher with the great rack.

"Watch out!" I cried. A pair of unmoving green lights were coming right at us. Liam swerved just in time to avoid a head on collision.

"Idiot," I hissed, shooting him my dirtiest glare. I pulled my scarf away from my mouth a little so I could speak more clearly. "I suppose we ought to talk about this crazy plan of yours. I have to say, it doesn't feel right—just offering you up like that. Redcap is a monster, what if his first wish is to kill us all? Ya know, no witnesses. Mobsters generally like that sort of thing."

Patsy smiled. "Oh, don't you worry about that. I've been in this business a long time, and you can bet your life he won't ask for that. Trust me, he'll have given this a lot of thought, and will already have his three wishes lined up. He won't be wasting them on vengeance when there are greater things in his grasp for the taking. Not unless he's a complete fool."

"Maybe, but I'm not sure I'm willing to bet all our lives on that. We don't know all that much about him really. He could be as nutty as a fruitcake." And yet I didn't think so. Our meeting had been brief, but my one lasting impression was that the master goblin knew exactly what he wanted, and always weighed the cost of getting it before he struck. Cold, callous, and cunning, yes, but not stupid.

"You have nothing to fear," Patsy said. "Trust me on this."

"Okay, so we sneak in, see if we can locate them, and if all else fails, trade you for Derek and Harrison. Assuming they're still alive, of course. And if he tries anything funny after we make the exchange, or if he's hurt them in any way, I'll hex his goblin ears off."

Patsy laughed. "I just bet you would."

I still felt uneasy. "And you're sure you don't mind being traded? I mean, Redcap is a nasty piece of work. As bad as they come. What if he does something bad to you?"

She shrugged. "The badder, the better. I love the evil ones. They always, always reach too high, and their wishes turn on them as curses. It really is rather fun to watch. The super greedy ones are such silly creatures."

Patsy said all this with such glee, I found myself glad she was our friend, assuming she was, and not our enemy. I had a feeling she could be a real terror if she wanted to be.

Liam, who had been silently steering the boat, eased off the throttle and began pulling up to a shared pier that connected The Rotting Corpse and its neighbor, The Barbecue Baron. The Barbecue Baron was directly in front of us, and was dark and silent, the last of its customers having left hours ago. At least, so we hoped. There was some activity over at The Rotting Corpse, but then paranormal establishments generally kept later hours and we'd expected this. "All set?" Liam asked as soon as the engine was silent.

"It's now or never," I said. "Are you sure you want to come? You being a police officer and all. I don't want to get you in trouble."

"I won't be, not if we find what we're looking for. But more important than that, I'm not letting you go in on your own. You need back up. So shut it. I'm coming with you."

"Well, if you're sure."

When we'd been given 'the tour,' I'd noticed two sets of access doors to the lower level of The Rotting Corpse. One was wide enough for river-side deliveries; the other was just a regular door; possibly just a fire exit. "I suggest we try the smaller door. If I recall, it opens near the storerooms."

"Agreed." Liam had already hopped out of the boat and was busy securing us to a mooring. There was a dimly lit sign over his head, that read, *Free docking for patrons of The Rotting Corpse and The Barbecue Baron. All others will be towed. Or sunk.* "I just hope it's not alarmed."

*Amen to that*, I thought. We scurried along the wooden boards; the pier wasn't well lit, but we were still at risk of being seen, so far out in the open. I could hear voices above us; perhaps they weren't as rambunctious as they had been last time we were here, but the bar was obviously in full swing, so hopefully the outer doors were still open. I grasped my wand firmly and pointed it at the door.

"*Exarmaueris!*" I whispered, figuring it was safer to whisper the disarm spell rather than to risk it. For a second the door pulsed a faint amber, and then was dull again. I tried the knob and eased the door open.

My wand still high, I peered around the door. All was quiet. To my right were the large, copper kettles, although this time they were unmanned, and just beyond them was the door to Redcap's office. There was no glimmer of light under his door, but still, I would take no chances. Perhaps he just liked to work in the dark. Without looking back, I motioned for the others to follow me in.

Slowly they slipped through the door and stood on either side of me. Liam gazed at me expectantly, and Patsy looked like she'd just walked into her favorite store, during a sale.

"*Ostende arcanum tuum!*" I whispered.

"What's that?" Liam asked.

"A spell to reveal anything hidden by magic."

We all watched as the spell that came from my wand adopted a serpent-like shape and began to crawl and slither around the room. It paused at every window and door, box and crater, but quickly moved onto the next object. Then it crawled over to the copper kettles, passing the first and the second without changing its pattern. When it came to the third, instead of slithering on it as it had done before, it began to circle the kettle, then rose up on its belly like an angry cobra, its tongue flicking as it swayed back and forth.

"Come on," I whispered. "There's something there."

Ever so slowly, with my ears pricked for any sudden change in atmosphere, we inched across the room toward the last copper kettle. The snake ignored us as we each examined the onion-shaped base of the kettle.

"What do you think it means?" Liam asked.

"I don't know." With a flick of my wand, the snake disappeared, and I stood on the spot it had been circling.

At the base of each of the kettles was a small door; I supposed this was where they put the hops to make the ale. It looked heavy duty, surrounded by copper studs that put me in mind of a porthole on a ship, only this door raised vertically from the base by about a foot. I grabbed the handle and was surprised when it yielded so easily. I'd been expecting a big heave-ho.

"Well, I'll be!"

The hole into the kettle seem to yawn and groan, until it was twice as large as it had been before. Instead of liquid, as I expected, I saw a ladder going down to another level. Since the space was now large enough for a body to pass through, I hoisted myself up and put my foot on the first rung.

"Are you sure that's a good idea?" Liam asked. "You've no idea where it leads. And what if the hole shrinks again? You'll be trapped!"

"Well, you can stay here and keep watch, if you like," I said. "But I'm going after my partner."

Before he could object again, I started to climb down.

"Ooh, this looks fun." Patsy climbed down right behind me, and though he sighed, I heard Liam's heavier foot on the ladder right after that.

I just reached the bottom and had stepped away from the ladder when Liam said: "I've got a really bad feeling about this."

And sure enough, as soon as he said the 'magic' words, I heard a scratchy chuckle, echoing from somewhere above, and then the metallic clang of a heavy copper door as it crashed over our heads, and we were left in utter darkness.

## Chapter Eleven
# A PARTY

"You had to say it!" I shook my head though I knew no one could see me do it.

"Sorry," Liam said.

I sighed and raised my wand. "*Lux!*" I whispered. A faint glow emanated from the tip of my wand. I pointed it toward the top of the ladder where Liam was still trying to pry open the door.

"No use, it's locked," he said, his teeth gritted as he put his back into the task. "We're stuck down here in this giant onion thing until we die or turn into alcohol fumes or something."

Lowering my wand, I turned slowly. We were in some kind of tunnel. The walls were bare, and I surmised we were at the far end of whatever it was since there was nothing but a brick wall behind the ladder. It smelled damp, and there was a dull echo when we spoke. I thought maybe this might have been dug under the river when the Rotting Corpse had been built, hence the dampness.

"It's never a dull moment with you two," Patsy said cheerfully.

"Thanks," I replied. "Come on, let's see where this goes."

As soon as Liam climbed down the ladder we set off.

"Which way do you think we're going?" Liam asked.

I looked up and tried to picture the layout of The Rotting Corpse above our heads. "Hmmm. I could be wrong, but I would say we're heading toward The Barbecue Baron. Sneaky little bugger. No one who raided The Corpse would ever think of looking in The Baron. Smart. Very smart."

"But," Liam argued, "The Baron is owned by some overseas dude with an Irish name I can never remember. He's supposed to hate Redcap. Are you saying he's in on Redcap's racket as well?"

"Maaaybe? Maybe not. What if he's just a paper owner and Redcap runs them both? It's not exactly a big leap of faith, and you could check it out easily enough back at the station. Or maybe he's not so much 'overseas' as weighed down somewhere out there in the Delaware River. But I'd bet a witch's hat something like that's going on here. If we ever get out of here alive to bet one, that is."

There were noises at the other end of the tunnel and we all instinctively slowed.

"Looks like the party's just getting started," Patsy said. She was not wrong. Up ahead a door opened, and a lone figure stood in the doorway. I recognized her at once from the hands on her hips and the dripping disdain of her posture. It was Emily.

"And you're the guest of honor," she said. She must have heard Patsy. Those big goblin ears. "Come on in, we've been waiting for you."

Well, there was no going back now, so we all three marched forward. Me with my wand held high, Liam with his gun pulled from his holster, and Patsy, smiling happily as if this was someone's birthday party.

As we approached the door at the end of the tunnel, Emily stood to one side so we could pass. She must have seen Liam's gun and my wand, but she didn't bat an eyelid.

Beyond her was some kind of storage area, full of stainless-steel baking trays neatly stacked on shelves, boxes overflowing with chef's jackets in various sizes, rows of plates and cups and boxes of cutlery. It was cold, too, perhaps even a few degrees colder than out in the tunnel.

To our left were some industrial sized-refrigerator doors.

"Follow me," Emily said, opening one of the doors.

"We're not going in there," I said. "Do you think I was born yesterday?"

"Suit yourself," Emily said, and walked in anyway.

Liam, Patsy, and I exchanged glances. What else could we do? Liam went first, closely followed by Patsy.

"Oh heck," I said, and followed them all inside.

The refrigerator was choc-full of different sized boxes; Emily marched past all of these and seemed to be heading for the back wall. As expected, the room came to a dead end, but unperturbed, Emily pushed aside a box labeled premium baby back ribs and swished her hand over the empty cold shelf. The wall seemed to be eaten away by frost, then opened up to reveal a secret room behind it. Hmmm. So, the girl had some magic in her. Who knew?

The room before us was heated by a blazing fire, with two long sofas running either side of the mantle. Bookcases adorned all the walls, and the main source of light seemed to be candlelight, though I noticed the bookcases were discretely lit by under panel lighting. I felt like I'd suddenly entered a gentleman's library from the eighteenth century or something. There was a small, toddlers cage over in the corner. Nice to know someone cared.

Liam looked as confused as I felt, though Patsy clasped her hands in delight.

"Take a seat," Emily said. "Redcap will be here in just a moment."

I half expected Emily to leave at this point, but instead she took a spot at the end of one of the sofas nearest to the fire and quietly stared into it. She looked lost in thought, almost as if she'd forgotten we were there. She was covering the back of her hand, but her efforts were futile—I'd already seen the bruise on the back of it. I wondered what she'd done to Redcap to deserve that.

Patsy happily dropped onto a sofa, and I sat down beside her, more cautious than the jinn. Liam stood behind us, ready for action.

I noticed Liam kept his gun in plain sight, and I twirled my wand in my fingers, wondering where all this was going to lead, and hoping, praying for the best.

We didn't have to wait long. After a while we heard footsteps, then one of the bookcases swung on its hinges and Redcap came into the room, accompanied by a burst of voices and music coming from somewhere above, which cut off abruptly when he closed the bookcase behind him.

He looked shorter than I remembered him, and his nose was red-raw with cold. The season was definitely not agreeing with him. His nasty red cap was pulled down low over his head and looked bloodier than ever.

"Back so soon, Miss Cruz and Detective Wells? And I see this time you've brought a friend. How delightful."

His gaze landed on Liam's gun, then on my wand. The corner of his mouth crinkled into a cynical smile for just a fraction of a second but was soon gone. He sat down next to Emily who barely shifted to accommodate him. I wondered how she could stand having him so close by.

"How could we resist?" I said, mimicking his flat tone. "It's your famous baby back ribs."

Redcap took a moment to look around him. "Ah yes, I see you've divined where you are. Well done, Miss Cruz, what an excellent detective you are." His tone dripped with so much disdain, I expected to see it pool on the floor by his feet. "But alas. You haven't introduced your friend. Let me begin. My name is Redcap, and this lady is Emily Applegate. What is yours?"

Patsy crossed her long legs, and I could sense Liam fighting the urge to check them out, even here, when we were up to our neck in danger. *Did the man know no limits?*

"My name is *Sasu-Khons-Pa-Set.*"

"Well, that's an interesting name. Where are you from, uh, Sasu... cons..?"

"Sasu-Khons-Pa-Set," said Emily, earning her a look from Redcap.

"Oh, I'm from everywhere," Patsy said. "Mostly Arabia. Although I spent a thousand years in India once. That was fun!"

"Huh?"

"She's not human," Emily said.

"Oh no, I'm not human, goodness me no." Patsy chuckled.

"Then what are you?"

"I am jinn."

"What the who now?" Redcap's confusion was a joy to behold.

Emily was way ahead of him. "She said she's—"

"I heard what she said!"

"Anyway, my friends call me Patsy. You, however, may call me Sasu-Khons-Pa-Set."

From the way he squirmed I thought the little goblin was going to poop in his baggy purple pants. Even the cold and unfeeling Emily shifted in her seat, and for the first time I turned to take a proper look at the girl. Whatever had stirred her, she mastered and was in control of herself again.

I thought it best to strike while the goblin was wrong-footed. "We've come to make a deal. If a deal can be made. We will give you the jinn if you return Harrison and Derek to us."

The look of astonishment left Redcap's face and settled back to his usual distrusting cunning. I could see he suspected a double-cross.

"So, you're going to hand me the jinn, just like that?"

"As I said, Patsy will surrender herself to you of her own free will. The moment we are all safely out of here, you can get what is coming to you."

Emily's eyes narrowed. Redcap pinched his nose under his eyes and began a flat, diabolical laugh. "I see. Do you take me for a fool? If she is, indeed, Jinn, why doesn't she just wish for you what you desire? I believe that's how it's supposed to work, isn't it?"

It was my turn to look uncomfortable. "Well, I would have, only, err—we already used the wishes on something else."

Redcap's brow darkened. "Let me suggest another option. I am guessing Detective Wells that your little visit here tonight is not sanctioned by your department. I wonder, would they even miss you if you disappeared?"

Liam raised the gun, and though he didn't point it directly at Redcap, it served as a good reminder that he had it. "Aren't you forgetting something?"

"Hmm. A gun in a house of magic. I'm shaking."

"You're forgetting this, too," I said, lifting my wand. "You can't just disappear us, Redcap. We're armed and dangerous. And we have a jinn."

Redcap's laugh was truly genuine this time. "A jinn who, by your own admission, you have rendered totally useless to you. Come, come, Miss Cruz, you and your friends will have to do better than that. In any case, as I told you, we don't know anything about your missing persons. No, all I know is that we've apprehended some trespassers who are here in my premises without a warrant. I have a good mind to call the police."

"No, don't," Liam said. "Listen to Dionne. She's not kidding."

"And neither am I. My offer is real." Patsy stood up from the sofa, and with a click of her fingers, she disappeared into a fog of black-green smoke. The smoke swirled upwards, bathing the ceiling of the room in a dirty soot, and then she reformed in a shimmer of golden sparkles, back to her beautiful towering self.

I could almost imagine Redcap's toes curling inside his squat little goblin boots. Emily's eyes grew an even deeper shade of green than usual.

When the dust settled, Patsy pulled her plait to the front and readjusted her harem pants. "I have to say I prefer the other outfit, but if this is what it takes to persuade you, then so be it!"

Greed crystalized in Redcap's eyes and in that moment, I knew he would do whatever we asked to get what he wanted.

"Name your price," he said, unable to take his gaze off Patsy. "Ask for anything I have, and it shall be yours."

Emily sat at the end of the seat, no longer caring whether I noticed her bruises or not. "Could this be some kind of parlor trick?"

Redcap finally broke his stare and turned to Emily. "How can we test her?"

"You can't," I said. "Not without wasting one of your wishes. So, it comes to this—either you trust us, or you don't. If you don't, fine, we'll leave, but we'll be back and trust *me*, we will get what we want in the end. Or you can be thankful we brought you the thing you most desired, and just give us Harrison and the warlock and we can all go our merry ways. It's up to you, Redcap. What'll it be?"

Redcap was silent for a moment, and I could almost hear the cogs in his brain turning as he considered my argument. But then he apparently came to a decision because he rose from the sofa and took a step toward me.

"Emily. Summon the Pukwudgies and their charges. Well, Miss Cruz. It seems you have got yourself a deal. But if I find out you've tricked me in any small way, I'll come after you, and things will get very, very ugly. You have my word on that."

Thankfully he didn't offer his hand or spit in it to seal the deal because that would have been too gross. Especially given his cold. Emily must have realized Redcap meant what he said, because she immediately stood up and left the room.

My heart began to race. Redcap had met our terms, and that surely meant only one thing. Derek and Harrison had to be alive! But one thing still bothered me, and I decided to suspend my celebrating until I had the answer to that as well. And the question was —what exactly were the Pukwudgies?

## Chapter Twelve
# THE PUKWUDGIES

I didn't have to wait too long to find out. The Pukwudgies, whatever they were, couldn't have been too far off, because within seconds I heard Emily's heels clacking on some hard surface, accompanied by the oddest whooshes and squeaks and puffs.

When the door opened, I shuffled to the edge of my seat, curious to see who would come through it. And for good reason, because two very small little creatures, no taller than my knees, shuffled through. They were bizarre little things, dressed in shabby jeans held up by loose belts holding little arrows. Both had bows slung over their shoulders. Like a horse's mane, their wild, unruly hair grew down their muscular backs to the base of their spines, and though I wouldn't be so rude as to call them ugly, I could hardly call them pretty. They reminded me of Neanderthals, but with large, bulbous noses and slightly better sets of teeth.

From the tips of their fingers came a sheet of pure white flame, forming a co-joined circle between them. The flames shot up and down, hiding anything from view within its fiery heights. Then I caught a glimpse of two shadowy outlines. My heart jolted as I realized Harrison and Derek were probably inside it.

I almost missed Emily, who was right behind the sheet of fire, but then she closed the door and stood to one side, a cruel, yet satisfied sneer on her face. Something was seriously wrong with this dame if she was getting a kick out of this.

The slightly larger of the two little figures puffed out his chest and bowed, placing his free hand on his heart. It was a surprisingly graceful motion, given his diminutive height and odd appearance. "We have brought the prisoners as you requested," he said. His voice was high-pitched and reedy, reminding me of the brownies in Willow. But at least it didn't need to be magnified.

"Thank you, Puk," Redcap said. He looked smug, clearly enjoying our confusion and transparent hope. "And you too, Wally."

The smaller pukwudgie bowed, though I noticed his bow was shallower, and his hand didn't quite reach his heart.

"You will release the prisoners into the care of Miss Cruz here, but though your fortress of flame may drop, you must continue to suppress their magic until you hear from me."

The two pukwudgies bowed again. "Miss Cruz has made a deal for their lives, and only when I'm sure she's made good on her part of the bargain will you release them. If there has been trickery, any at all, you can shoot them both with a poison dart." Redcap turned to me. "I trust I have made myself clear."

"Crystal," I said. My eyes remained glued to the wall of white fire, desperate to see my partner again. I was itching to poke it with my strongest spell, just to see if it would stand up to the test, but since neither Harrison nor Derek had been able to best it, I doubted I could, and in any case, why blow the deal now? I was this close to getting what I wanted and was done with games and theatrics. "Can we get this over with? I'm gagging for a Big Mac and fries."

Unperturbed by my sass, Redcap nodded. At his command, the two small creatures waved their hands in a regal-like flourish, and the wall of flames came crashing down.

And there they were. A little dirty, and they looked like they hadn't slept, but they were otherwise unharmed. The second the wall collapsed, Derek and Harrison, bound together by a magical circle, started looking frantically about them, evidently oblivious about where they were. Their eyes landed first on Redcap, and their struggle intensified, but then they saw Liam and me, and their expressions became confused.

"Are you okay?" I asked.

Harrison nodded, though Derek kept his focus on Redcap.

"What's going on?" Harrison asked.

"It seems you have friends who think your life is worth something," Redcap said. "They've paid quite a price for your release."

Confused, Harrison looked to me for an explanation. I, in turn, motioned to Patsy. "He wants the jinn we found hiding in the kettle Derek gave me. She is giving herself to him for your freedom."

Blood drained from Derek's face, such was his shock at hearing the words, and for a second I thought he might try a verbal hex, but then he caught whatever it was he was about to say and his face relaxed.

"If I were you," Redcap said, "I'd toddle off before I change my mind. Get them all out of my sight. Not her," he said, indicating Patsy. "She's coming with me."

Patsy beamed, like she was the first pick for a netball team, and she looked at me expectantly. She raised her arm, and as she did so, a silvery band with a slightly green tint appeared in the air and circled her arm three times like a snake, covering the paler skin near the top of her arm. At the same time, a similar band wrapped itself around Redcap's wrist.

"By Erlking's teeth, what is this?" Redcap exclaimed. "Get it off me!"

"If you wish me to, then of course I shall," Patsy said. "But I would think carefully before you waste your first wish on something so trivial. The bands merely mark our agreement, each turn will fade as a wish is spent. When the band is gone, our association will be at an end. Do you still wish me to remove it?"

For the first time Redcap bent his head, humbled. "Um, no. I understand now." He toyed with the band on his wrist in wonder, and I could only imagine the dreams of power and untold wealth running through his head as he coveted it.

"What about them?" I looked at the pukwudgies who made no attempt to leave.

"Consider them insurance," Redcap said. "Until you're safely off the premises."

It was time to go.

The two pukwudgies led the way back through the bookcase doors. And although the wall of flame was down, Derek and Harrison were still constrained by their circle, and progressed awkwardly between the small creatures, bumping into each other and seeming to trip over their own feet.

Grumbling profanities I didn't quite catch, the small troop marched ahead, leaving me to follow with Liam.

As the last out, I looked back, nodding one final time to Patsy, and catching a final seething glare from Emily. *Had I done something to offend her?* And then the door closed behind me, and they were gone.

In silence, we trundled along a short passage to another set of stairs that led up to the Barbecue Baron.

My anxiety intensified the closer we got to freedom. I didn't know what these creatures were capable of, and I still didn't trust Redcap. That he was capable of untold trickery was a given, and I'd be a fool to let my guard down.

Liam's expression told me he was thinking along the same lines, that, and he still hadn't holstered his gun.

Two flights of stairs later and we had reached the main floor of the Barbecue Baron. I took a peek through some windows into the main dining area. It looked pretty upscale for a barbecue joint.

The restaurant was very dark, lit only by the ambient light of the full-service bar in the center of the room. I had thought the place empty, but then I heard the scrape of a table. On alert, I raised my wand as a shadowy figure approached. I noticed Puk and Wally merely slowed their pace.

Out of the shadows came perhaps the most handsome creature I had ever seen. Like Emily, he looked mostly human, but like her, the downward slant to his eyes betrayed his goblin heritage. He was dark, with a strong jaw and just enough stubble to be appealing but not scruffy. *Hello*, my ovaries thought.

He wore no obvious weapon, perhaps he was a manager, not muscle, and I wondered what he'd been doing there, sitting all alone in the dark. Right now, he was blocking our way forward.

"He's letting them go then?" he said, giving Derek and Harrison the once-over. His gaze lingered on Harrison for just a while longer. My partner just glared back in return.

"How is that any of your business?" Wally replied.

The man's incredible looks were marred by his look of amused disdain. I wanted him to give me that look. I wanted him to give me a lot of things.

"I guess that means you'll be tied to his books again. I bet you liked playing the gangster, if only for a little bit. It sucks to have such aspirations when you're no higher than an ottoman. Poor you. Poor Wally."

Wally gave him an ugly look.

"Back off, Jordan," Puk said. "Or you'll wake up one day with one of my stickers in your ankle."

Jordan sneered, but I noticed he didn't badmouth Puk as he had Wally. Instead, he stood to one side, and with a flourish of his arm, like he was giving us permission, he allowed us to proceed to the building's exit.

I noticed him checking me out as I passed him. He smelled oh so good, but since all I wanted to do was get the hell out of Dodge, I lowered my head and passed by him as quickly as I could. While wishing he'd call me back and kiss me passionately and invite me out for dinner sometime, was that really too much to ask for? Stupid hormones.

With a wave of his hand, Puk opened the exit leading directly onto the dock. I breathed in the night air, as much from relief as anything else. Our boat was right in front of us. Heck, they'd probably spotted us the second we'd docked. But it didn't matter now.

The two pukwudgies stood by the Genesis, pointing inside the boat. Some unseen force propelled Harrison and Derek into it, and the two landed in an untidy muddle on the deck. But now they were free of restraint.

Instinctively, the two looked back to where their captors were still on the dock, but the pukwudgies were now armed with bow and arrow, and had darts aimed at the two men.

"Hey, there's no need for that!" I tapped Liam's gun down which was aimed at Puk. "We just wanted our friends back."

"And there they are," Puk said, "Now skedaddle!"

"You guys need to find yourself a better class of boss," I complained, as Liam and I stepped into the boat to join Harrison and Derek. "Before you get yourself killed."

"Point taken. Now get off our dock."

With a purposeful grin, they retreated in unison to the open double doors, never breaking eye contact, and swinging their bows from Harrison and Derek to me and Liam just in case we planned to do anything crazy.

Only when they were safe back inside the Barbecue Baron did Puk lower his weapon, and with a click of his fingers, the double doors closed, and they were gone.

## Chapter Thirteen
# THE VOICEMAIL

AFTER GETTING OUT OF THE BOAT, HARRISON AND DEREK HAD BOTH taken off to shower and change, but since neither of them had anything to eat, I'd offered to buy everyone breakfast. Not out of the kindness of my heart, but because the '*official*' story had been lacking in pertinent detail, and I wanted to get the full Monty, off the record. We all agreed to meet at the local deli in an hour's time.

While Liam went downtown to file his report, I'd tried calling Mom, but given the hour she was probably sleeping, so I decided to let her rest. I ordered a cup of coffee and checked my email while I waited for the others to arrive.

An hour later and we were all lined up in a row at the cafe bar. Everyone was famished, but Derek and Harrison had practically ordered the entire menu. There were numerous plates of bacon and eggs, cinnamon buns, hash browns and pancakes scattered in front of us, not to mention juices, coffee, and a whole jug of iced water. For a while the two of them tucked in, saying nothing and chomping like there would be no tomorrow. I nibbled thoughtfully on a rasher of bacon, going over everything that had happened in the last few days.

"So, what did you tell them?" I asked Liam.

"Oh, not much more than we discussed. Once they heard the two missing men had turned up safe and unharmed, the rest was easy enough."

"So, it's over?"

"More or less. I was able to keep Redcap's name out of my report, so all you need to do, Derek, is put in an insurance claim and the matter will be considered officially closed, at least as far as downtown is concerned."

"And Redcap?" Derek asked "Who's gonna keep us safe from him?"

"He made a deal," I said. "He won't renege on it. The price would be too much even for Redcap to pay."

So, it was over. Apparently. *Yay!* Never mind that he had Patsy. I couldn't bear to think what he might be doing with the naïve, sweet-natured jinn.

Harrison was the first to down his fork, so I turned my attentions to him. "Seems I can't leave you alone for five minutes without you getting yourself into trouble."

"Yeah, well, what can you do?" Harrison said.

"So, how long after I left the store did this all happen?"

"Haven't we done this already?" Harrison downed a glass of OJ in a single draft, but then he sighed and stared at some spot on the wall behind the counter. "I dunno. Not long. The police had just left, and Derek and I were just chatting when the goblins came."

"Didn't you see them come in?" I asked.

"No. We had our backs to the door, and I just thought it was one of the officers returning for something."

"Then what?"

"Then nothing. There's nothing much to tell, really. I kind of remember half turning and then, *bam!*" Harrison mimed someone whacking him on the back of the head. "The next thing I recall is we're trapped inside this flame thing with no idea who put us there and no way to get out."

Our server leaned across the counter, refilling the coffee mugs, though Liam put a hand over his mug indicating he was done. Derek and Harrison picked theirs up eagerly, downing them faster than they should have, considering how hot they were. They clearly both had asbestos throats.

Derek buttered some toast and pulled the cover off a pat of jam. "I'm just surprised we're not dead," he said. "All the time we were in that fire thing I kept wondering why he was keeping us alive. I mean, I know *now*, but I didn't *then*. I had no idea what was in that damned kettle."

Harrison said nothing. It was strange. I knew my partner well, and I sensed he was brooding on something. But what though?

"I still don't understand why they took you both. I mean, *you* I get," I pointed to Derek. "They clearly thought you knew about Patsy, even if you didn't, but why *you*?" I said, looking up at Harrison. "Knocking you out I get. I'd have done it myself given half a chance, but why take you along for the ride? It doesn't make any sense."

Harrison downed the last of his coffee and sighed. "I dunno. You're asking me what was on their minds? How should I know? Derek and I have been trying to riddle this thing out ever since we were taken, and we're still none the wiser."

It sounded like a good lawyer's argument more than the truth. I knew in my blood there was more to it than that, but Harrison was too cagey to be tricked into saying something he didn't want to. But what could it be?

Then I remembered something. "Derek, you were expecting someone when we came into your shop. You're not telling me now that you had no clue something was going down?"

"Oh, come on, Dionne, isn't it obvious? This is Philly. I was being shaken down. You don't blab about that kind of thing, not even to your friends. I figured that was all this was about. I really hadn't a clue about the jinn. I swear to you, no matter what anyone may have told you. Or how Redcap could even have known about it."

Yeah, that had been bothering me, too.

Liam, who was sitting beside Derek, yawned and then stood up. "Look, I gotta go get some sleep."

He searched in his pockets for money, but I held a hand up. "I told you this was on me."

The shadows under his eyes were telling and I felt bad for him. And my questioning was getting us nowhere.

"Sure, dude, go get some sleep. I'll be in touch, okay?"

He slipped his jacket off the back of his seat, then nodded respectfully to the others, patting Harrison on the back. "Good to have you both back with us." And then he left.

Shortly after Liam left, I felt myself flagging. I popped my plastic down on the bar, beckoning for our server to settle the bill. It was late, and I wanted to get home to check on Mom.

Staring down at my phone, a voicemail alert flashed on my screen—from Finn. Why my phone hadn't bothered to ring was another mystery. It looked like I'd only just missed him. Hmm, if he was looking to cash in on another C from me, he could think again. If anything, I was surprised he hadn't already heard that Harrison and Derek were alive and had been released. Finn was typically sharper than that.

"Excuse me, guys, I have to take this. Back in a sec."

Not even Harrison knew who my informer was, and since his goblin ears were even sharper than mine, I didn't want to take any chances. While they finished their meal, I slid off my seat, and tapped my card before I left, just to remind Harrison it was there.

He nodded and I slipped outside and strolled a little along the street, ensuring I was out of range of even the acutest of ears. Then I listened to Finn's voicemail.

"Redcap is dead. He was found face-down in the Delaware a few minutes ago. From the blood all round his head it don't look like no suicide. So much blood it was. The police are on their way, and we be going into lockdown. Your 'friends' might wanna skip town. Don't call me. Like, really bad timing, could be dangerous for me."

The message ended.

Redcap was dead? But we'd just seen him. I was not going to play hypocrite and mourn his passing but hot damn. Someone hadn't wasted any time sending him to the Hereafter.

Harrison gleaned something had happened from the look on my face and turned anxiously on his stool to hear what it was.

"I got good news and bad news," I said. "Redcap swims with the fishes. Someone put a sizzler in the back of his head from the sound of things."

"What's the bad news?" Harrison asked, shoveling the last of a syrup-laden pancake into his mouth.

"Good," said Derek. "Looks like someone beat me to the punch."

"Don't say that," I said.

"Why?" Derek asked.

"Because you're a potential suspect, idiot! And my informant suggests you both get out of town and lay low for a bit."

Harrison laughed. "You're not telling me they think *we* did it?" The laughter faded from his face when he realized I wasn't kidding around. "Come on, Dionne, we've been with you since we left him. They're not gonna pin this one on us, that's absurd. We haven't had any time."

It sucked having to play Devil's advocate, but there was no point not telling it like it was. "Sure you did. You were both gone for an hour to wash and change. I don't know exactly when Redcap was killed but if it was while you were gone, you could have done it. In fact, I don't know for sure that you didn't do it."

"You really think that?" Harrison asked, incredulity written all over his face.

"Of course, I don't," I lied. "But they will argue that. Come on, Harrison, you know how the system works. You had motive and opportunity. The cops are gonna be all over you like sunscreen."

"So, what do you suggest we do?" Derek asked. I could tell he was mad, heck, who wouldn't be? They'd just been subjected to a terrible ordeal, and now this. "I live at the shop, and it's been blown to smithereens!"

"Just hang tight for a bit. I'll go on down to The Rotting Corpse and see what I can find out."

Dang, why did Liam always leave just when I needed him? I started typing into my phone. REDCAP DEAD, CALL ME WHEN YOU'RE AWAKE.

"So, you want us to make a run for it?" Harrison asked.

"No, no I don't." I shook my head vehemently. "Then you'll look guilty for sure. Right now, no one knows it was Redcap who kidnapped you both, although word will be out soon enough. Someone at The Corpse will blab, I'm sure. Just, don't be too accessible for a bit, ya know? Lay low. Stay off the radar. In fact, why don't you stay at my place? No one will expect to find you there, and if nothing else, Mom will keep you supplied with coffee and donuts, if you don't mind her talking your ears off."

"You sure you or your mom won't mind?" Harrison asked.

"Nah. She'll probably love it. Look, give me a chance to find out what happened, and we can go from there. Right now, neither of you are officially suspects of anything, so you're free to do whatever you please. But that could change in a heartbeat, so, let's settle up and get the hell out of here before the cops come looking for you."

Harrison picked up the receipt and handed it to me to sign. I signed it off with a flourish and left a ten dollar note on the counter for the tip.

With heavy sighs, Derek and Harrison rose from the bar, and though they looked better for having eaten a hearty meal, they both sounded tired and hounded. I owed it to them both to clear this up quick.

"I'm gonna try and reach Liam again," I said, the moment we were back out on the street. "I'll need him if we're gonna to find out anything fast."

The Philly police knew me well enough, but they would close ranks in a murder case, and, without Liam, I'd be lucky to get anywhere near the pub, let alone the crime scene.

"Sounds good," Harrison said. "Bloody goblin. If it turns out he's not dead, then I'm gonna kill him for sure."

I couldn't say I blamed him. I slipped my card back into my purse, and checking I had everything, took my leave, and walked flat out over to my parked car. I was tired and cranky. And Liam was about to bite my head off. What joy was mine?

## Chapter Fourteen
# NUTS

I WAS RIGHT. THE POLICE HAD CORDONED OFF THE PERIMETER OF The Rotting Corpse and the place hummed with squad cars and media crews. Liam pulled up behind a bright green ParaTV truck. He hadn't said a whole lot on the way down, and the dark rings forming under his eyes made me feel guilty as hell.

"You want me to fix you something?" I asked. "I can conjure up a lovely little *wakey, wakey eggs and bakey* spell if it'll help you shake it off?"

Liam shook his head as he put the car into park. "I'm fine. It's not like I haven't done this before."

The truth was, as much as Liam loved to see me perform magic, he never wanted my wand turned on him. Deep down I supposed he was a teensy bit afraid of it, even the good stuff. Oh well, what could you do? He wasn't the first normie to be wary of all the hocus pocus, and he sure wouldn't be the last.

Liam sighed as he stared at the Black Ford SUV parked on the other side of the road.

"Anyone you know?" I asked.

Liam's fingers tapped thoughtfully on the steering wheel. "That's the captain's car. I was just wondering what the heck I'm gonna tell him if he hears about last night."

"You mean, breaking into Redcap's place?" I asked.

"Yeah."

"I've been thinking about that myself," I said. "Maybe you should just come out and say it?"

Liam shook his head. "I'd be off the case in a heartbeat. Heck, you and I would go straight to the top of the suspect list if I said anything. No, it's better no one hears about it, trust me."

"If you say so. But what if one of Redcap's people blab?"

"We'll deal with that when it comes to it."

Hmm. Tricky. Suddenly I was nervous. What if Liam lost his job over last night's shenanigans? Lord, I'd never be able to forgive myself. After all, it had been my fault he was there in the first place. If it came to it, I'd find a way to take the bullet for him. I just prayed I wouldn't have to.

"So, who do you fancy for it?" I asked, changing the subject.

Liam rubbed his eyes and stifled a yawn. "The murder? Heck, it could be anyone. I'd have done it myself after what they did to Harrison and Derek. But there's a lot of people out there who hated his guts. Redcap was no Mother Theresa."

"Ain't that the truth," I agreed.

"Who do you think it was?"

"Me?" I thought about it for a second. "I fancy Emily for it. She looks the type."

Liam laughed. "You always think it's the woman. Come on, let's get this over with."

To get over to the Pub we had to fight our way past frantic reporters, who were pouncing on anyone who arrived on the scene, desperate for any news. I grimaced and pitied any poor journalist who might try for Liam as a source. Not in his current mood.

Sure enough, just as his foot hit the tarmac, a waif-like elf with ginger hair tied up in a messy-do and more attitude than common sense stuck a microphone in Liam's face. She wore a ridiculously tight, low-cut green dress and stylish white leather jacket that was at odds with her sensible, clog-like shoes. I figured she must be freezing, dressed like that, with no gloves or scarf to protect her from the elements. At any other time, she'd have been just Liam's type, but this just wasn't going to be her day.

"Detective Wells! Can you tell us anything about what's happening?"

she said, walking quickly to keep up with him. "We're hearing rumors that Redcap, allegedly Philadelphia's most notorious crime boss, has been gunned down in a brutal murder. Can you confirm whether or not what we're hearing is true? The public needs to know! Is Philly at war? Will there be repercussions?"

Liam continued at a brisk pace, his eyes on the ground as he deliberately avoided the provocative cleavage thrust at him. If she'd have known him one little bit, she'd have given him a wide berth but no, this one was a pit bull and determined to get what she wanted.

"Can you tell us anything about the victim's family? Did he have one? Who will mourn the passing of the goblin some have called the most vicious mob boss of all time? Did he have a dog? Or a puppy, maybe? Come on Detective Wells, give me something!" When the woman finally paused to take a breath, he rounded on her.

"Will you get out of my face, Caroline, I've got a job to do!"

"So have I. Come on," Caroline said, trying pouty helpless since sexy determined wasn't getting her what she wanted. "I could use a break. Help me out here, please."

Liam wasn't taken in. "No comment, Caroline. You know I can't talk about an ongoing investigation."

The determined elf was not to be put off, and she ran a few steps ahead of Liam. "But don't you think the public has a right to know? I mean, if the Mob King is dead, who will replace him? Are we looking at grand scale mayhem? Will there be war on the streets, will innocent people be able to risk leaving their homes?"

Liam paused and pushed her mic out of his face.

"Didn't you hear what I just said? Anyway, we just got here, and I know as much as you do. Now if you don't mind." He straight-armed Caroline and we were rescued by a uniformed cop who pushed her back into the crowd.

"Aww, gimme a break!" the angry elf cried.

The cop was about to do the same to me when Liam touched his arm.

"It's okay, Murphy, she's with me."

Murphy nodded and allowed me to pass.

"HEY, HOW COME SHE GETS THROUGH BUT I DON'T?" Caroline squealed behind us.

I recognized some of Liam's colleagues standing on the deck outside the main entrance. Liam made a beeline for them and I stayed close, not risking being kicked off the site.

"So, what's going down?" Liam said, helping himself to one of the coffees one of the juniors was passing around. "We got a witness?"

"Sure." I recognized First Base as one of the officers who had been at our office after the goblins broke into it. I caught *the look* as Liam and I approached together but was too preoccupied to set him straight on that. Geez, did these guys ever have anything else on their minds? "Got a... *I dunno what-you-call it* back there, who says he saw it all. Short fella. Hair all down his back, goes by the name of Puk."

"He's a pukwudgie," I said. And just as likely as anyone to want to see Redcap dead, I thought.

"What the h—!" Murphy, who had come over to join us, caught himself just in time. "Sorry, Ma'am. I mean what on earth's a pukwudgie?"

I smiled inwardly, not wanting to share that I had to look them up myself.

"They're wood creatures—you don't see too many of them in town. They're sorta related to goblins, way back in the day. These guys seem especially short, but don't let that fool you. You'd better watch out for those darts hanging off their belts, they're lethal."

"Huh. Good to know."

"Was Puk alone when he found him? Redcap?"

First Base sneered, like he didn't want to deal with someone not police, but one look from Liam set him straight on that.

"He says he was buying tacos from a truck when he saw Redcap." He pointed over to a silver and green Haunted Habanero truck parked a little further down the river. "The driver," he paused to check his notes, "Juanita, confirms she had to get out of the truck to hand him his food," First Base snickered, "and they both spotted him at the same time."

"Where did they find him?" I asked.

"Over there." First Base pointed to the side of the building just beyond the truck still parked right by the water's edge. I could smell the onions from here.

"Where are all the other potential witnesses?" Liam asked.

First Base jerked his thumb over his shoulder to the Pub. "Captain says no one leaves until he gives the okay."

"No worries, we'll find 'em."

Liam edged past his men and since he had a coffee in one hand, I opened the door for him.

As soon as we were inside, I spotted a bunch of people over by the bar. There was a dark and silver-haired, chubby woman, banging her fists on the table.

"Look, if you keep me here much longer, all my dinners will be ruined! Who is gonna pay, huh? You?" Then she mumbled something in Spanish even I would blush to repeat. I guessed that was Juanita.

Other customers were sitting around, frustrated and clearly desperate to leave. A junior officer was busy taking statements, and by the way he kept scratching his head I guessed he was having a pretty rum time of it.

Emily was sitting at a table by the window, a laptop open in front of her. She glanced over in our direction as we came in, but she said nothing. Jordan (*be still my beating heart*) sat beside her, looking unruffled as he drank a large cappuccino.

I spotted Puk standing on a stool, leaning over the bar, reaching for something. He straightened up and starting nibbling at it. I tapped Liam's arm and together we headed that way first. I could smell the distinct aroma of peanuts as we got closer.

His eyes narrowed when he saw us approach and his free hand subconsciously or otherwise caressed the feather on one of his darts. I knew he wouldn't dare attack either Liam or me in front of witnesses, but he must have been thinking of our last encounter, and he looked ready for anything. My hand sought the outline of the wand in my pocket in response.

"You string that dart to your bow, then you and I are going to have a serious falling out, my friend," I said.

"What do you want?" Puk said, turning on his seat. I thought he might climb up onto the bar so he could look Liam in the face, but he stood his ground and eyeballed him from the stool. "Ain't you got some little old lady you need to help across the street?"

Liam pulled a notebook from the back pocket of his pants. "Just a few questions," he said. "I heard you were the one who found him."

"Yeah, that was me all right. Me and Juanita over there. What of it?"

"Don't be a wise-ass," Liam said.

I could see the two men weren't exactly hitting it off. The little creature exuded a ton of testosterone for something so tiny. Time to try a different tact.

"We were wondering how you found him?"

The contempt never left Puk's eyes, but he turned to me and tossed in another handful of nuts. He took his time to chew them, then his expression changed, and I knew he'd decided to talk to me.

"He was face down in the water, but I knew it was him, all right. His cap for one thing. And I recognized his clothes."

"Where exactly was he—in the water I mean? How far was he from where you and Juanita were standing?"

Puk shrugged. "Just a few feet, I guess. He'd got all caught up on a pier support. Good thing really, or he'd have drifted downstream, and we might have missed him. I don't think he'd been in the drink too long."

"Why do you think that?"

"The blood was still oozing from his head. Any longer and it would've all bled out into the Delaware."

"You're a forensic expert now?" Liam asked. I nudged him in the ribs.

Puk snarled at him. "I've seen a few go in my time. I know how it works. It was a fresh kill, I tell ya. A minute or two, tops."

"Did you hear a gunshot?"

"Nope, nothing. Not a darn thing."

"What did you do then? Did you try and pull him out?"

Puk smiled at that. "Look at me, lady." He pointed his finger up and down the length of his body. "I'm two feet bloody tall. You really think I'm gonna be able to pull a waterlogged goblin out of the river?"

"What about Juanita? Did she try?" I asked.

Puk laughed a high, reedy laugh that made my skin crawl. "Juanita was too busy screaming her busty chops off to be much use to anyone. After she'd done running around the tarmac like a lunatic, she finally pulled herself together and called it in."

"What did you do then?"

Puk stared at me like I had two heads. "What did I do? What do you think I did? I hung around and waited for your lot to show up. If I'd have legged it, you'd have found a way to pin this on me, I know how this works. Shoot. I never did get that damn taco. Now if you'll excuse me."

"Any idea who would want to kill him?" I asked.

"Witch, take a number. You be better off asking who didn't want him dead. As for me, I kinda liked him. He kept me and my brother, busy, ya know?"

"Talking of your brother, do you know where he was while you were down at the truck?"

"How should I know? I'm not my brother's keeper. He was probably cooped up in Redcap's office someplace, counting beans as usual. You'll have to ask him."

Puk shoved another handful of nuts into his mouth and stared at me thoughtfully for a moment. "Listen to me. Don't try too hard to find his killer. I wouldn't mind a stab at him myself, *capiche*? Now get lost, 'cos I gotta find me a new sponsor."

"Wow, you're a real bleeding heart," Liam said.

"So, sue me. Now scoot, or maybe I'll tell your boss what you and your lady friend were up to late last night..." He cast a nasty glance over to the exit, where Captain York, a bald man with a straight back, had just come into the pub and was talking to one of the uniforms. "From where I'm standing it looks as if *you* might have had something to do with Redcap's happy little accident. So, nuts to you both." Puk plopped down on his stool, and swung round to face the bar, signaling the interview was over.

Liam and I exchanged glances. I doubted there was much more we'd get out of him for now. And we had a load more people to question.

Liam snapped his book shut, and in a show of intimidation, leaned right across Puk to deposit his finished coffee cup on the bar. "Don't leave town without letting me know."

"Yeah, yeah, don't call *me*. I'll call *you*," Puk said.

## Chapter Fifteen
## BEEF EMPANADAS

"What now? Didn't I just tell that idiot over there everything I know?" Juanita motioned to the poor uniform, who was currently sitting with Emily and, from the looks of him, he was getting nowhere fast. Jordan was no longer with her and had settled at another table closer to the exit. "Look, I wanna see whoever's in charge. Who's the big boss here? I'm not talking to anyone else; I've got a business to run!"

Juanita stood alone in the corner of the bar, a set of strong, strangler's hands on her girthy hips while she tapped her foot impatiently on the floor. I sure as hell didn't fancy tackling her but tackle her we must.

"We just have a few questions," Liam said, notebook at the ready.

Juanita didn't even look at him. "And I have answered all the questions I plan to, so if you'll excuse me."

She was just about to brush Liam aside when I stepped in. "If you like, we can have a quick word with the captain for you. If he has everything he needs, he might let you go."

Juanita stopped in her tracks and seemed to notice me for the first time. "You would do that?"

"Sure." I glanced up at Liam and he nodded. "There are just one or two things I need to clarify, first."

"Yeah, like what?" Juanita's foot looked set to start tapping again.

"Exactly how long was Puk with you before you discovered the body?"

Juanita's gaze shifted to the right while she thought. "I dunno, three minutes, maybe four, something like that. I cook all my stuff fresh; you know—only the best for my customers." She said this so loud a few people seated near us glanced in our direction.

"And you could see him the whole time? Puk? While you were still inside your truck" I asked.

"See him? No, Hear him? Sure. Puk's a big talker. I was busy at my grill, and he's only a little guy, but he's a regular and he likes to chat with me."

"What did he chat about?"

"Oh, you know, this and that. His kid brother Wally, mostly. They're very tight, those two. I don't see the brother at my truck much. Redcap kept him pretty busy and Puk typically ordered for them both."

"Busy doing what?" I asked.

"How should I know? I sell burritos."

"Did Redcap like your burritos?"

Juanita laughed. "Are you kidding? The only time he ever came out of The Corpse was to shoo me off. He didn't like my truck parked here and threatened to get me towed."

"When was that?" Liam asked.

"Oh, I dunno, a few months back. Check your files, it'll be in there. I got a permit, anyway, so there was nothing he could do. My food is as good as his, better if you ask my opinion, and I don't charge the earth to eat there." Her voice raised again, and I sensed the curiosity behind me. "Can I go now?"

I had to ask myself, how would a gangster like Redcap not arrange for Juanita's truck to mysteriously end up in the river, with or without her still aboard? Was she protected? Liam's pen paused as he took notes, and I imagined he was thinking the same thing.

"Last question, I promise," I said. "Puk told us he never heard any shots. Did you?"

"Nah. Not a thing. But I had the radio on so it's hard to hear anything going on outside. So, is that it?"

After jotting this down, Liam closed his notebook. "Wait here, I'll go and see if the captain will let you go."

"Good," Juanita said, pulling her shoulder bag up over her shoulder. "Those tacos won't cook themselves you know."

Liam disappeared for a moment, and I smiled. "You think I should try one of your tacos, then?"

Juanita grinned. "Absolutely. Though Emily says my beef empanadas are the best in the business. I told her it's all in the quantity of raisins."

I glanced across to Emily who was now sitting all by herself again. Somehow, I couldn't quite picture the snooty half-goblin ordering lunch from a food truck. She came over as more the five-star dining type. Wonders never ceased.

"Was she a regular, too?"

"*Sure.* Emily knows a good thing when she sees it." Juanita stood a little taller. "We're related you know, on her mother's side. Of course, there's no goblin blood on my side of the family—excuse me, I meant no offense—"

"None taken."

"But we're all very proud of how well she was doing. She has a good eye for business."

I raised an eyebrow at this. Emily was the hostess in a dubious mob-run restaurant. She wasn't exactly dancing with the stars, but then everyone's perspective was different.

"I guess a lot of people like to come to your truck to talk?"

"A fair few."

"What did Emily like to talk about?"

"Oh, just the food, mostly." Juanita eyed me suspiciously. "She never talked shop, if that's what you're getting at. She was far too smart a cookie for that, and frankly...." She lowered her voice for the first time. "...I wouldn't really want her to, know what I mean? We all knew what Redcap was. A loose tongue could get you killed. No, I took the wise monkey line. See all, hear all, say nothing, that's me."

"You hear anything else that might be able to help us?"

Juanita shook her head. I suspected she wouldn't tell me if she did, after what she just said.

Over by the door I watched Liam's captain share a few last words with him, and then he came back to join us, armed with a fresh cup of coffee.

"The captain says it's okay for you to go," he said. "We have your number and if anyone has any more questions they'll be in touch."

"At last," Juanita said loudly, drawing more attention to herself as she puffed out her chest.

"Keep it down," Liam said, motioning to the people seated at the tables around us. "There are still a few people we haven't gotten to yet. They'll all want to go."

"Whatever you say, detective. Just get me out of here so I can go make a living."

Liam nodded and stood to one side, allowing her to pass.

"Learn anything new?" he asked as soon as she was out of earshot.

"Only that she's distantly related to Emily who has a thing for beef empanadas." I sighed. "You?"

"Yeah. I talked to the captain and went over what they've got so far. I've gotta say, it ain't much."

"Not like that's a surprise," I said. "Redcap might be dead, but no one likes a talking idiot. These people have long memories."

"Don't they just?" he agreed.

"Who do you want to tackle next?" I asked.

Liam looked around him as he took a quick swig of coffee. Emily was busy typing something into her laptop.

"Groan," I said, but it had to be done.

"After you." Liam gestured for me to lead the way, but this time I could have stuffed his gallantry where the sun didn't shine.

"You're too kind," I said, sarcastically.

"Hey, what about us? We've got lives too, ya know?" A tall, athletic looking elf in a business suit jumped up from his table and barred our path. Like the others, he'd watched Juanita go and I supposed he was hoping for the same treatment.

"Sorry, pal, cool your jets," Liam said, ushering him back a pace. "We'll get to you all as soon as we can."

I noticed Jordan had moved to the elf's table, and the cool half-goblin stared at me in an almost amused fashion, as if weighing up how I was dealing with this. I pretended not to notice, while making sure he got my best side.

The angry elf stared hard at his watch but then slumped back down in his seat, allowing us to pass. This was turning out to be one heck of a morning. And it hadn't even begun yet.

## *Chapter Sixteen*
## EMILY

EVEN THOUGH EMILY'S ATTENTION APPEARED ABSORBED AS SHE TYPED something into her laptop, she closed the lid as Liam and I approached the table. She did not get up, but instead sat back in her chair, examining us from beneath hooded eyes.

"Please don't tell me they've sent *you* to interrogate *me*," Emily said. She laced her fingers together and lowered them to the lid of the laptop. The bruise on the back of her hand was yellowing at the corners. "How funny is that?"

"You think so?" I said, keeping my tone even in case she thought she was getting under my skin.

Her gaze flitted over to the captain who was just out of earshot, talking with First Base. "Your friends are well, are they? Settling down now they're back at home with their loved ones? How nice for them."

"That's really none of your business, now, is it?" Liam said.

Emily arched her eyebrows and turned from us to look out of the window. Outside, new people were gathering and talking to the cops in the parking lot. "Look. How long is this going to take? We've got staff arriving who don't know what to do and we're supposed to open in a couple of hours. Life goes on, you know?"

"Then let's get on with it and you'll be out of here all the faster," Liam said. "I don't have many questions for you. You told the officer that you were working in the kitchens earlier this morning."

"Yeah. What of it? You can ask any of the kitchen staff and they'll tell you I was there all the time. Go ask them."

*They'll tell us whatever you told them to say,* I thought.

"I will," Liam said. "Were you still there when the body was found?"

"All the way up to when we heard the sirens. Is that it?"

"For now," Liam said.

He closed his notebook, ready to move onto the next witness, but a thought occurred to me.

"What were you doing in the kitchen? I thought you were the hostess. Isn't that a little lowbrow for a woman of your um, standing?"

I wouldn't say she leered at me, since she only had one expression where I was concerned, and that was dripping disdain. But her gaze intensified a little.

"We're short staffed. I always muck in if they need me. Once we're open, I stay in the restaurant, but when we're closed, I do whatever I have to. Working in the kitchen—answering emails—overseeing the accounts." She tapped the top of her laptop. "Happy now?"

"Almost," I said. "There is just one other thing."

"And what's that?"

"What exactly was your relationship with the deceased? What other extra curricular activity were you up to when the restaurant was closed? Or even when it was open?"

"Now wait a minute!"

It was kind of fun to see Emily's blood boil like that. At least it proved there was a beating heart buried somewhere under that cold exterior.

"My relationship with Redcap was strictly professional. How dare you suggest otherwise."

"Even when he beat you?" I looked down at the yellowing bruise on the back of her hand.

Emily self-consciously covered her bruise and glared up at me. "That was an accident. In the kitchen. Redcap never touched me."

"So how did it happen?" I asked. "That's an odd accident for the kitchen, isn't it? Cuts and burns I get, but how did you manage that little beauty?"

"I forget," Emily said dryly. "Accidents happen all the time here. We're very busy."

"Do they?" I responded.

"Did you report it in the accident book?" Liam asked.

Emily looked at him with something akin to amusement. "Now really. Do you honestly think I have time to record every little thing that happens? Of course, I didn't. I don't even remember banging it, so why would I take the trouble to write it down?"

"But you do encourage your employees to follow the rules?" he asked.

"Absolutely. One hundred percent of the time. I even oversee the First Aid cabinet in the kitchen and handle all the accidents and work comp claims myself."

"Aww, you're a regular Florence Nightingale," I said.

"Why are you asking me questions anyway? You're not a cop." She looked at Liam. "Are you really so desperate?"

"Thank you, Miss Applegate," Liam said, jumping in before this could escalate. "That will be all, for now."

"What about Patsy, where is she? Do you know what happened to her?"

Liam paused long enough to let her answer.

"I have no idea. Sorry."

Not sorry, more like.

"Okay, that's enough," Liam said.

I wanted to think up a thousand more questions just to keep her there and get under her skin, but Liam was right, we were done for now. Emily picked up her laptop, eyeballing me hard as she brushed past me.

"You two are so much in love you could be sisters," Liam said, watching her with interest as she stomped off.

"Funny guy. She's been giving me dirty looks since the moment we met, and she's hiding something. You should have asked her who she's working for now Redcap's dead, but all she's worried about is his restaurant opening on schedule."

I thought about Finn. I really wanted to talk to him, but not here. Even under the illusion I was working with the police, it would be too dangerous to confront him. But I had so many questions he might have answers for. If we were lucky, the uniformed policeman had already interviewed him, which meant Liam wouldn't have to. But still, I wanted to.

I looked around, thinking I hadn't seen him since we got here. But then he was kitchen staff. From what I could tell all of those were waiting in the back, not allowed to leave but at least working.

"You wanna talk to this Jordan guy? Or leave him for now and go talk to the kitchen staff?"

"No need," Liam said, consulting his notes. "All the kitchen staff were interviewed first. Let's do Jordan, then we'll finish up here and call it a wrap."

I looked around the room, growing anxious. "Where the hell is Patsy? And Wally for that matter? I haven't seen either of them since we got here. Have you?"

"Maybe they weren't here when it happened. Some people like to sleep regular hours, if you know what I mean."

"Wally, perhaps, but what about Patsy? Do the jinn even sleep? When we're done here, let's checkout Redcap's underground library place in case she's caged up or something."

"We can do that," Liam said. "Have you tried calling your mom? Maybe Redcap's death released her, and she returned to the comfort of her cozy kettle."

"Hmm. And maybe she saw who killed him."

"Or she killed him herself," Liam said, half snorting.

It was meant to be funny, but I wasn't laughing. Instead, I pulled out my phone and wandered over to a window where I could talk in private and get a reasonable signal.

The phone rang a few times at the other end, and then Mom answered.

"Hey, Mom, it's me. Umm, I don't suppose Patsy's there, is she?"

"Hey Dee-Dee! Why yes, she is! We're just having a little natter over a cup of tea. Did you want to speak to her?"

"Yes, please. Put her on, will you?"

There was a slight rustling sound, and I heard Mom say, "That's okay, dear, I'll make you another cup while you talk to Dee-Dee."

"Hello, *Dee-Dee*," Patsy said with emphasis. "How are you, sweetie?"

"Great. I'm down at The Rotting Corpse investigating Redcap's murder. Remember Redcap? Your new, err, Master?" *What would she call him?* "Is there anything you think you should tell me? Maybe?"

"No, not really," Patsy said, as sweetly as if she were counting kittens.

"Ooh, do you have any more of those biscuits for me to dunk? Thank you! Err, no, the second he passed into the beyond the band on my arm turned to smoke and I knew he was a goner. So, I zipped back here, watched a movie with everyone, and now I'm having a nice cup of tea and a natter while the boys take a nap."

Only someone as sweet as Patsy would consider Harrison and Derek—*the boys!* "And that's everything? You didn't happen to see what or who shot him, or go and check on him to see what was going on?"

"Nope? Why would I? It's not like I cared about him or anything. I'm a jinn, not his girlfriend. Alas, I know nothing about it, and wouldn't help you if I could. You've got this, Dionne, trust me. You don't need jinn or magic to solve this. You're wonderful. Shall I put your mother back on? The darling just made me a fresh cup of tea. I do love being pampered. This is so much nicer than being cooped up in that old kettle. How is your day going?"

Bewildered, I shook my head. "No. Tell Mom I'll be home late and to maybe get in some groceries. I imagine we're pretty low on everything in the fridge."

"I will. Have fun. See you later."

The line went dead. I glanced over to Liam who was talking to the angry elf. I guessed he'd probably blocked his path again the second my back was turned. Now probably wasn't a good time to interrupt him, and I needed a moment to gather my thoughts.

Really, what was the point of having a jinn for a buddy if she couldn't help you solve mysteries or do anything amazing? I pictured her, Mom, Derek, and Harrison, all with their feet up in front of the T.V. watching *Days of our Lives* with a plate of sandwiches, mugs of cocoa, and a box of Kleenex.

That was three suspects right there, sitting in my house, eating me out of house and home while I was down here, surrounded by the scum of Philadelphia, eating hatred pie. This was getting beyond a joke.

"Having fun?"

I almost jumped out of my skin because I'd been so wrapped up in my own thoughts. Jordan stood behind me, his smoldering hotness dangerously close to throwing me off my game. I reeled in the hormones and found myself wishing I was wearing lipstick.

I slipped my phone into my pocket. "Working, as always. What can I do for you, Jordan?"

He smiled, a dangerous, conspiratorial smile that put me on my guard. "You remember my name? Good, Dionne. As you can see, I've already learned yours." There was a hint of sauciness lined with threat. He was trying to wrong-foot me, and I knew it.

"Before you even open that pretty mouth of yours, you should know that I'm a truthsayer. If you lie, I will know." I hope he didn't realize I was the one who was lying. But it was worth a shot.

Jordan's smile didn't falter. "So charming."

"You know, I can't quite figure out how you fit in here," I said. "So why don't you do me a favor and fill me in?"

I suspected Jordan must have been used to ladies fluttering their eyelashes when he honored them with his attentions, because my directness made him pause, and he appeared to be searching for a new line of attack.

"I—ah—I'm Redcap's IT and systems guru. And I run the security around here," he said.

I raised an eyebrow. "I'd be careful about putting that on my resume if I were you."

Jordan had the grace to blush and began examining the cuticles on his left hand. "I confess, I was a little off my game on this one. I suppose everyone has a bad day from time to time."

"That's the understatement of the century, isn't it?" I looked beyond him to where Liam was still busy talking to the elf. He might have preferred me to wait for him, but I saw no reason not to put forward a few questions of my own. "So where were you when your boss took a couple of slugs to the head?"

"Gunshot wounds have been confirmed then?" he said, his eyes narrowing.

It was my turn to be wrong-footed. "Do you have any reason to suspect they won't be?"

"I never heard a shot. Whatever ideas you might have in your head, we don't hear a lot of gunshots down here, so when we do, people tend to notice. Nobody I've spoken to heard anything. Anyone confirm it to you?"

"I'm afraid I couldn't say."

"I'll take that as a no, then," he half-snorted.

"You have a theory of your own?" I asked.

"Me? No. Whoever it was knew our routine, though."

"What makes you say that?"

Jordan slid into a seat and beckoned for me to do the same. "Every Friday, first thing, I meet the armored car that comes to collect the takings. It's really the only time I'm not watching the restaurant, or the bar—"

"Or Redcap?"

"Indeed."

This was helpful. These guys would keep accurate times of pickup and delivery, and we'd be able to pinpoint the exact time Jordan spoke to them, and if he was telling the truth, maybe even the time of the murder.

"We'll need the name of the armored truck company and the driver to corroborate what time you were with them."

"Easy enough. I have their number in my phone some place. I'll text you their contact information." He pulled a Galaxy from his pocket.

I wasn't about to give him my number. "Just give me the info and I'll look them up."

He grinned. "Whatever you like."

"How long have you worked here?" I asked as he checked his contacts.

His cocky grin lit up his face and he looked at me with amusement. He knew something I didn't, and I could tell he was enjoying the sensation. "Worked here? Oh, you've got it wrong. I don't work here, not in the way you're thinking. I'm a managing director."

I looked at him sideways, a little confused. "Say what?"

He smiled and sat back confidently in his seat. "Redcap and I were partners. Didn't you know? He was my brother."

## Chapter Seventeen
# COFFEE AND SANDWICHES

"Your brother? Really?"

"Half-brother actually. Different dads. *Mine* was a human" Jordan said with sneering emphasis. I wondered what he had against humans. "It wasn't common knowledge."

Filial love at its finest, I thought. Did any of these people have a beating heart?

"I see his death hit you hard," I said, with more than a hint of sarcasm. Jordan's expression didn't alter. "So does that make you the sole owner of all this?" I swirled my finger in a quick circle. "The King is dead, long live the King, is that it?"

A hint of a smile crept over his face, and his forefinger began to tap the table, lightly. Good to know he had a tell, smug smoothie, I thought.

"You'll be wanting to know all the principals, won't you?" he said, inspecting his nails. Had I really thought this guy was hot? My opinion was changing by the second. "After all, we're all going to be high up there on your suspect list, aren't we? You're all dying to find murder suspect number one, and each one of us is going to do very nicely out of his death." He sighed, as if this entire investigation was boring him.

"Are you talking yourself into the electric chair?" I asked.

His smile faltered, and leaning forward, he looked at me like something he might examine on the bottom of his shoe. "Miss Cruz—perhaps that might be the case—if I were guilty. But I assure you, I am not."

"Well then, I suppose I'd better just cross you off my list," I said.

"Sooner or later, you will. Now, I've been extremely patient with your questions." He looked over to where Liam had finally extricated himself from the angry elf. "So, I suggest we wrap up with your boyfriend, and bring this fiasco to an end. My brother is dead, and whether you like it or not, I have family business to attend to."

"Liam isn't my boyfriend."

"Sure looked like it last night. You know he wants you, right? You can see it in his eyes. The hunger."

I was about to retaliate when Liam appeared at my shoulder. "I'm sorry to keep you waiting."

"Not at all," Jordan said, his plastic smile sliding easily back into place. "We were just killing time, weren't we, Miss Cruz?"

"I was just consoling Jordan here over the death of his brother."

"His brother?"

"That's right," I said. "As you can see, he's racked with grief. It makes a fascinating tale. Trust me, you'll need a hanky before he's done."

Jordan looked more amused than annoyed by my revelation. I guess he thought he'd rattled my cage, but it was deeper than that. Half-goblins had a bad rep at the best of times and his cavalier attitude did nothing to dispel it. And that ticked me off.

Liam sat down across from Jordan. He was holding up well, considering he hadn't slept in forever, though I noticed he was clinging to yet another cup of coffee for dear life.

"Good grief, do you really expect me to go over this again? Can't you people coordinate your interviews? Stop wasting my time—everybody's time!"

"I'm sorry, sir, it won't take long."

Jordan slouched back in his chair, resigned to the inevitable, and while he brought Liam up to speed, I got up and wandered over to Murphy who was propped up against the bar, sweet-talking a pretty elven waitress who had made some fresh cups.

"Can I have one of those?" I asked.

"Sure," the elf said, putting a white mug down in front of me. She had pale green eyes, fair, almost transparent hair, and a classic elven waif-like figure. She also had an easy, kind smile, which looked completely out of place in this joint. "Cream and sugar?"

"A little cream please. No sugar."

My mind emptied as I watched the cream swirl into the coffee. I had to admit, I was pretty tired myself and was picturing my comforter back home and how wonderful it would be to slide into it right now.

"Thanks," I said, when she was done pouring. I touched the mug but sensing it to be too warm to drink just yet, left it on the counter. "I'm looking for Wally. Any idea where I might find him?"

Her smile faltered a little. "No, sorry. Hold on, I'll be back in a sec." She disappeared for just a minute, then returned with a tray laden full of ham and turkey sandwiches which she set down on the bar just beside me. "Jordan thought your men might be hungry," she said to Murphy who was still standing right beside me. She motioned over to where Jordan and Liam were still talking. I had to admit, I was surprised by his thoughtfulness, but then my meaner, inner goblin, figured he was probably trying to butter everyone up.

"Cool," said Murphy, helping himself to a turkey sandwich. "I'll tell everyone." He took a bite and his eyes widened. "Holy moly, this is the best sandwich I ever tasted. Marry me."

"I don't think Wally's here," said the elf, ignoring Murphy as he took off, chomping away. "He wasn't here when I came in this morning. Want me to ask someone? Did you ask his brother, Puk? If anyone knows, he will."

I looked around for Puk, but he had disappeared some place. The odds of him talking to me again were slim, and I certainly didn't want to risk him complaining to the captain. "Thanks."

"Puk? Captain York let him leave," Murphy said, who had just returned to the bar and was reaching for another half sandwich. "Family emergency or something. A likely story if you ask me. Hey, these are real good." He winked at the waitress who remained determined to ignore him. "Sorry, I couldn't help overhearing."

I looked over to where Captain York was wiping his forehead, overwhelmed by the number of customers pressing their case to leave. The words, "sorry," and "short-staffed," caught my ear, and I wondered if this was why he'd turned a blind eye to me helping out. Or maybe he just hadn't gotten to me yet.

At that moment, he looked my way, and I'd have ducked if there had been anywhere for me to hide. He didn't look too thrilled about me talking to people, and I sensed if he wasn't so bogged down with angry bodies, he'd stomp over and give me my marching orders. I knew that's what I'd do if I were in his shoes. I turned from his gaze and assumed a more casual chatting posture.

"Oh, I see," I said. "I was just hoping to talk to his brother." He appeared to hesitate, so I added. "Detective Wells will certainly want to talk to him, anyway."

The busy waitress left us again, and Murphy turned his full, Irish-ancestry charm on me. I could feel his eyes running up and down my torso in a most offensive way, and I would have cut him dead if I wasn't so desperate for information.

"Wally's not here. He worked late and went home to sleep I heard. He was nowhere near the place at the time of the murder. Say...." I saw it coming before he said it. "What are you doing when you get out of here?"

"Going to bed. To sleep," I added. "Do you have Wally's address?"

Seeing he had hit a brick wall his tone went flat. I got the impression he struck out a lot. "Yeah, I got it someplace. Hold on." He fished out his notes and flipped through a few pages. "Here it is. You got something you can write it on?"

"Sure." I swiped my phone and went straight to my navigation nap. "I'll type it right in here."

"7715b Lower Walnut."

"Hmmm." I didn't know it, and frankly I was struggling to imagine where a pukwudgie would live. I figured them for raccoons, dwelling among trash cans, which was probably unfair stereotyping, but that was the vibe they gave out. Not exactly something you could plug into a GPS. "Is that all of it?"

"I said the exact same thing but apparently that's it. Good luck." Murphy snatched another sandwich off the tray and winked at the waitress who was rinsing a few returned mugs behind the counter. I had to give him ten out of ten for trying.

The scraping of chairs a few feet away told me Liam was done. Jordan treated me to a smug smile as he strolled on past me, and I watched as he moseyed out of the restaurant and into the kitchens.

Liam joined me, returning his used coffee cup to the bar. "That's everyone who was here," he said. "Word is, Captain York will be letting everyone leave in a few."

"Does he know about the tunnel to the Baron?" I asked.

"Yes."

"You?" I asked.

"No. Word got out though. Our people have been all over it. No sign of Patsy or anything."

"She's at my place with Mom."

"Oh. Well, that's something at least. Did she see anything?"

I shook my head. "No. But I got Wally's address from Officer Murphy. Can we go over there now? Shake him up and down by his hairy toes?"

"Sure. Sleep is for wimps. Let me just have a quick word with Captain York before we go."

He snatched one of the few remaining sandwiches and headed over to the captain, who was giving orders to a few uniforms, and making noises like it was time to wrap this up. Everyone around me could sense this and the level of anxiety in the room was double what it had been just a few minutes ago.

I turned to the waitress, who was still cleaning up just behind me.

"Is Finn in today?" I asked as casually as I could.

"Finn, yeah. You want me to get him for you? He's out the back."

Totally. But as much as wanted to, I suddenly thought about how it might look if I singled him out in particular. If he was as shrewd as I knew him to be, he'd know I was here already. If he needed to talk to me, he'd find a way. Plus, I knew he'd blow a gasket if I summoned him especially. "No, that's okay. Come to think of it, I think he was interviewed already."

"Fair enough." She put her head down, and started loading a dishwasher behind the bar, all thoughts of Finn forgotten.

Liam came back, looking ready to go.

"How did it go with Jordan?" I asked. "Learn anything new?"

Liam's expression hardened in an instant. "Well, that was a waste of time and energy. He sure thinks a lot of himself. I thought you and him were hitting it off, I didn't want to interrupt you. He seems just your type.

Hey, I don't mean the mixed blood. I'm not species-ist. You like 'em tall and handsome, that's all." He held up both hands in a placating gesture, maybe because he sensed I was about ready to sock him one.

"He is not my goddamn type," I spat through clenched teeth.

"Noted. Shall we head out, then?"

I couldn't have been more relieved. I was sick of this place, of its seediness and devilishness, and was suddenly desperate to breathe some fresh air into my lungs. I downed my cooled coffee is a single gulp.

"Thanks," I said to the nice elf bartender, who took my empty mug and smiled back.

"You're welcome."

We were almost at the door when my phone went off, and looking down, I saw the call was from Gayle, down at the morgue.

"Hold up, I need to take this," I said.

Liam had the door half open when he paused.

"Hey Gayle, what's up?"

"I heard you found your friends," she said.

"Yes, thank goodness. They both turned up hale and hearty, barely a scratch between them."

"Well, that's good to know. Hey, I also heard you were on the Rotting Corpse thing, down at the docks. Is that true?"

"Yes," I said, my curiosity piqued. "In fact, I'm still here right now. What have you got for me?"

"I've got a body," she said, her voice full of a perverted kind of mortuary glee. "A goblin brought in with reported gunshot wounds to the head."

Redcap, she meant Redcap. A shudder ran down my spine, then ran back up it again. "Oh, what of it?" Me, trying to play it cool. My heart was pounding against my ribcage.

"Just a bit of a mystery, that's all."

"Oh?"

"Yes. There was hardly any blood on his head, and I guessed everyone supposed the river had washed all the blood away, but here's the thing...."

"Yes." It took me all my control not to shout at her.

"When I peeled that nasty nasty cap off him, I found his skull was perfectly intact. Not a gunshot wound there at all."

"Really? So where was he shot? Or wasn't he? Did he drown or something?"

"We'll that's the intriguing thing. You see there were no gunshot wounds at all. Apart from a few scrapes most likely caused by the fall into the river, his body was completely intact. Not a single unaccounted-for hole in his tiny torso. How deliciously mysterious is that!" I was reminded that Gayle loved mystery novels and whodunnits. It was how we'd met.

"Then what do you think killed him?"

"I haven't the foggiest!" she said, her voice rising an octave or two with glee. "We'll have to wait for the postmortem to know more—see if there's any fluid in his lungs or whatnot. Will you want me to let you know?"

"Of course, yes," I said. "Thanks for keeping me up to date."

"Any time!"

The call ended. Liam had caught the gist of the conversation, and stood expectantly, his hand still on the door.

"Son of a goblin!" I exclaimed. And without further ado, I began filling him in.

"Detective Wells, aren't you going to introduce me to your charming companion, who you have allowed to speak to witnesses without my authorization?" said Captain York, his huge shadow looming over us like a harbinger of doom.

I cringed. We should have left when we had the chance. We were so in for it now. Liam closed the door, and we both turned to get what was coming to us.

## Chapter Eighteen
# THE BROWNSTONES

"MISS CRUZ, DO I HAVE TO REMIND YOU, YOU ARE NO LONGER POLICE, and the privileges once extended to you no longer apply?"

"Of course, I'm aware, Captain York," I said, a little surprised he knew my name. "But I am here by invitation and I'm in no way interfering with your investigation. I haven't used magic once."

"It's not just magic that makes evidence inadmissible. I've had complaints, several, and it's totally unacceptable."

"Sir, if I could...." Liam interjected.

"As for you, you should know better. You're lucky I don't take you off this case right now."

"But...."

"Don't you 'but' me, Detective Wells. All l wanna hear from your sorry backside is *yes, sir*. Are we clear?"

Liam bowed his head, subdued. "Yes sir." But then he still came back with, "But sir, Dionne is part goblin, and this is a goblin-mob related crime. She has insights we don't, and I thought—"

"Enough," Captain York said, raising his hand. "When your badge has captain or higher on it, then you can contradict me. Right now, just do as you're told and follow my orders."

"Sir..."

"That's enough! Now get off my crime scene before I have your friend thrown in jail for interfering with a police investigation. And I'll toss you in the cell beside her."

"Liam? On what charge?" I asked, incensed at his heavy-handedness.

"For being a pain in my backside. Now get out of here."

Liam was about to argue again so before he could say another word, I ushered him out of The Rotting Corpse before his ego got him busted back to street patrol.

"I was handling it," Liam said as the doors slammed behind us.

"Yes, you were, but we have stuff to do and time's getting on. I just wanted to keep things moving."

Liam harrumphed, ready to argue with me, but I knew it was the sleep deprivation talking, so I nudged him over to his parked car.

I noticed a long line at the Haunted Habanero, now reopened for business, and imagined Juanita was having the time of her life juicing up the news along with her spicy tacos and burritos. She saw me and waved. I waved back.

"You got the address?" Liam asked.

I held up my phone. "Already mapped in. Let's get out of here before something else happens and Captain York decides to yell at you some more."

Without another word we marched over to the car. As soon as we were seated inside, I looked down and saw my fingers were red with cold.

"Liam, if you don't turn the heating up full, right this second, I am going to die. Do you understand?"

He opened the glovebox and pulled out actual gloves. He tossed them to me, and I slipped them on. They were rather on the big side, but they were lined with fur and my hands immediately felt warmer.

"Bless your kind heart. I've no idea where this place is, do you?" I asked, awkwardly pulling up the direction details and trying to identify the location.

"Never heard of it," he said. "But the GPS found it okay, so it has to exist."

"I guess so."

We drove in silence through the streets, interrupted only by Yoda, the voice of my GPS system as he uttered things like, "turn right, you must." I loved the humor but right now was too tired to appreciate it. Both of us wanted to get this over with, and I was relieved at how soon we were pulling up outside 7715b Lower Walnut. At least I thought we had. Though I looked along the brownstone row homes numbered 7713 and 7717 on one side of the street, and 7714 and 7718 on the other, I could not see a 7715b or a 7715 period, for that matter.

"Where is it?" I asked Liam. "You see it?"

"Nope," he said, pushing the driver's door open. "Come on, let's go look. It's got to be here someplace."

I forced my tired legs out onto the quiet street. The cobblestone was slippery with black ice, and I took care not to fall or trip over.

There was a bald maple tree right beside me, so I held onto its bark for support. It was so cold. I imagined Redcap's body lying face down in the icy Delaware and felt a sudden twang of pity for him. I would hate to die in the cold, alone.

The brownstone row houses in front of us were three stories high. They were sinisterly elegant, impossible to price, and I wondered that I'd never been to or heard of this street before. Maybe it was like Brigadoon, it only appeared every so often, or you only found it when you were looking for it.

Each home was clearly labeled with a bright white plaque denoting the house number. But no matter how hard I looked, none of them said 7715.

"Where the heck is it?" Liam said, frustration in his voice.

I pulled out my wand.

"What's that for?" Liam asked.

"I'm checking for concealment charms. If the house is hidden, this will find it. *Ostende arcanum tuum!*" I waved my wand between 7713 and 7717. The cobblestones seemed to wobble beneath my feet, and a large bubble appeared between the two houses which got larger and larger A small annex jutted out into the middle of the street, no taller than a single story, but this was divided into three sections, each with its own front door labeled 7715, a b and c. A set of steps ran up the middle of the three homes, Wally's would have been in the center.

There was a solitary clay flowerpot outside his door with an unseasonably red daisy in full bloom sticking out of it. His front door looked tiny, and though I imagined I could probably fit inside, I knew it was going to be a tight squeeze.

"You'd better wait here," I said to Liam.

"Nuh-uh, if anyone's going in, then I am."

I shook my head, determined. "No Liam, not this time. You don't know what's on the other side, and you have no magic." He opened his mouth to protest but I laid my hand gently on his arm. "It'll be fine. In any case, I doubt you'd be able to squeeze through that front door. All those donuts, catching up with you." He looked down at his belly, even though it was nicely flat. "Don't worry, I'll call for you if there's any sign of trouble."

"I don't like it, Dionne," he said. "You don't know anything about these pukwudgies, not really."

"Neither do you," I pointed out reasonably. "And besides, you're way too big. You might step on one accidentally."

Reluctantly he nodded, and I put away my wand away to avoid intimidating anyone. This was Wally's home. I should at least begin with a show of respect.

Leaving Liam on the pavement behind me, I advanced cautiously up the tiny steps, holding onto the surprisingly sturdy wrought iron railing as I climbed.

The front door looked expensive, cut from a heavy wood and would have looked awesome on many a homemaker show if it had been larger. I grabbed the ornate brass knocker, that looked unsettlingly like Redcap, and gave it two heavy raps.

A moment later, the door opened, and Wally stood inside it, dressed in a long black robe that covered him from head to toe. He was smoking something that smelled of licorice.

"What do you want?" he said in his high, reedy voice, though he didn't look surprised to see me at his house. Bad news traveled fast.

"Can I come in?"

Wally looked around me, to where Liam was waiting for me over by the maple tree.

"Why? What do you want?"

"I just had a few questions about Redcap's death. I presume you've heard?"

"Yes, yes of course I have. Why you? Why not him?" Wally asked, motioning toward Liam. "He's the cop, isn't he?"

"We didn't think there would be room for two."

"Hmm," Wally said. "You have a point. Not that I want either of you inside my home. I just had it cleaned, so I did."

He didn't see me raise an eyebrow because he turned to go back inside, leaving the door open for me to follow if I chose to. I bowed my head and went in after him, if nothing else, curious as anything to see how a pukwudgie might live.

That said, it was hard to take in anything at all. At two-feet tall, Wally would have considered his home a mansion, but I was having a total Gandalf moment, with my head bowed against the ceiling, trying not to bump into the light fixtures or knock any of his ornaments off the shelves on the wall.

Wally sat down in a comfy-looking armchair by a warm log fire and took a few puffs on his tiny pipe. He was clearly enjoying my discomfort and didn't say anything for a while as I tried to make myself comfortable. There was another chair, but it was so small I would have smashed it to matchwood if I'd sat down. I guessed he didn't have too many big folk dropping by for coffee. I made do with sitting cross-legged on a rug on the floor instead. Wally nodded approval of my choice.

"*Herne toonder fash*," I said, giving the traditional pukwudgie house blessing—I'd looked it up on the way over. It was the equivalent of thank you for inviting me into your warm abode, may Herne watch over you and keep you safe. They pack a lot of meaning into their language. Wally raised an eyebrow, but then solemnly nodded acknowledgement of my greeting.

His room was beautiful, full of expensive-looking art, including an ornament of jade elven girls, dancing in a circle, and a magnificent collection of tiny poison darts, hung in an elder wood cabinet on the wall. The rug I was sitting on, on his polished wood floor was made of some kind of dwarfish fabric, judging by the interlocking scrolls in the weaves. The crystal in his cabinet looked almost like water. This guy had a lot of moolah.

"Is this going to take long?" he asked, his tone laced with amusement.

"I'll get straight to the point, shall I?"

"Yes, I think that would be a good idea."

Satisfied at last that I was safe from breaking anything, I took a deep breath.

"Can you tell me exactly what you did after Liam and I left last night?"

"If you like, I've nothing to hide. I went back inside to find Redcap. Our business with the prisoners was done. My brother went off some place, and before you ask, no, I don't know where he went. But I went to have a word with Redcap, I did."

"What about?"

"I'm sure you've heard—I do the books for him. I'm pretty good with numbers. All this," he motioned around the room with his pipe, "is bought and paid for, cash. I know money. I know how it works and how to make it. Redcap liked me handling his affairs, so he did."

"You and he talked about the books after what happened?"

"In a way."

"What does that mean? 'In a way?'" I asked.

Wally took a long draught from his pipe and stared at me through the plume of smoke he exhaled. "Hmm. I don't suppose it matters now that he's dead. I didn't think it was a good idea him letting you all go, so I didn't."

*Jumped up little toilet-brush—what was it to do with him?* "You didn't, huh? And why was that?"

Wally smiled, the kind of smug, self-congratulating smile a person has when they know something you don't. "Because we'd gone to so much trouble getting him in the first place, handing him back like that seemed stupid to me, and I told him as much, so I did. I thought it would be bad for business."

"But we gave him the jinn. He got what he was after. I don't see why releasing the warlock would bother you."

Wally sat forward in his chair and glared at me. "Not the warlock, you idiot. Your partner."

"My partner?" Now I was really confused. "Surely you mean the warlock Derek?"

"No." His voice was higher than normal; this was clearly amusing him. "I mean your partner, the goblin Harrison. Redcap intended to blow Derek up, why would he care if he was alive or dead? He could have blown him to smithereens, then his soldiers would have waltzed in after the bombing and swept up the jinn, that would have been easy enough. But Harrison. Wow. That was just a stroke of pure goblin luck, so it was."

"How do you mean?"

"The soldier who threw in the spell-bomb just happened to recognize him as he turned around. So, he hung about, waiting to see if Harrison survived, and when he did, he got word back to Redcap. And well, the rest you know."

"I'm sorry, no I don't. Why did they want to kidnap my partner? What has he got to do with anything?"

Wally chuckled. "I guess you don't know. Wow. You goblins and your secrets. Harrison is part-owner of The Rotting Corpse. That and other ventures through some common relative. Redcap learned about it quite by accident—I don't think anyone wanted him to find out given his taste for violence. It was supposed to be some big secret, but Redcap got wind of it somehow, he always does, and would have loved to cut Harrison out of the picture—goblin style." He made a chopping motion with his hand, cutting his own neck. The picture was crystal clear. "He'd been after him long enough, so he was. Harrison was also shielded by his police brothers, but not anymore, not anymore. What a chance wasted." He shook his head.

"So why did Redcap change his mind and let him go?"

"I dunno. That's what I wanted to know myself, so I did. Maybe since he had the jinn, he was feeling generous and decided to let him live after all. If you want to know for sure, you'd have to ask Redcap, won't ya."

A nasty, twisty little grin contorted his features, and he began refilling his pipe, clearly enjoying how much this was unsettling me.

While my brain tried to wrap around everything, I shifted uncomfortably, almost knocking a lamp off a small table beside me.

"Be careful, won't you? That lamp cost me more than you make in a month."

Something wasn't right. Why was Wally telling me all this? Redcap's people were known for their silence and even though the goblin boss was dead, Wally was spewing this all out without the slightest prompting. Nobody liked a tattletale. Snitches get stitches, as the saying goes. And how the hell was the little guy so wealthy? He was just the muscle for a mobster after all. That is, when he wasn't doubling as an accounting clerk.

"I'm not buying it," I said. "If my partner had money, I would know about it. He would tell me; I know he would."

"Would he now? Why? Are you two married?"

I hesitated to mention that Harrison was gay—no need to spread his personal business around. "No. But he just would."

"Suit yourself if that's what you want to believe. But you came to me, remember. I have no reason to lie. No, I don't."

I remembered Wally's less than respectful bow to Redcap and wondered why he had less admiration for his former boss than his brother.

"I take it you didn't like Redcap?"

"No. I'm an investment genius, and he treated me like a scummy bean counter. The man had no finesse, and when I complained, he made the work even more menial. *Inventory the pantry!* he says. *Tell me how many eggs I have!*" He spat into the fire. "I despised him, I did."

"Enough to kill him?"

"Ugh no. I can wield a bow, but I prefer to leave the um, dirty work to my brother. And no, Puk didn't kill him either. He worshipped him too much. He can be an idiot sometimes, can Puk."

"So why didn't you leave him? Redcap?"

"No one leaves Redcap. Unless you plan to exit by the river. And I for one can't swim. You really think he'd let me walk away, someone who knew every aspect of his business? Down to the number of eggs in his pantry? You're not thinkin' straight, *ma-naab*," he added, using the pukwudgie equivalent of colleen. I wasn't insulted. The ma- honorific meant sweet.

"I still don't understand why you're telling me all this. Your kind doesn't like my kind."

"You don't? It's quite simple, really. Your lot will want to pin Redcap's death on gang warfare, it's what you always do. But this time I suggest you look a little bit closer to home. Your partner had more motive than anyone to do this. Let's see." He mocked counting on his fingers. "Kidnapping, starvation, oh, and a serious pot of gold at the end of it. How sweet is that? A hell of a lot more motive than two insignificant pukwudgies who are now out of a job, don't you think? So, you see, Miss Cruz, I want *that* on the record. Now, if you don't mind, I'd like to finish my pipe in peace. You can see yourself out, can't you?"

I stared at Wally in disbelief. The idea that Harrison was somehow tied up in this business just baffled me. Up until now, I'd been happy with the wrong place, wrong time theory, but this was a slap in the face. And yet, everything rang true in my ears, and this would certainly explain Harrison's reactions to a lot of things.

"Thank you for your time," I said, my own voice sounding lame in my throat. "You've been very, um, helpful."

Wally puffed on his pipe and stared into the dying fire. "*Aye ey toonder, Miss Cruz.*"

I had to think what it meant. *May your journey be a safe one.* Was it a simple politeness, or a warning that I was navigating a dangerous part of the woods? I bowed my head in thanks.

Carefully I got up from the floor and I backed out of the room, and only really breathed again when Wally's heavy door closed tight behind me. Liam had left the tree, but I could see him waiting inside the car with the engine running. Good, at least the heater would be on. And I needed something warm to get the chill out of my heart, which had little to do with the weather.

## Chapter Nineteen
# BUBBLE AND SQUEAK

WE PULLED UP OUTSIDE MY APARTMENT BLOCK. LIAM SET THE CAR IN park and took a deep breath. I'd told him everything that Wally had told me, leaving nothing out. I was sick and tired of secrets and betrayal.

"You want me to come in with you?" he asked.

Yes. And no. Liam was exhausted, and there really wasn't anything I could think for him to do. I had to confront Harrison alone on this one. But I'd gotten used to having him around and it was hard saying no. But I had to.

"Thank you, I'll be fine. Go home and get some sleep."

He never betrayed his relief, but I knew he had to feel it.

"Alright. But if you need me, call me. Don't think twice, okay?"

*Not a chance. You need the sleep.* "Sure. I'll call if I need to."

I opened the passenger door and slipped out. I knew Liam wouldn't get going until I was safe inside, so I huddled up against the cold and made a dash for it. As soon as I was in my apartment building, I turned, and watched as he drove away.

Sleep. We both needed some badly, but I had a job to do first. One I didn't relish in the slightest. As Liam's car faded from view, a peculiar sensation came over me. A sudden tremor ran down my spine and all my senses jumped to high alert.

"Is anybody there?" I said into the dark corridor behind me. I could see the outline of the mailboxes, lined up against the wall, but it was so dark. Why? The entranceway was usually well lit. I pulled out my wand, pointing it into the darkness. "Hello. Who's back there?"

Before I knew what was happening, a powerful blast of wind howled along the passageway, tearing my wand from my hand. I heard it hit the tiled floor and the trickle of wood as it rolled away into the shadows. I lunged for it, but I couldn't reach it in time, because before I knew what was happening, a second wind hit me, and though I felt no pain, the dim light faded, leaving only darkness. And I knew nothing more.

---

I could smell vinegar. The air was ripe with it. Was I in some kind of factory? A kitchen perhaps? Wherever I was, the stench invaded my nostrils and made me feel light-headed. But I could feel nothing. I was floating in some delicious dream, a happy euphoria, where there was no pain, and no emotion to unbalance me. I was drifting along on a sea of contentment, and it wouldn't be such a bad thing to stay like this forever.

I was moving now. How, I couldn't tell. I reached out, and my fingers framed something soft and gel-like. It wasn't sticky exactly, but it stretched the skin on my fingers as I pulled them away. How odd. Whatever it was, I was encased inside it. Was I in a hospital? Was this thing protecting me? Carefully, I raised my hand to my face. My skin felt smooth under the tips of my fingers. I seemed sound enough. I found no tubes, no wires, no *beep* from a life support machine. All of which was great news.

Why was everything so dark? I blinked, just to check my eyes were open and they seemed to be working fine. Sleep seemed like a nice idea. I could drift off to a lovely dream, and I seemed to remember needing to sleep, before, in the other world.

The smell of vinegar faded, and I heard a door open, and then the sound of planks, and then I went down head-first, and found myself bobbing and spinning, like some wild water raft at a Disney attraction. How fun. Still, I would rather sleep.

From somewhere far away I heard a voice. "Don't sleep, Dionne. You must wake. You must wake now!"

I licked my lips and closed my eyes. "Maybe later, Mom. I'll get up for school soon. Just five more minutes."

"Wake up. Open your eyes, you must wake up!"

I didn't want to. I felt so good. I liked this sensation of floating, just drifting along without a care in the world. I felt so at peace, why would I have to snap out of it? Why?

Something was rocking me, side to side, like a mother, nursing her baby. Lovely. Odd though because I wasn't a baby. Not really. But then something deep inside me woke up, adding its own voice to the far away one.

"This isn't right, Dionne, this isn't real. Something is wrong. Wake up, sweetie, wake up." And then more forcibly, "Snap out of it sunshine, 'cos if you don't, you're going to die!"

That got me. I took in a deep breath, and shook my head, as if that would wake me out of my stupor. Nothing. Slowly I put my hand to my pocket, reaching for my wand. It wasn't there. I vaguely recalled it rolling away someplace and I groaned. I could do a few minor spells without it, but nothing significant.

I closed my eyes, fighting off the powerful desire to just roll over and take a nap, and tried to focus on a point of light burning faintly in my head. My inner witch sense told me this was what I needed to do, so I put all my energy into staring at it, wrapping my chi around it, embracing it.

At first, nothing happened, and I felt my hold slipping away. Perhaps I should just go back to sleep after all. But then I noticed the white flame had grown a little larger, so I mentally shook off the growing lethargy and renewed my efforts.

The ball of flame intensified in my head, and my lips parted, and I whispered, "Lux." The world around me lightened for just a second, but then faded back to black. Hopeless.

*"Your power lies within and may be tapped at will."*

Patsy's voice rang in my head as if she were lying here in this happy space with me. I had failed her then, or failed myself, more like.

I had to try again. Patsy believed I could do it. Why couldn't I?

"Lux!" I said, with a little more emphasis, ignoring the inner voice that called me a big wuss and placing all my trust in the jinn. It was working. A sensation like water trickled through my fingertips. Suddenly I was surrounded by light, and slowly, somewhat painfully, I opened my eyes, willing my pupils to adjust to the intense brightness that lit up my surroundings.

"*What the*—!" I squealed. I was in some kind of clear bubble, floating on water. I turned, sharply, forcing the bubble to tilt upward and almost overturn. It was the Delaware, I was sure of it, and my heart filled with terror. I couldn't swim, I was going to drown the second we collided with something sharp enough to tear into us. Panicked, I looked around me. There were boats everywhere, sailing up and down the dark waters. Fear swelled in my heart as I realized that with no light, they wouldn't see me, and even with the light, we were so close to the surface they probably wouldn't even notice me until it was too late.

Just to prove my worst nightmare, my stomach jolted as a tugboat floated by, and the bubble rose on the crest of the wave and then plummeted, forced further into the center of the river and into the heavier stream of traffic. The light went out, leaving me almost invisible in the blackness of the night waters.

My phobia consumed me, but I didn't scream. I had to beat this. I had to do something and—and fast! —or I would be as dead as a dodo for sure. I was not going to die here. I had no plans for a cold and watery death.

"Help me, Patsy," I whispered into the night, hoping somehow that she might hear me.

"Help yourself," said a voice in my head. Was it her, or someone else, or was it my imagination talking?

Shaking, I rolled onto my belly. Through the skin of my bubble, I could see the water beneath me; the bubble protected me to some degree from its icy wetness, for now anyway, but I knew nothing could survive in such intense cold for long.

To my left I could see the riverbank, with boats lined up in a marina. That meant I was just a little north of The Rotting Corpse, drifting toward it.

To my right was just a large mass of water. All kinds of commercial and private boats cruised through the lanes. The river was especially wide and deep here, and if I drifted out much further, I would be lost for sure.

It was so cold. Whatever spell had numbed my senses was gone now, and I could feel the full measure of my peril. My movement was slow; I hadn't known it, but I'd been freezing to death.

I stared back to the marina. Somehow, I had to maneuver this bubble toward it, but the tide was against me, and I was drifting further and further away by the second. Shelving my terror, I looked deep inside, remembering every spell I had ever uttered, and every spell I had ever learned.

There was a large sailing boat docked not too far away. A loose dingy was propped up on its side. I couldn't see all of it and could only hope it was unsecured.

"*Veni ad me!*" Nothing. "*Veni ad me!*" I cried, only louder this time. Still nothing. Although my magic worked in the confines of my bubble, the water blocked any magic beyond it.

Whatever I did, it would only work inside the bubble. What could I do?

To my horror, I could hear a small cargo ship cutting its way through the waves. Looking up, I saw it was heading straight for me. There was no time. I had to think quick, I had mere seconds before the thing would cut my bubble, and quite possibly me, in half. If only I had learned to swim.

Desperation took over, and a million spells swarmed at once inside my mind, each jumbling into the other in my panic. Terrified, I shouted out the first words that formed properly on my lips.

"*Sic faciet avolare!*"

The same sensation of water teased my fingertips, and the bubble began to expand, stretching out until it was the size of a large ball. It began to inch out of the river, and I watched with terrified impatience as the water of the Delaware dripped off its side. Up and up it went, and my heart thumped loudly against my rib cage. "Come on, come on!" I cried, willing it to rise faster.

The cargo boat was much closer, when I was just a few feet in the air, it sailed by me, clipping the edge of the bubble, and sending me into a wild spin across the surface of the river.

Round and round I went, twisting and turning until I was almost sick. But then the spinning slowed, and the ball came to a gradual stop, floating just on the surface. It never rose out of it again.

But things had only become worse. Although I was clear of the path of the cargo ship, by winging the bubble, it had catapulted me right into the heart of the river traffic. It would take more than a slow rising balloon to get me out of this mess.

Perhaps magic wasn't the answer. With some difficulty I stood up, supporting myself against the side of the bubble. I turned to the lights along the riverbank, and as fast as I could, I began to walk the bubble back to dry land.

It was tricky, my hands were like ice, and I constantly slipped and slid against the gel-like interior of the inner surface. Just to confound things, the sludgy, ice-riddled waters made my going super slow. But inch by inch, I got closer to the docks, and apart from a few near misses, and the ever-present danger of jagged driftwood on the surface, I made it back safely.

Ironically, the tide had pushed me back to the pier of The Rotting Corpse. I didn't want to get wet; I didn't want the feel of the ice water on me at all, but I had to get out of this see-through prison. With as much strength as I could muster, I rammed myself into the old timber of the dock, hoping to snag the bubble on some rough surface.

Sure enough, as soon as it hit the rough wood it burst with a loud *pop!* I had hoped to grab the ladder and save myself from falling, but the *pop* disconcerted me, and I was plunged into the icy depths. The pain was intense, and the cold waters filled my ears with their mighty roar. My feet scrambled to make purchase, but I couldn't latch onto anything. Horrified, I realized that after all my trouble, I was going to die mere inches from the dock.

But then something grabbed me, and a second later I had broken the surface of the water and was gasping for air.

I felt myself pulled from the river and was cradled in someone's arms. At first, I was too busy coughing and spluttering, trying hard not to be dead to realize who had saved me.

"What the heck do you think you're doing? Are you crazy? What did you think you would find down there? A murder weapon? For goodness sake, someone get her a blanket or a coat or something before she freezes to death. I've never seen anything so stupid in my life!"

I half-recognized the male voice, and looking up, almost died again when I realized who had fished me out of the river. It was Jordan.

"Here, take my coat!" someone shouted. I recognized Juanita, bless her.

The coat was wrapped around me, and I huddled under it, shaking like a baby as Jordan carried me off the docks and headed back toward The Rotting Corpse.

I had never been so happy to see a potential murder suspect in my life. But I couldn't tell him, my teeth were chattering too much.

## Chapter Twenty
# SWEET TOOTH

APPARENTLY, I'D ATTRACTED A SMALL CROWD, AND SO TO AVOID further disruption to the day's business, Jordan had carried me straight downstairs to his late brother's office which had, among other items of furniture, a warm sofa and a hot stove.

Emily followed behind us, and after closing the door to Redcap's office, she hovered above me as Jordan planted my sodden and shivering body down on the sofa.

"Emily, grab some of the spare uniforms over there," he said. "She'll have to strip out of these wet clothes before she catches pneumonia or something. And see if you can find some towels."

He started fussing with the settings on the stove, and totally missed the death stare she gave him. Then she looked down at me, her expression an odd mix of frustration, dislike, and concern.

"What were you doing down at the docks this time, Miss Cruz? Trout fishing? You're quite an oddity, I must say. What were you looking for now?"

"N-n-nothing," I said through chattering teeth. "I w-w-was t-t-thrown inside a b-b-bubble and left for d-d-dead."

My teeth were rattling so hard I could barely speak. Emily turned to a stack of boxes on the shelves beside Redcap's desk and began sorting through some cellophane packs. She pulled out some Rotting Corpse tee-shirts and some slacks, then threw them my way.

"Occupational hazard, I suppose," she said unkindly. "Jordan."

Jordan turned to see what she wanted.

"Miss Cruz is about to get undressed?" Emily said.

I half expected him to say something ridiculous and crude, but he merely looked at me. "Oh, right." He did half smile but made nothing more of it and left the room.

"Wait here," Emily said. "I know where I can find you a towel so you can dry off before you change. I'll be right back. And don't touch anything."

Touch anything? I could barely move I was so frozen. The door closed behind her and for a moment I was all alone. Everything about me was knocking, from my teeth to my ribs, to my very knees. I was appreciative of the warmth of the heater, which Jordan had cranked up to max strength, but hugged myself tight, not wishing to lose even an ounce of body heat. Touch anything indeed!

I looked around Redcap's office. He had shelves full of ledgers, which I would have expected, a large screen television which was turned off, and a few lockable cupboards that at this time were slightly ajar. His desk had been cleared since I last saw it, which was unremarkable since business had to go on. I wondered if Jordan had stored his brother's personal items somewhere, or just tossed them into a dumpster. He was certainly strong enough to have tossed Redcap into the Delaware. Had they had an argument, a falling-out? Would I ever know?

Emily reappeared, this time laden with some towels, a plastic bag, and what smelled like a mug of hot chocolate, which was very kind of her. "I'll just close the door," she said, placing the mug on the table. "No one will disturb you down here while you get out of those things. You can put your wet clothes in this bag. I'll be back in ten minutes." She turned away and headed for the door.

"Emily?"

She looked back over her shoulder. "What?"

"Thanks."

She didn't reply, she just went out and closed the door behind her. At least she didn't scowl at me.

I didn't want to get up, the cold was crippling, but I had to. They had shown me a ton of consideration, more than I would have hoped for from these guys, but I needed to dry off and get out of here. Someone had done this to me, and I wasn't going to find out who and why, sitting on my butt. Slowly, with my hands shaking, I unraveled and began to undress. My flesh was colder than I'd ever known it to be, and I huddled for a second inside the towel as my body temperature restored. I didn't think I would ever feel warm again. But now that I'd peeled off my freezing cold clothes, things were already feeling a little better.

I threw my sodden things into the plastic bag and hung Juanita's damp coat on the back of the door. I remained wrapped in the towel for a minute, letting the heat from the stove take the chill from my bones.

I used the time to study Redcap's collection of ornaments. His tastes were typical for a goblin. There was a pygmy skull studded with jewels and decorated for the day of the dead, a few macramé feathers hanging from a pine rod that looked like they'd been dipped in blood—that was *so him*—a series of books, mostly about the history of human sacrifice, with titles like, "Moloch Is Hangry: Phoenician Death Cults And Their Practices" and, "I Left My Heart In Tenochtitlan - The Bloodthirsty Aztec Gods"— and more than a few cookbooks, suggesting the late mob boss had a thing for unusual gourmet foods.

As I thumbed through his collection, I caught the faintest whiff of vinegar, and curious, I pulled open a cupboard door that had been left slightly ajar. Inside was an assortment of some very nice, candied delicacies, including several packs of goblin chocolate malt balls, tarantula-web licorice, lickable frogs—it was clear Redcap had quite the sweet tooth—and a half-eaten mason jar of home-made pickled eyeballs.

Still, it was probably a coincidence, the vinegar I'd smelled earlier was much more pungent, but then maybe my mind had been playing tricks on me, after all I was totally out of it then. And Redcap wasn't the only creature in the world with a passion for pickled foods—each to their own. Or so I told myself, even as the goblin part of me wondered what they must taste like.

Time was ticking, so I closed the door as I'd found it, and pulled on the clothes Emily had brought for me. They fit snugly, she had a good eye for size, and I was beginning to feel more like myself again.

I was just drying my hair with the towel and pondering my soaked boots when there was a knock at the door and Emily arrived carrying a pair of sneakers.

"These might be a little big, but they will get you home."

"Um, thanks," I said, and then blurted, "You're being very nice all of a sudden."

Emily sat down behind Redcap's desk and looked at me as if I were an ignorant child in need of instruction.

"Miss Cruz, let me explain something. Regardless of what you might think of us, we're not animals. We have a city to run, that's all, and though you might find our methods a little harsh, I can assure you, they're quite effective and prevent a lot more crime than you probably imagine."

I didn't know, I could imagine quite a lot. Even so. "Kidnapping and murder, a little harsh? Well, *excuse me*."

She shrugged and opened up a drawer to look inside. It dawned on me she looked quite comfortable there, sitting in her late boss's seat, as if it wasn't the first time she'd sat in it.

I laced up the last sneaker and grabbed the bag of damp clothes.

"Um, thank you again," I said, awkwardly.

Emily didn't respond. Instead, she just stared at me, waiting for me to leave.

"Do you mind if I ask, where did your late boss get his eyeballs? I've rather a thing for them myself."

Even though Emily was part goblin, just like me, the suggestion appeared to make her gag. She looked beyond me to the cupboard, thought for a moment, then shrugged. "I've no idea. Some local vendor got them for him, I guess. I'm sure if you go online, you can Google it. I never eat candy or treats myself."

Looking at her svelte figure, I didn't doubt it.

"I assume you know the way out," Emily said.

I supposed I had overstayed my welcome. And a new thought occurred to me. Whoever had put me in that death bubble then dropped me into the Delaware had been at my apartment. What if they went back there? Did they pose any danger to Mom or Harrison?

"Any chance I could use your phone before I go?"

Emily sighed, but sat back in her chair, leaving me room to use the office phone. I smiled at her with an exaggerated sweetness, then called my apartment.

After a single ring, Mom answered.

"Hey Mom, is everything okay?"

"Dionne! Yes of course it is! Where have you been? I cooked meatballs for you. I thought you said you were coming home? Isn't that your car parked outside? I've been worried sick."

"I was, and yes, it is, but I um, had a little distraction. Are you sure everything is all right?"

"Why wouldn't it be, Dee-Dee? I'm surrounded by two very capable men in a spell-bound fortress with a jinn who likes playing rummy. We've all been lying low, just as you told us to. I was showing Derek your baby photos earlier. He really is a lovely warlock. Perhaps you and he…."

"Mom!" I cut her off before she could say anything I might regret forever. But I was glad she was okay, and I didn't want her to worry.

A smile curled Emily's lips as her sharp goblin ears picked up everything Mom was saying.

"Something came up, that's all, and I had to leave the car behind," I explained. "I'll be home in a bit once I've called an Uber or something. Keep those meatballs warm, 'cos I'm positively starving."

I heard the door open behind me and turned to see Jordan standing in the entrance.

"I gotta go, Mom. Rub Scratchpoop for me. See you in a bit."

"Did I hear you needed a lift?" Jordan asked. "I can take you home if you like."

Emily looked at him sideways but said nothing.

"I um—" I wasn't sure I wanted Jordan to see where I lived, but that was juvenile, he could find out easily enough if he wanted to. And I certainly needed a ride. I shoved a strand of damp hair behind my ear. "Sure, that would be helpful. Thank you."

"Follow me, then."

I smiled at Emily, and she almost cracked a smile in return, but then thought better of it.

"Um, Juanita's coat," I began, pointing to the coat on the back of the door.

"I'll take care of it," Emily said.

I wondered what she made of me heading out with Jordan. I wondered if they'd ever had a thing. Not that I was about to ask him. How bad would that look? But they would certainly look good together; both ridiculously attractive; both had goblin blood, it seemed like a no-brainer to me. But perhaps the chemistry just wasn't there. Or maybe they'd had a thing, but it hadn't worked out, which might explain the dark looks she'd been giving him. Whatever. None of it was my business.

"I just need to grab my coat," Jordan said as we climbed the stairs. I could see the damp patches where I'd dripped all over the place, and then felt a stab of something else as I recalled him carrying me in his arms. I'd been as appreciative of it as an ice-pop at the time, but now that I was all toasty again, the memory gave me the tingles.

"Thank you for pulling me out of the river," I said as we reached the top of the stairs.

He pulled a black leather jacket off a hook at the top of the steps and oozed into it. "What? You think I'd have let you drown?" He shook his head and laughed ironically. He looked like a sexy demon, but there was something else. My goblin sense was telling me not to trust him any further than I could throw him, but the witch part of me was in complete disagreement. Her voice was whispering for me to trust him, that he wasn't so bad after all.

I must have been standing there with my mouth open or something because he looked at me strangely. "Are you sure you're okay? Did you bump your head or something when you went down?"

"Yeah, peachy," I said. "I was just thinking about stuff. It's all good."

Jordan reached up and pulled a slightly smaller jacket from a second hook. "Here, this is Emily's. You're both about the same size. It'll keep you warm while the car heats up."

"Do you think she'll mind?" I asked, gratefully slipping it on.

"Probably," he laughed. "But I'll get it back to her before she notices it's gone."

I nodded. My hands were cold, so I slipped my hands inside the pockets, hoping to warm them. My fingers brushed against something weird, and without thinking, I pulled it out. Odd. It was a pacifier. I didn't know Emily was a mom. I remembered the cot I'd seen in the library room. I slipped the pacifier back inside the pocket before Jordan noticed I'd found it.

"Ready?" Jordan asked.

"As I'll ever be."

I didn't like the punch of cold that socked me when the door opened. Jordan noticed my hesitation and grinned. "Good thing my car has bum warmers. Shall we?"

I followed Jordan out into the parking lot, dashing to the small Merc that double beeped as we exited. There were no rear seats, so I threw the bag of wet clothes in the small space at my feet and squeezed in, loving that the dark leather was already warming up behind me.

"Nice wheels," I said, my goblin heart admiring the complicated dash that lit up in front of me as the engine roared on.

"Yes, she's a beaut, isn't she?" He grabbed the steering wheel with affection. "Where am I going?"

"Oh. I have an apartment down by the Schuylkill, on Boathouse Row."

Jordan arched his eyebrows. "Oh, very nice. I didn't know snooping into other people's business paid so well."

"It's a small place," I said, defensively. "Not that my income is any of your business."

He laughed dismissively, driving off at a speed that felt oddly right in his snazzy sports-car.

"So, who do you have pegged for the murder?" Jordan asked as he stopped at a stop sign.

I shook my head.

"Oh, come on, you must have some idea."

I knew from his tone he was half serious, half-messing, but it would take more than a few warm clothes and a ride home for me to open up to him. As far as I was concerned, he was still up there on the suspect list.

"What's the deal with Emily?" I asked, as he sped forward.

"How do you mean?"

"I can't make her out. One minute she's a kitchen drudge and the next she's running the show. What gives? Was she Redcap's whipping girl or something? Is she related to you all, too? The wicked goblin stepsister or some such?"

Jordan was silent for a minute as he thought about his answer. "No, we're not related, although I've been told I look like her, so who knows? Maybe dear old Mom or Dad were playing away, no one can ever be sure, can they?"

I smiled. "I guess not."

"Redcap took her on a few years back. She started off bussing for us, but it soon became clear she was cut out for much more, so Red promoted her a few times. We all secretly thought they had a thing, but my brother was always very private about his affairs. It was only by accident I discovered—"

"Discovered what?"

Jordan looked at me, weighing up something in his mind. But then he shrugged, and took a resolute breath in. "I discovered quite by chance what they were into. Each to their own, I guess."

"Tell me!" I was almost on the edge of my seat, needing to know.

"I think they call them, um, Littles,"

"What's that mean?" I asked, wondering where this was going.

Jordan grinned like a naughty child. "Um, well, you know?"

"No sorry, I don't follow."

"Okay, well, one day I walked in on them. Didn't mean to, it just happened. Emily had Redcap bent over a stool. She was wearing a gingham apron and nothing else, he was dressed up like a little schoolboy. She was caning his naked butt."

"Oh my God, she was not!" I laughed out loud; I just couldn't help it. Then I remembered the pacifier and laughed some more.

"Yep. Redcap didn't see me, he was looking the other way, but Emily did. I zipped my lips, promising her I wouldn't say anything, and backed out of the room. But she knew I knew. She was never the same to me after that. I guess maybe she resented me knowing about their little secret."

I wiped tears from my eyes. "So that's what 'Littles' means. I'll have to remember in case anyone asks me for it."

It was Jordan's turn to laugh, and it was a gorgeous, deep laugh that made my spine vibrate, in the best possible way. I bit my lip and looked out my window at the passing world, thinking all kinds of unprofessional thoughts.

I remembered the bruise on the back of Emily's hand and realized

Redcap hadn't been brutalizing her at all. She'd got that backhanding him for some naughtiness or other.

"After I found out, they were still pretty private about everything, but one thing I will say about Emily, was I think she really loved him."

"Oh? How so?"

"Well, when he was sick, and trust me, my brother was a real pill when he was under the weather, she would go way out of her way to look after him. She insisted on preparing his medicines herself. So, you see," Jordan continued, "she's probably the last person in the world who would have wanted to see my brother dead. She had all the power in the world while he was alive. And now, well, she's just an employee. Of course, I'll make sure she's taken care of, my brother loved her after all, but everything has changed for her. Try and understand her if you can. She has a good heart underneath all that bravado."

"And gingham."

We both chuckled some more.

Well, I'd asked for the truth, and he'd given it, if only to clear Emily's name. But the goblin mob boss of Philadelphia, *a Little*? That was a lot to take in. But why would Jordan lie about that? What could he possibly hope to achieve?

"Look, I'd appreciate if you'd keep that bit of information to yourself," Jordan said. "My brother is dead. No one needs to see his dirty laundry as well."

I nodded. I could sense how this was paining him and was grateful for his trust. "Thank you," I said. "I'll do what I can to keep that part secret," I said, trying not to laugh.

"Thanks," Jordan said, with feeling.

Funny. It was like driving with an old friend. Not quite as comfortable as being with Liam, but up there. Jordan certainly knew how to press my buttons. I'd gone from fancying him, to disliking him, to feeling gratitude, to liking him, all in the space of a few hours. *He's a murder suspect, Dionne, don't forget that too.*

Jordan slowed down as we got close to where we were going and cocked his head to get a better view of the houses. I pointed to my apartment block right at the end of the row. "That's it, right there."

"Nice," he said.

"Thanks. And thanks for the ride."

I grabbed my bag of wet things, then slid out of Emily's jacket. "You better get this back to her before she misses it." I looked at the short distance from the car to the entrance to my apartment. "I've got this from here."

My hand was on the door handle, but I remembered what had happened the last time I'd run inside. Still, at least the lights were back on in the lobby. It was probably okay.

Jordan must have seen me hesitate.

"Is this where the balloon thing happened? You want me to check everything's okay before you go inside?"

"No, it's fine, I'll just—"

But he was already out of the car, a gun in his big paw—where had that come from? —and his other hand wrenching the door open to check inside. I know I was supposed to be a strong master of the universe, but God I loved the way he wanted to protect me.

I rushed inside, anxious to get out of the cold.

"Well, thank you again," I said, as I rubbed my arms which were once again feeling the cold.

"My pleasure." And he left.

This time I didn't wait to watch Jordan leave, I was shivering, and sure as day didn't want to hang around in the lobby.

I glanced around the floor, looking for my wand. I vaguely remembered it rolling off in the direction of the mailboxes, but it wasn't there. My gaze fell on a little trash can in a shadowy corner. I went to it and breathed a sigh of relief when I found it nestled in with the discarded mail. I pulled it out, and after wiping it on my trousers, ran upstairs to the door of my apartment.

"*Submitte defensiones!*" I said, more to check my wand was undamaged than anything else. My front door pulsed then settled down again. The door wasn't booby trapped or anything, which was a relief. Nor was it locked, which it should be, *dammit Mom*. I opened it and went inside.

It was strange, walking back into a place so familiar after everything that had happened. Mom was over at the stove, and Derek and Harrison were watching something on the television. Both looked very sorry for themselves. I guessed they were going stir-crazy; being cooped up in a small apartment with Mom was probably no picnic.

Harrison acknowledged me with a wave. I desperately wanted to fill my partner in, but I was shattered, and after all, what could he do now? Maybe I would give him a rundown of everything just as soon as I'd had a bit of dinner and a good night's sleep. Well, maybe not all of it. After all, my friend and partner had kept a few things back himself. Could I even trust him now? I hated that I'd just had that thought.

"There you are, Dee-Dee," Mom cried, as I put the bag of wet washing down on the kitchen table. "I was just getting ready to turn off the pasta again. I'm sure it's quite ruined." She looked me up and down, confused. "What are you doing in those strange clothes? Have you taken on a job in a diner?"

"No, Mom, look it's a long story, but my clothes are all wet. How long will that food be? I'm starving."

Mom brightened up and dashed back to the stove. "I'll have it all plated up for you in a jiffy. You just sit yourself down and leave everything to me. And take that bag of dirty washing off the table, were you brought up in a barn?"

I was too tired to do anything else, and so I slid on a stool and waited for Mom to dish something up, just like she used to when I lived at home. Scratchpoop jumped up in front of me and I rubbed his ears affectionately.

"Did you miss me?" I asked.

He head-butted my hand and flopped on his side, exposing his belly. I gave him a good rub there, too.

"Where's Patsy?" I asked, looking around and not seeing her.

"Oh, she went back into her kettle for a bit of a nap. She said she'd catch you later. Oh, and I almost forgot," she said. "A woman called for you."

"What was her name?" I asked, rubbing my eyes that were getting desperate to close.

"Her name was Ginny¬—no wait—Judy—no, that wasn't it. What was her name?"

"Gayle?" I suggested, making an intuitive leap.

"Yes, that's it. Anyway, she said it was urgent."

My body felt like a lead brick, but I slid off the seat and picked up the house phone. Luckily, I knew the city morgue number by heart. I strongly suspected this might be why my social life was non-existent.

After a few rings, my call was answered.

"Hello, city morgue, Assistant M.E. Brightflower speaking."

"Hi Gayle, it's Dionne. Mom said you were trying to reach me?"

"Oh hi, Dionne! Yes, I've been calling your number all night, but it keeps going into your voicemail."

"Err, yeah, um, my phone got a bit wet. What's up? Do you have the autopsy result?" That got Harrison's and Derek's attention.

"I do, I do," Gayle exclaimed cheerfully. "The official cause of death was heart failure caused by the introduction of Batrachotoxin into his cardiovascular system."

"What's that in English?" I asked, although the "toxin" part already gave me a clue.

"Poison. The cause of death was poison."

## Chapter Twenty-One
# GIRL TALK

"What kind of poison is that?" I asked. "Where would a poison like that come from? Who would have access to it?"

"It's a pretty nasty one, you get from certain species of bird, frogs, and beetles. It's very popular in Columbia with the Chocó I believe. The frogs excrete it through their skin you know, and it's insanely lethal. The goblin wouldn't have stood a chance."

"How did it get inside him?" I asked, thinking of Emily's little medicine bottles.

"Well, these toxins were typically used for poison darts. It comes off the skin of little yellow frogs. Lethal stuff. It'll bring a deer down in seconds. And there's no known antidote for it."

"Err nice," I said, suddenly off the meatballs Mom had shoved in front of me. I pushed the plate away. Poison darts, huh? Had Wally killed Redcap after all? Or Puk? Puk seemed to have worshipped Redcap, but what if there was something I'd missed? It wouldn't exactly be the first time.

"Actually, it's pretty easy to come by," Gayle continued. "There's a black market for everything these days. If someone wants it, someone supplies it."

"How did it get inside him?" I asked, thinking about those nasty little darts. "Where were the puncture wounds?"

"No, I checked every square inch of his body, including his scalp and his, uh, nether regions, but I couldn't find a thing. He had no tattoos, which was good because it's impossible to spot little punctures there. Not even his ears were pierced. No, my guess is he probably drank it, unless of course, someone *made* him drink it, but there were no signs of bodily violence. Nope, one quick swig and the goblin would have been down in seconds. That stuff acts that fast. Anyway, that's everything I know. Oh, one last thing."

"Yes?"

"There were traces of a sticky gel on his clothes. It was pretty degraded; but it wouldn't have killed him, so it might be nothing at all. I just thought I'd mention it."

"Thanks, Gayle," I said, my mind racing. "I owe you one. Whenever you're up for it I'll buy you a horn of frothy mead down at The Fairy Barn."

"Yup, good call. We're totally overdue for a girly natter. Call me when you have a free night."

"Will do. Thanks again." I hung up the phone.

Derek and Harrison were both sitting in front of me, all ears. "What do you two know about frog poison?"

They both gazed back at me with blank expressions. "Know about *what* poison?" Derek asked.

"Frog. As in *ribbit*. You know—Kermit." I pulled my plate back to me and twirled some spaghetti around my fork. I guess I was still hungry after all.

"Is that what killed him?" Harrison asked.

"Your *other* partner? Yes." Maybe I was being blunt, but I wanted to get to the bottom of this.

"Oh. Then you know," Harrison said, his voice flat.

"Of course, I know. They threw you under the bus the first chance they got. Rather you a suspect than them. When were you gonna tell me, huh? We're supposed to be partners."

Harrison frowned. "It's not something I'm proud of. I'm in the finding missing people business, not the extortion or killing people business. But the money came in handy for some things."

"Like what?" I snapped.

"Well, like it paid for the deposit on our office."

I winced at that.

"You can't get started in this city without a bit of cash," Harrison continued. "I just figured I'd keep my mouth shut and take the payouts until I could tell 'em to stuff 'em where the sun don't shine."

"You still should have told me," I admonished.

"I'll put the kettle on, shall I?" Mom said, anxiously.

"What, and wake Patsy?" I sighed and stabbed a meatball. "Can I get a glass of hot milk?"

Suddenly I was exhausted. While Mom warmed milk in a pot, I forced in another loaded fork of spaghetti, but it was getting harder and harder to swallow. I was just too tired. I pushed my plate away again, done eating.

"Here's your milk, sweetie," Mom said.

"I'm off to bed," I said, taking the glass. "And I need company."

Everyone looked at me confused, but I swept the kettle up and tucked it under my arm. "*Smart* company," I said, frowning at Harrison. "See you all in the morning. Don't wake me up before noon."

I yawned, almost spilling my milk. "Oh, and Mom."

"Yes, Dee-Dee?"

"Would you mind running that through the wash?" I asked, indicating the bag of wet clothes.

"Sure."

"Just make sure you pull my wallet and phone out of my pockets. They've had enough of a soak for one night."

Mom looked confused but I didn't hang around for any of her questions. I had way too many of my own to contend me, and I needed space to think.

As soon as I was safely inside my bedroom, I closed the door and took a quick shower to get the stench of the river out of my hair. After that I felt a little better and slipped into my pajamas before climbing into bed. Then I grabbed the kettle and gave it a quick rub.

Patsy performed her usual dramatic entrance, filling my room with green tinted smoke and flame. Luckily, it was all for effect, nothing actually caught fire. She was gigantic and loomed over the bed, having to bend double, before shrinking to handy human size again. Her hair was braided into pink pigtails, and she wore green flannel pajamas, and furry slippers topped with baby goblins balls on the front. She looked like she was staying over for a slumber party. All that was missing was the pillow.

"Good evening, Miss Dionne," she said pleasantly, floating cross-legged above my bed. "How lovely to see you again. What can I do for you?"

"I need someone to help me clear my thoughts. And no, I'm not asking for a wish. I just need a good listener."

"Listening is one of the things I do best," Patsy beamed. "What would you like to talk about?"

"This case," I said. "My thoughts are all in a jumble and I need someone to bounce them off to get them straight."

"Excellent!" Patsy said. "I'm all ears. Give me the um, what do you call it?"

"Rundown."

"Yes, give me that!"

"Okay." I cleared my throat and tried to focus my thoughts. "Well, we just learned that Redcap was killed by poison."

"Roger that," Patsy said, drawing a glowing tick-mark in the air alongside a picture of a brown glass bottle with a grinning skull painted on it. Very useful.

"So now I'm thinking about all the suspects."

"Okie dokie. Fire away."

"Well, first off, there's the pukwudgies. Wally, we know despised Redcap, but he wasn't even there when he died, and Gayle said the poison would have killed him in seconds."

"True," Patsy said, "but he might have planted the poison in something earlier. He didn't have to be there to do it."

"Yes, he did. If it killed Redcap immediately, how would someone as small as Wally get his body into the river and so quickly if he wasn't even there?" Hmm, this prompted a thought —maybe the killer used a bubble to transport the body, then popped it over the Delaware! Of course—that would explain the gel! Heck, anyone who can employ bubble magic could have done the deed. But then, who could do bubble magic?

"Ooh, good point," Patsy said, sounding all serious. She drew a picture of Wally in the air, then drew a big red X through this.

"His brother Puk had opportunity, but he was loyal to Redcap, at least as far as I know, and I haven't been able to establish any ulterior motive."

Patsy nodded solemnly, following all this. She conjured a picture of Puk, and crossed it out with another red X.

"Then there's Derek and Harrison, well, both had clear motives, but dart poison? Derek, we know for sure had no time to plan this, and dart poison isn't exactly easy to come by, so I figure it isn't likely to be him."

"True," Patsy agreed, "but he has a magic shop and knows a lot of people. Who knows what he was able to get his hands on?"

I thought about it for a second but shook my head. "Nah, this was planned. Derek wouldn't have had time to come up with something so elaborate, and well, he's a known pacifist, he had peace signs all over his shop. Murder hardly seems his style."

Patsy drew Derek's scowling, bearded face in the air, then applied a red X over it. Derek's expression changed to a beatific smile. I almost laughed. Above him, the images of Wally and Puk had become animated, they were arguing with each other, one looking down, the other looking up, both shaking their little fists. She was quite the comedienne, our Patsy.

"What about Harrison, then?" Patsy asked, nodding toward the door.

"Hmm, well, he had motive and opportunity, but dart poison? That was a little too sophisticated for him, don't you think? No, if Harrison wanted to off Redcap, he would have banged him over the head with a baseball bat or shot him in the chest. He's pure goblin through and through, blunt and to the point. I can't imagine it was him."

"Liam could have done it."

I laughed. "Why, what possible motive would Liam have?"

"Isn't he a bit in love with you?" Patsy said sweetly. "He'd do anything for you, I know he would. And if he thought you were in some kind of danger...."

"No," I smiled. "Liam knows I can handle myself," I blushed, thinking about how I'd been abducted, "and in any case, he was down at the station giving his testimony at the time, so unless he can move like the devil himself, he wouldn't have had a chance to do it."

"If you say so," she said, snickering and drawing a red X over a picture of Liam. His eyes rolled up so he appeared to be staring at Patsy with what could only be called frank admiration. I wanted to slap him. I was over here.

"So that leaves me with who, Emily and Jordan?" A picture of Emily appeared, scowling at me, and then Jordan, smiling as if he knew I was a sure thing. She side-eyed him but he seemed oblivious to this. I'll be damned if he didn't wink at me. Or maybe that was just my sleep-deprived brain. *Hmmm.* I grabbed the glass of hot milk and hid behind it for a second so Patsy couldn't read me so clearly. I had to admit, if it came to a choice, I secretly wanted it to be Emily, because maybe, when all this was over, maybe Jordan and I...

No, that was stupid. I had to get back to the facts.

"Well, Emily had opportunity and sure as heck had means. Redcap was sipping that medicine she was dosing him like cranberry juice. She could easily have slipped some poison into it."

"Okay, but why?" Patsy asked.

"That's what I'm trying to figure out. I wish I knew." I pondered telling Patsy about Redcap's predilection for playing baby, but I suspected she already knew. She seemed to know pretty much everything that was going on.

"That leaves..."

"Jordan. With his brother out of the picture he'd gain full control of The Rotting Corpse, and all their other sordid ventures. The only thing is, he's not the only partner, but it could be him. He had opportunity, means, and a motive."

"You think he would choose poison to kill him. He wouldn't just shoot him?"

"Maybe, if only to throw the scent onto the others, who might appear much more likely to use poison to kill him."

"But you're not sure?" Patsy observed.

I tapped my gut. "No, not in here. He's not shown much remorse over his brother's death, but he's a goblin. Goblin men rarely show their true feelings. He could be hurting like crazy, and we'd never see it."

The image of Jordan darkened, and his brow looked tortured and heartbroken.

"On the other, maybe he is just a cold and callous murderer, just waiting for a chance for the other goblin gangsters to gather and pledge loyalty to him as their new godfather, the capo di tutti goblins. I could sure as heck see Jordan doing that."

The image of Jordan changed again, and this time, a hoard of goblin soldiers bowed down before him, kissing his hand. But there was no red X though.

"So, what are you going to do?"

"Good question." I drained the last of Mom's warm milk then parked the glass on the bedside table. "I think I'm going to have a word with a little friend of mine."

"Who's that?" Patsy asked.

"Finn."

"Ooh, I don't think I've met him yet, have I?"

"No, not yet. He's my, um, eyes and ears. Anyway," I said sleepily. "It's getting late. I'll just call him in the morning."

"Okie dokie!" Patsy clasped her hands. "I liked this game. We should do it again sometime."

"Yeah," I said, already out of it. I slid down under the covers and closed my eyes. It had been one hell of a day. "Thanks for your help, Patsy."

"Was I really useful?"

"Yes, you were, you really were."

"Oh, goodie. Sleep tight."

The images Patsy conjured all popped.

And I slept.

## *Chapter Twenty-Two*
# PICKLED EYEBALLS

THE SMELL OF GRILLED BACON FILLED MY ROOM. NOTHING COULD HAVE dragged me from my bed faster, and after a quick wash I was out of my bedroom and in my kitchen, hoping the plate of bacon and eggs at the vacant seat was mine. Harrison and Derek were already chomping down, and Scratchpoop was up on the counter in front of them, staring them down, hoping they would notice him and share their feast.

I paused, wary of how cozy this all looked, and began to wonder if any of them were ever going to leave. Except Scratchpoop of course. He just had some retraining to do.

"Ah, Dee-Dee! Last one up again!" Mom said, flipping a pancake over in the pan. "That plate's for you. Do you want a side of pancakes, or will the bacon and eggs be enough? Where's Patsy?"

"Just the bacon and eggs," I said, yawning. "Patsy's in her kettle as far as I know."

"Morning," Harrison said warily, as I slid into my seat. His skin was his full-on green today, which I preferred, and I began to suspect he might know that. I took hold of Scratchpoop and lowered him to the floor. Unimpressed, he walked off, tail straight and rigid in a huff.

I didn't answer immediately, because Mom slipped a mug of coffee my way and that took precedence over everything. If there was any doubt about my goblin heritage, my mornings proved it. Talk to me at your peril.

When I came up for air, I growled a polite, "Good morning," and set about mashing my bacon into the runny yolks. I had my egg-smothered fork half-way to my lips when the house phone rang. Typical.

"Can you get that, Mom? Or someone?" I asked, looking at the two men around me who had done little except sit on their behinds since the moment they'd arrived. Mom flipped the last pancake onto a flat plate and slid it over to us. Harrison tucked in right away and began buttering up a stack of six. Boy that goblin could eat.

Derek began to get up, but Mom beat him to the punch and sweetly ushered him back down into his seat. "Don't worry dear. I've got this. You just enjoy those pancakes." Anything rather than ruin her breakfast. "Hello. Dee-Dee—I mean Dionne Cruz's residence. How can I help you? Why yes, it is— Oh hello—Yes—No, I'm afraid she's eating—Yes. Absolutely. Bye for now."

She hung up. I stared at her expectantly, my mouth full of protein, wondering who on earth she'd just been talking to.

"Such a nice man," Mom said.

"Who was it?" I asked.

"It's a pity he's just a human," she continued, dreamily.

"Mom!"

"Oh, that was Liam, dear. Who else would it be? I don't know anyone else. I thought you were a detective."

Derek almost choked on his hash browns and even Harrison managed a smile.

I ignored their snark. "Was there a message?"

"Yes, dear. He's on his way over. I told him I'd tell you."

"Did he happen to say why?"

"No, Dee-Dee. Why would he tell me anything? You're the one he wanted to speak to."

I almost dropped my face into what remained of my eggs so I could drown in them. But the others were watching me, and I didn't want to give them the satisfaction.

I shrugged and picked half a rasher up from my plate.

"Fingers, dear," Mom remonstrated.

I shoved it in my mouth and licked my egg-stained fingers for good measure. Mom just shook her head, hands on her hips. "Headstrong, just like her father."

Mom sat down beside me and began working on what looked like a dry piece of toast. She always had been a light eater whereas I could put it away when I wanted to. Dad genes as well, I guessed.

"Where did you put my phone and stuff?" I asked Mom, looking around the kitchen for both my phone and my soggy wallet. "Does anyone know a spell to dry them out?"

"No need," Mom said. "Everything's dandy. And your phone's probably working just fine now."

I looked at her curiously. "What did you do?"

"Well, I thought about sticking it in the microwave…"

"Oh no, you didn't?" I gasped, horrified.

"Well, I thought about it but then I had a better idea."

"And what was that?" I said, covering my eyes with my palm. I had nasty visions of her running it through the tumble dryer or sticking it on a baking tray in the oven and heating it under the grill.

"Well, since you ask, I turned it off so it wouldn't short out and stuffed it in a Ziplock bag with a cup of dry rice. It's over there, on top of the microwave. I cleaned off the rice earlier. Go check it out."

I dropped my hand in surprise. That was a seriously smart thing to do. Curious, I slid off my seat and went over to retrieve it. It looked cleaner than it had in a long time—Mom had polished it up good. I had a moment's trepidation while I waited for it to power on, but power on it did, and I saw I had a number of missed messages pop up at once, all from Liam.

"Cool, Mom. Thanks."

"You're welcome, dear."

"I um, just have to make a quick call," I said, heading toward my bedroom. "I'll be right back."

Once inside my room, I closed the door gently behind me and sat on the end of my bed. This was one call I didn't want anyone else to hear.

I pulled the phone from my ear as his high-pitched whine almost shattered my ear drum. "This is Finn. I is not here, ha ha. Leave a message—I might call you back—if you be lucky."

I called again and got the same. I said, "Hey Finn baby, it's Ivanka, you wanna good time this weekend? You know you do. Call me, kiss kiss."

Finn would know well enough who it was. I doubted anyone else had this particular number. The Bucca was far too careful about things like that.

My call made, I went back into the kitchen where Mom was cleaning up after breakfast, and the two guys were hunkered down in front of the television, so situation normal. My throw pillows were all tossed on the floor and unused blankets were crumpled around their feet. I knew they had no place else to go but was already looking forward to the day when this was all resolved, and I had my apartment back to myself. I also noticed the two of them were certainly very chummy, sitting very close to each other. I wondered if Harrison had gotten lucky after all.

"Everything okay, dear?" Mom asked, steering me into the hall.

"Peachy. What's up?"

As soon as we were alone, she whispered, "They watched all the Lord of the Rings movies. Now they're binge-watching Game of Thrones. Derek keeps covering his face and whimpering. Harrison pauses it until Derek's got up the courage to watch more. I haven't the heart to tell them they only have one more season to go."

"Don't worry, Mom," I whispered back. "They'll be gone soon enough."

"If you say so, Dee-Dee." But she sounded none-too-convinced.

I gave her a quick kiss on the cheek. "You're a rock star, Mom. I'd be totally lost without you. Thank you for everything."

Her eyes sparkled with delight. "Come on," I said, steering her back to the kitchen. "I just need to look something up on the Internet. Don't mind me." I grabbed what was left of my breakfast and my coffee and settled down in front of my laptop.

While the front room reverberated to Good Morning America, I Googled for poison dart frog supplies, since I couldn't remember the name of the actual toxin. I was gob smacked by the number of breeders, YouTube videos and suppliers that popped up, like Supernatural Frog World and Bad Bart's Dart Emporium. I added Philadelphia to narrow the search.

*Wow.* I'd expected a hunt but was amazed by how easy it was to find what I was looking for. Websites showed social media accounts, and vendors accepted major credit cards and cash apps, with discounts and coupons for regular customers. How easy it was to come by the actual poison was another matter, but a determined murderer would have no trouble getting his hands on enough to wreak havoc.

*Hmm.* The sites were a wonder of low-level illegal live contraband, like hellbenders, fire salamanders, and hedgehogs. Gray market dealers specialized in this stuff, flying right on the radar line, remaining too low-key to attract law enforcement but definitely dealing on the shady side of legal.

There were three suppliers in this area alone, so I pulled up those sites and made a note of the addresses and phone numbers in between nibbling my bacon and sipping my coffee.

Since Liam wasn't here yet and I had a bit of time, I did an internet search for pickled eyeballs. After all, why not? My inner goblin was just dying to try one after all.

*Hmm.* Wow again. It was amazing what you could find in a mason jar on Etsy. Again, I added Philadelphia to the search and clicked on the first link that popped up in my feed. Eyeball Junky - pickling eyeballs since 1983.

A whole series of multi-colored eyeballs came up, some of which were clearly macabre candy, others looking a lot more like the real thing. I scrolled through the feed, enjoying some of the more elaborate creations, at least in a visual way. As I suspected, none of these were really eyeballs, and the pickled ones were just mollusks shoved inside reptile eggs. I added a couple of jars to my cart.

On the purchase page I noticed the contact address of the seller. The address looked oddly familiar, and I cross checked it to the three addresses I'd written down just a moment ago. "Interesting!" I exclaimed. I had a match. Coincidence maybe? Not if my instincts had anything to do with it. I resolved to check out that dealer first.

"Find something, sweetie?" Mom asked.

"Maybe, I'm not sure," I said truthfully. "I was thinking if I found the supplier, they might help me nail the killer. And I might have just found them."

Harrison got up and came to look over my shoulder.

"Oooh, pickled reptile eyeballs. I haven't had those since I was a kid. My mom gave them to me all the time."

"Mine didn't," I said with a hint of regret. But I smiled inwardly at the fresh reminder of Redcap's fetish.

"Nasty, smelly things," Mom said. "I wouldn't allow them in the house."

"Any closer to the killer?" Harrison asked.

"Not yet," I said, truthfully. There was no need for either of us to mention he was still on the list of suspects. "I've been checking out all the local suppliers of frog dart poison. I never knew it was such a big thing. Check this out."

I moved aside, allowing Harrison the opportunity to scroll through at his leisure. The big green goof was like a kid in a candy store, chuckling at all the ghoulish things they had on sale. Some items appealed to me, like the pickled eyeballs and the sugared or salted troll toenail clippings, big as bananas. Others not so much, like the slug gum you could chew for hours, and jellied snail poop. Those I would happily pass on, real or otherwise.

"Oh, ha, I used to do that," Harrison laughed. He had pulled up an image of a young goblin boy licking the back of a rather surprised looking frog. "That was a lot of fun. All the boys used to do it."

"Well then," Mom said, curling up her nose as she stared over his shoulder at the screen, armed with a carafe of coffee to freshen Harrison's mug, "I'm so glad I had a daughter. I'd never allow one of those nasty looking things in my house. How do you think witches get their warts?" She put a hand to her face just to check her complexion. "Ugh!"

Harrison and I both laughed, and he moved aside so I could finish what I was doing.

"Well, when you find Redcap's killer, tell 'em thank you from me," Harrison said. "Saves me the trouble of doing him myself."

I was just about to reply when a buzz vibrated through the apartment. I looked instinctively over to the door. "That'll be Liam. Would you buzz him in?"

"Sure." Harrison went over to the front door and pressed the button on the intercom. "Hello—Yep, come on up."

A minute later there was a knock at the door, and after checking through the peephole, Harrison opened it, allowing Liam in.

"Hello," Harrison said.

Derek waved but immediately turned his attention back to the television.

"Ah, Liam, let me fix you a cup of coffee," Mom said. No wonder these guys never leave, I thought unkindly.

"Thanks," Liam said. "I'll take it black if that's okay?"

"Lovely," Mom beamed. "And how about a nice bacon sandwich?"

"No, thank you, I just had breakfast."

Mom looked deflated but went about fixing his coffee.

"Hey," I said, not getting up as I quickly finalized my purchase using my cash app. "What gives?"

"I just wanted to give you an update," Liam said. "The tests on all of Redcap's medicine bottles came back negative for any signs of the Batrachotoxin."

Hmm. I imagined Patsy's image of Emily getting another big red X. Shame. But then she could have dropped the incriminating bottle into the Delaware, right beside him. The X disappeared. She was back on my list again.

"And the poison darts?"

"Probably another dead end. The samples we tested were potentially lethal, but the tips were coated in curare."

"What's that?"

"It's a vegetable-based toxin that paralyzes the victim's diaphragm and causes asphyxia. You'll be glad to know that goblins have a natural resistance to it. The stuff will make you sick as a pig, but it shouldn't kill you."

"Oh, right. You know you could have told me all this on the phone and saved yourself a trip."

"I could have. But there's something else I thought you'd want to know."

"Yeah?"

Mom interrupted at that moment to give Liam his mug of coffee.

"Thanks. Redcap's funeral is this afternoon, down at the 'Slug and Swamp Cemetery.' If you want, I thought we could take a ride over there and check out who shows up and see how they react."

Goblin funerals were odd events. Not so much a mourning of the dead, so much as the official stamp on his division of minor assets. The goblin himself was generally tossed in an unmarked grave, not much bigger than the goblin himself, and the mourners would chuck all manner of nasty stuff in after him, like rotting eggs and vegetables, all to hasten the decomposition process.

"Good idea. I'd better change," I said, staring down at my retro Killing Joke tee and black sweatpants.

Liam took a tentative swig from his coffee, then winked at Mom. "Hits the spot, Mrs. Cruz."

Mom beamed.

"Yeah, maybe you should," Liam continued, looking me up and down frankly. "Where's Patsy?"

Without knowing why, I left without giving him an answer. As I closed my bedroom door, I tried really hard not to think about Jordan. And more importantly, what would be the most appealing thing to wear, while still remaining respectful at a funeral for the goblin dead?

## Chapter Twenty-Three
# THE GOBLIN DEAD

Half a foot of snow had fallen overnight. I shivered as I zipped up my black leather jacket and wished spring would come sooner rather than later. Ahead of us were the black iron gates leading into the Slug and Swamp Cemetery. It was the only place in Philly where goblins could get a decent burial.

We moved forward with the mourners, stepping carefully along the slush-strewn, salted path. Dirty flecks of the nasty mess coated my black slacks, and the soles of my boots were caked in mucky snow. Yet the mood was upbeat and festive; all goblins loved a good funeral, and the death of a mob boss was absolutely chart-topping in that regard.

Most of the mourners carried the traditional goblin-green disposable garbage bags, chock full of all the nasty things like spoiled tomatoes and moldy bread we liked to throw at the body. I had a bag of my own, and though I'd kept nothing especially moldy at home, I'd filled it with some turning potatoes found at the bottom of my potato bin, along with some ham a day or so past its best-before-end date.

"Is this your first goblin funeral?" I asked Liam as a short goblin with a rather pungent bag passed us on the path.

"Sure is," Liam replied, pretending he was only scratching his nose so as not to appear impolite. "I have to ask, what's with all the garbage?"

"Ah, well, goblins believe in reincarnation. The sooner a corpse decomposes, the quicker the soul can return for another round. Anything that can speed up the process of rotting is considered a good thing. It's very eco-friendly, in a macabre sort of way."

"If you say so." Liam looked none too convinced.

I was not surprised at the size of the crowd come out to show their support, even in this weather. I recognized more than a few of the faces and I was sure Liam did, too. There was Steely, the one-eyed mob boss from Pittsburgh, and Missy Grendell, the goblinette boss from Allentown, both looking to muscle in on the late goblin's action. And of course, Jordan. Although the half-goblin might inherit his brother's primary assets, it was no sure thing he would head up the organization in his place. That position had to be earned.

If I had to choose, my money was on Missy Grendell; she was younger, stronger, and a thousand times nastier than both her chief rivals. It would be a bad day for Pennsylvania if she became capo di tutti goblins. Time would tell.

"So, is there like a priest or something?" Liam asked as we made our way through the graveyard, passing all the pebble mounds that marked the sites of the dead.

"No, nothing like that," I said. "He'll be carried in by his soldiers and dropped feet first into his grave. It's really pretty basic. No decent goblin would toss good money after the dead. That would be disrespectful. Better to give it to the living."

"No one says anything? You know, about the dead."

"There might be a shaman, but he doesn't cost anything."

Liam raised an amused eyebrow but said nothing. We took up a spot near a leafless weeping willow. The ground was slightly raised there, affording a reasonable view of the burial site, though very little shelter from the falling light snow. The grave was already dug out, and we watched as the arriving mourners gravitated to the left, where Steely had camped, or to the right, showing their support to Grendell, or to the head of the grave, where Jordan and his followers had camped. Emily stood beside him, dressed respectfully in dark green, her veil-covered head bowed in thought. Jordan's gathering of followers looked the smallest, Steely had just a handful more, whereas Grendell looked positively delighted with the number of goblins who went down on one knee to pledge their support.

"Well, Jordan doesn't look too bothered," Liam observed. "Do you think he really wanted to succeed his brother?"

"Hard to say. Neither of us know him that well, and you know how good my kind is at masking."

"Well, if hand kisses are anything to go by, then Long Live Queen Grendell."

I nodded. "It certainly looks that way."

I scanned the faces of the crowd, looking for Finn. There were plenty of goblins, hobgoblins, demons, and sprites. As was the tradition, there were a few cardboard boxes with unwanted items belonging to the deceased left out for the mourners to squabble over. I watched as one hobgoblin squealed with delight when he pulled out a long string of pearls. Almost immediately, the hobgoblin beside him leapt onto his back, making a play for the necklace which the first kept at arm's length. They began to spin wildly, the one trying to shake the other off, but the second hobgoblin had his claws in him good and wasn't about to let go. Desperate, they fell to the ground, fighting like madmen. Inevitably the string broke, and both hobgoblins squealed at the top of their lungs as the pearls went flying, then they thrashed around in the snow, trying to recover what was lost.

Other items, such as framed pictures of Redcap with family or I presumed old girlfriends, were left untouched on the snowy ground. Boy were there a lot of them!

There was no sign of the Bucca. I really thought he would be here, just to pay his respects. It would certainly be expected if he intended to keep his job. But he was nowhere in sight. I checked my phone to see if he'd called me back, but so far, nada. "Expecting someone?" Liam asked.

"Err, yeah. I have a friend I haven't heard from in a while." Come to think of it, I hadn't heard a whisper from him since the morning of the murder. I truly hoped he was alright.

"You want me to look into it?" Liam offered.

"Err, no, I don't think he'd like it."

"Oh, it's a man, huh?" Liam's eyes twinkled.

"Nothing like that," I said. "But I *am* getting worried. If he doesn't show up soon, I'll let you know."

"Sure. Just tell me if you change your mind and I'll see what I can find out."

After a while, a hearse pulled up a few feet away, followed by a few regular cars. For a minute or so, all we could hear were the slams and bangs of doors as they opened and closed.

Jordan, as the nearest blood relative of the deceased, rose to take his place by the hearse. Puk and Wally climbed out of the rear of the first car, then stood respectfully in front of the hearse, while soldiers of the late boss pulled out a stretcher from the rear, wearing dented top hats with black silk ribbons that sat at an awkward angle on their goblin heads.

Lying on the stretcher was Redcap, fully clothed, dressed in his finery, a green suede jacket with gold braid, bellbottom pants, and matching green snakeskin boots, his red cap washed and ironed and respectfully returned to his head. Jordan, who was considerably taller than the true blood goblins, began to walk back toward the grave. He was flanked by the two pukwudgies, then the soldiers carrying the body.

The mood remained upbeat, more like a wedding than a funeral. Someone turned on a ghetto blaster the size of a small car. 'Stayin' Alive' by the Bee Gees played at full volume, echoing across the cemetery. Goblin humor and irony all in one. I bowed my head and tried not to snicker. That would have been rude.

When they got to the grave, Jordan and the pukwudgies stood aside and the soldiers advanced until they stood at the end of the freshly dug grave. Those at the back raised their end of the stretcher, tipping it up until Redcap slid into his final resting place, feet first. He made a dull, wet thumping noise. *Adios, Redcap.*

Out of nowhere (I hated other people's magic) came the shaman, wearing a cloak and headdress made of crow feathers. He made a big show of raising his fists and screaming at the sky. "Great Ogg, I call on you to visit bloody vengeance upon Redcap's murderer, who is still unknown to us. Straighten his teeth, weaken his eyes, and cover his face in warts!"

And then he disappeared again.

"That's all you get for free, I suppose," Liam said.

I tried not to chuckle.

One of the soldiers handed Jordan his green bag, and Jordan walked to the edge of the grave and dumped a whole ton of rotting vegetables on his late brother. He then stepped to one side, allowing others to come forward.

One by one the mourners dropped in their rubbish, and if it wasn't for the cold weather, I imagined the place would pong like high heaven. As was custom, the visiting goblin bosses held back, allowing the rank and file through before paying their respects themselves.

It was time for us to do the same, so I nudged Liam and we headed over to the grave. As I dumped the contents of my bag, I caught Jordan's eye for the first time. As ever, he remained inscrutable, betraying nothing of what he was feeling. He acknowledged my presence with a slight nod. Emily's face remained cold, though I wondered if this time it was to mask her grief. Who could tell?

We were just about to leave when Steely appeared beside me. He was a typical goblin, about Redcap's height, with a broad stocky physique and a narrow waist. His fingers were long and knobby, and he had long, discolored fingernails that looked years old. After shaking out his offering, he approached Jordan, but unlike the goblin who'd just left him, he did not go on bended knee.

"Don't get any ideas above your station, half-goblin. Only a true blood can keep the peace. Try to step into your brother's shoes and there will be chaos. It will not go well for you."

"I don't take orders from a mountain goblin, Steely," Jordan countered. "Why don't you return to your pits and suck out what's left of the coal? Your kind is done, old man. Leave our business to those fittest to run it. The younger goblins."

"I couldn't agree more," came a gravelly voice from behind me. I turned just as Missy Grendell was shaking the contents of her bag into the grave. She was a slender, new generation goblin, with height born from solid nutrition, but a true blood, nonetheless. Her dark green skin was scarred heavily from fighting, but though her face bore similar scars, her eyes were too close together and her nose too long to be considered a beauty. It gave her a shrewd, calculating look, and you knew at once she wasn't someone to fool with. "Oh, by the way, nice job on your brother. I hear you have the normies running around in circles, trying to riddle this one out. Well done."

She looked at me as she spoke, a sneer of contempt distorting her already ugly features. I wondered if she knew who we were. Then again, I'd have been surprised if she didn't.

"I didn't kill my brother," Jordan said. "When I find out who did, you'll hear his screams all the way to Allentown." He said it with such sincerity that I couldn't help but believe him.

"That's unfortunate," Grendell responded. "Because you'd have risen in my esteem if you had. Steely is right about one thing, though."

"Oh?" Jordan said.

"Do you really think you have the guts to do what it takes?" Grendell clicked her fingers, and in a flash one of her soldiers appeared at her side, a solid slab of hobgoblin muscle. He looked as if he'd eaten The Hulk for breakfast. "This is Rorkell, one of my longest-serving, most loyal soldiers. One word from me and he'll jump in, right next to your brother, and will stay there as we cover him up. Somehow, I don't think you wield that degree of loyalty in your people."

Rorkell bowed his head, a grim but iron determination on his face, like he'd do anything to prove his loyalty, even if it killed him, the chump. That was goblins for you, poop for brains didn't even cover it. How we'd ever survived as a species was beyond me.

Grendell smiled. "Pity. But there it is. See you in the trenches. I won't be coming to the wake. I have a city to run."

"Nor will I," Steely said, although it sounded a tad pathetic after Missy Grendell's show of strength.

The two mob bosses left, leaving Emily and Jordan the last remaining mourners at the grave. Rorkell, realizing he wasn't required to commit suicide in the worst possible way imaginable, shrugged with what might have been disappointment, then turned and hurried after his boss. I felt kind of relieved. I hoped Grendell appreciated his gusto.

"Pity they can't come," Emily said.

"Why's that?" Jordan asked.

"I baked muffins."

I almost laughed. But then I wondered if she meant the muffins were poisoned. With the same frog snot that had killed Redcap. I'd been thinking Jordan might have killed his half-brother so he could control The Rotted Corpse and The Barbecue Baron… or Emily had done it because Redcap had refused her promotion and a stake in the business. But what if the two of them were working in cahoots with each other? Cahoots, I never got to use that word enough. What if they'd both had a hand in his death? Talk about fog on the river. If required, each could even provide an alibi for the other. But here was another potentially murderous twist. Were they hoping to wipe out the competition in one fell swoop at the wake? Clever, if that was indeed their plan. I made a mental note to avoid Emily's muffins.

## Chapter Twenty-Four
# THE WAKE

THE ROTTING CORPSE WAS PACKED. THE WAKE WAS AN OPEN invitation to anyone who knew Redcap. Drafts of Drunken Goblin ale were flowing, 'Ashes to Ashes' was booming through the speakers, and trays of sandwiches, sausages rolls, and muffins were doing the rounds.

Neither Liam nor I had officially been invited, but here we were, and we had to eat. I happily snatched what looked like a ham sandwich as a tray passed under my nose. Liam reached for a muffin, but I steered his arm clear.

"I'd stick to the sandwiches if I were you," I said.

He let them pass.

Jordan was standing in the corner looking uncharacteristically downcast. Like Missy Grendell, Steely had opted not to come to the wake, which was basically thumbing his nose at Jordan, and he knew it. Not that it made any difference to the numbers at The Rotting Corpse—free food was free food, and the miserly goblins were lapping it up. When the goblins got too rowdy, which was mostly when they fought over Redcap's goods, then Jordan would swoop in, bang a few heads, then resume his post at the end of the bar, just watching.

A young, quite attractive fairy dressed in a shimmering red dress was standing by him. She kept touching his arm and leaning into him, all the while fluffing her hair and trying to catch his eye, but no matter what she did, she just couldn't draw his attention. He seemed immune to her gold fairy dust, which was rare in any man.

Emily crossed the room and whispered something in Jordan's ear. He frowned and said something back. The excluded young fairy got the message and disappeared into the crowd. I could relate. My inquiries were getting nowhere, fast. It was time to up the tempo.

"I think I'm gonna have a word with our friend over there," I said to Liam, who was busy washing down the last of his sandwich with some free raspberry lemonade. He had his eye on the same fairy but for different reasons.

"Huh? Oh yeah, good idea," he said, half-listening. I rolled my eyes and left him to it.

Jordan looked up as I approached. Emily saw me, and after whispering one last thing to him, she made a hasty retreat out of the restaurant area.

"I just wanted to thank you for dropping me off yesterday," I said, shouting over the noise. "I was in a pickle, and I really appreciated it."

"You're welcome." Jordan's tone wasn't unfriendly, but he sounded harassed. I wondered if it was something to do with his earlier encounter with the mob bosses. "How's everything going?"

Jordan grunted. "Not bad considering we're so understaffed in the kitchen. We're down a few heads, dang turncoats. First whiff of trouble and they defected to the other side. Emily's back there now, fighting fires. Remind me again why I got into this crazy business?"

I thought about Finn. Maybe that explained his absence. Perhaps he'd already dropped to one knee to kiss Missy Grendell's proverbial ring. But then, why not tell me? I didn't care which mobster he worked for just as long as he kept his ear to the ground and remained my snitch.

"Who did you lose?" I shouted, trying to sound as off-hand as I could. "Any important err, positions?"

Jordan frowned and grabbed a frothy ale as a tray passed by us. "A couple of wait staff and one of the cooks," he said, pointing toward the kitchen. "Their timing sucks. They bailed right after the body was found and there just hasn't been any time to hire any replacements. Emily's just pulling in a few volunteers from the Baron."

"They all went together?" I asked. "Were they in cahoots, you think?" *Ha.*

"How should I know? Finn went first, and the others shortly after. Waiters are ten a penny, but Finn was a pretty good cook, they're really feeling the pinch. Anyway…."

Obviously, he didn't want to talk about it anymore. I bit my lip, wanting to probe but Jordan was no fool. If I pushed him on Finn, he'd grow suspicious, and if he wasn't dead now, he soon would be if word got around he was my snitch.

Emily appeared by my side. She glanced at me, then angled herself so I might as well not have existed. "The ale is playing up. Can you go down and have a word with Cranky, see if he can fix it? Oh, and we need some more chips. This crowd is going through them like butter. Can you bring up a couple of boxes as well? And some spare shirts. Medium I think."

Jordan nodded, downed the last of his ale and set the glass down on the nearest table. "Sure."

"Could you use a hand?" I'd learned next to nothing and thought maybe I'd find out more away from all this noise.

"I can manage," Jordan said.

"Oh, go on, I won't arrest you, I promise."

Jordan looked over to where Liam was busy talking to the pretty fairy in the red dress. "Really? I thought that was his job?"

"Darn, you're right, old habits die hard, sorry."

He headed over to the stairs, and when I followed, he didn't grumble. As the raucous dulled behind us, we descended the stone steps to the ale room and Redcap's former office.

A goblin was sitting on the ground, munching on one of the ham sandwiches and chugging ale from a large growler. He jumped up when he saw Jordan.

"Cranky, the taps aren't working upstairs, please see to it."

Cranky wiped his mouth. I didn't like the way he was looking me up and down. "Sure boss," he said. "How's it going upstairs?"

"Mayhem, but Emily's got everything under control," Jordan said.

"As always," Cranky snickered, as he began climbing to the top of an onion. "Not like the other one. She wasn't half as good. I knew she wouldn't last. No backbone. That Emily's something else."

In a flash, Jordan turned and shot Cranky a look that shut him up at once. Cowed, Cranky set about fixing the tap lines, mumbling something incoherent under his breath.

"What did he mean?" I asked, my inner detective not caring that Jordan didn't want this discussed.

"Nothing."

I laughed. "He must have meant something." I looked up to where Cranky was now hard at work, and somehow not catching my eye at all. "So, if it was nothing, why did you shut him up?"

Jordan dropped a bulky, but fairly light box labeled *Curdled Cheese and Garlic Chips* into my arms. And then a second box. I could hardly see over the top. Suddenly they weren't so light anymore. "Because someone's personal business, is none of *his* business. I don't encourage idle gossip among my staff." There was a loud roar above us, and Jordan looked up. "Now let's get back up there before they tear the place apart."

He led the way, balancing three boxes of his own topped by a handful of restaurant shirts still wrapped in cellophane, without waiting for me to respond. But a little bell was tinkling inside my head, and I couldn't ignore it. Whatever it was Cranky knew, Jordan clearly didn't want me to hear it, which meant I really wanted to know what it was. *Very well, goblin-boy*, I thought, *let's do it your way until I can get Cranky alone. And then, well, we'll see.*

Before I followed Jordan up the steps, I blew Cranky a kiss and whispered a little spell under my breath, *"Esse amicus meus!"*

"Excuse me?" Jordan asked, looking over his shoulder.

"These chips smell lovely." I said, holding the box ahead of me as I followed him back to the bar.

---

The wake went on into the night, and Liam and I had long since abandoned the pub and were sitting in his car, listening to Para FM on low, while watching as, one by one, the intoxicated mourners staggered, fell, or were tossed head-first from the pub.

The revelry and fighting had been endless, which was pretty much as good as goblin send offs went. Redcap would have been proud.

"Are you sure he'll come out the front entrance?" Liam asked. We'd been waiting for hours and still there was no sign of Cranky. "What if we missed him? There's half a dozen or so entrances, and he could have come out of any one of them."

"Maybe," I said, reluctantly agreeing with him. "But let's give it a little while longer. I want to nab him without Jordan around."

Liam stiffened in the driver's seat next to me. "What's so special about this Jordan guy?"

I smiled. "You mean apart from being gorgeous, wealthy, and totally unattached?"

"Yeah, apart from all that," Liam said. "I didn't think you were into the bad boy type."

"I'm not." And it was true. I'd prided myself on not being the cliché witch, falling for the wrong guy every time. But there was just something about Jordan. I couldn't quite put my finger on what it was exactly, he just seemed to tick all the right boxes, as well as all the wrong ones. Maybe all he needed was the right woman to guide him. Maybe I was that woman. Maybe that was why Emily was so curt with me. She knew it, too.

"Heads up, I think that's our guy."

Liam was right. Cranky was the first one in a while to actually walk down the steps, as opposed to tumbling or being thrown down them.

He wore an old Macintosh that was too big for him and trailed down to the floor. He paused, looking up and down the street, and pulled the collar into his neck to fend off the cold. His gait was slightly bent, giving him a shifty, dubious look, but I was surprised at the speed with which he took off down the road.

Liam waited for a while, then began to follow him slowly.

Cranky turned a couple of streets, and at each corner he stopped to look over his shoulder. I doubted anyone was following him (other than us), it was just the goblin way. He'd probably poop his pants if he knew he was really being followed.

I figured Cranky wouldn't live too far away, after all, he was heading home on foot, so I wasn't surprised when he turned into a rather seedy looking building with duct tape-secured windows and some old, beaten-up cars parked along the front.

I unbuckled my seatbelt and watched as he disappeared inside.

"Wait for me," I said. "I don't think this is gonna take long."

"Wait, what? You don't want me to come in there with you?"

I pursed my lips and shook my head. "Mmm, I don't think so. He might clam up if we go in gung-ho. I think he's more likely to talk to me if I go in alone."

"Yeah, but you don't know anything about this guy."

"Well, if I'm more than twenty minutes, come in and get me."

"You can be long dead in twenty minutes, Dionne."

"Oh, you party-pooper, you. I'll be fine." I didn't want to tell him about the befriending spell I'd cast on Cranky before I left. It was magic after all, and I knew he wouldn't approve. But it was only a minor spell, and I told myself it wouldn't make a difference if the case ever came to court. Which it probably wouldn't, but I knew Liam wouldn't want to take that chance.

I slipped out of the car before Liam could say anything else and jumped cautiously over the pile of snow plowed to the edge of the street.

A small lump of a creature with its head bowed, was crouched at the entrance. He didn't look up as I passed, but I'd swear I heard the thing growl at me. I didn't hang about to strike up a conversation with it.

There were about twelve apartments in the building. Hardly any of the intercoms were labelled, so I pressed the lot.

"Hey, what do you want?" said a voice.

"I'm looking for Cranky."

"Never heard of him." The line went dead.

"Who's that?" came another.

"Dionne. Looking for Cranky."

"Too funny, Buy yourself some Midol." That line died too.

"Hello," said a third voice.

"I'm looking for Cranky."

There was a silence. "Who's looking for him?" *Winner, winner.*

"I am. My name's Dionne Cruz. We met earlier at The Rotting Corpse." I knew my name triggered the spell, just as it would end it. This non-wand using was proving to be pretty cool.

"Dioooone!!! Oh my, I've been thinking of you all night sweet girl, come on up to the second floor!"

The door buzzed, and I slipped inside.

The thin carpet and peeled paint on the walls made the stairwell sound hollow. I climbed it as quickly as I could, not relishing the unsavory odors infused into the walls.

When I got to the second floor, I didn't have to figure out which apartment was Cranky's—his door was open and he stood there waiting for me, a huge non-typical grin on his face, his Macintosh gone, though he was still in his work clothes. My spell was working just fine.

"Hey, Cranky," I said, smiling like I was greeting an old friend. "Can I come in?"

Cranky looked like he'd swallowed a sunbeam. "Of course, of course." He stepped aside and I passed by him. His studio apartment was surprisingly neat—sparse, but comfortable, with a solitary armchair in front of a television that was currently playing an old black and white movie.

There was a pack of bacon and some bread out on the counter, clearly, he was just making dinner.

As soon as the door closed behind me, Cranky embraced me in a tight hug. "Dionne, Dionne! Can I get you something to drink? I have some coffee someplace, or I have ale? What would you like?"

"Um, I'm good," I said. "Thank you though. I'm sorry to interrupt your dinner."

Cranky looked over to the counter and waved dismissively. "Not at all, dear girl, think nothing of it. Now what can I do for you?" He smiled broadly, revealing a set of very sharp, goblin teeth that were somehow more cartoonish than threatening right now.

"Actually Cranky, err, may I call you Cranky?"

"Of course, of course! How delightful!"

"Actually, I was wondering about something you said earlier, when we were talking about Emily. You mentioned another person. I was just wondering who you meant?"

Puzzled, but happily so, Cranky put his forefinger to his lips and thought for a moment. And then something came to him. "Ah, I remember now! I was talking about young Fingal, the girl before Emily." His smile faded a little as he shook his head in sad remembrance. "Pretty little thing she was, such a shame."

"Who was she?" I asked, not failing to notice that he talked of her in the past tense.

"She was the girl before Emily. Tiny little thing, too, just a slip of a girl as they say. Too fragile and too dainty for Redcap's kind of play."

"What happened to her?" I asked.

Cranky wandered over to his kitchenette and pulled a frying pan out of a cupboard. "No one knows," he said, placing the pan on the stove and lighting the burner under the pan. He counted out a couple of rashers and dropped them in the pan. Even from here, I could tell they were well past their sell-by date. "I mean I could guess; it wouldn't be hard; I knew all about what went on downstairs. I get forgotten about, you know, down there on my own, sitting on those onion things. Sometimes I think I'm invisible."

"What did you see?" I asked, conscious of the time and not wanting Liam to burst in on us.

Cranky tapped the side of his nose, then pulled two slices of bread from the bag.

"Ah, well, Dionne, he liked to play certain games," Cranky said, being uncharacteristically delicate. "But I suspect Fingal wasn't into them. And Redcap didn't like it when people wouldn't play along, if you know what I mean?"

I did, all too clearly.

"Anyway, she disappeared. Not that anyone cared, that is. Well, her brother maybe, but no one else."

"Her brother?"

"Yep. He still works there. Well, he did, right up until Redcap died. He hasn't clocked in since. I hear there's been a right to and fro in the kitchen since he left."

As the puzzle pieces began to slide into place, I felt sick, and it had nothing to do with the sizzling bacon. "What was her brother's name?" I closed my eyes, not wanting to hear it.

"Oh, didn't I tell you? Finn, his name is Finn. Not that you would know by looking at them. Those Buccans are funny-looking things, but their women, mmm mmm, oh boy!" Cranky licked his lips in a way that would put anyone off their dinner. "Like I said, such a dainty thing, she was. Oh well. Are you sure you don't want to stay for dinner or something? I make a great bacon sandwich."

"Um, no, thank you. I'd better be going." I gestured over to the door. "Thank you for the chat."

Cranky's smiled faded. "Are you sure you won't change your mind, Dionne dear?"

"Nope, sorry, I have to run."

As I reached the door I glanced back to where Cranky was standing, a little down in the mouth and brandishing a pair of tongs in front of the stove.

"Have a good evening," I said, and ready to break the spell I added, "and remember, my name is Dionne."

I lingered just long enough to see the crazy smile glued to his face disappear, replaced by confusion, then anger. Before he could throw a rasher at me or worse, I shut the door quickly behind me and made a dash for the stairs.

## Chapter Twenty-Five
## THE WAREHOUSE

LIAM STARED AT ME, AGHAST.

"He's your what?"

I winced on the inside, even now reluctant to disclose the identity of my informant. It was just something you didn't do. "Finn's my informant," I repeated.

Liam gripped the steering wheel like he was having an aneurysm.

"Dionne, are you out of your mind?" he gasped. "Those things are horrible. Stab you as soon as look at you. What on earth were you thinking?"

"He knows stuff, Liam. He had his ear to the ground and in my book that makes him worth his weight in gold. Not all of us have access to police informants. We have to make do with what we have."

"You're lucky you're not dead yourself. It's a wonder he didn't kill you when he had the chance. Geez, don't you remember anything from the academy? There are just some creatures you should steer clear from. Buccas were right at the top of the list."

I shrugged. There was nothing I could do about that now. "Look, whatever, just call it in, will you? We need an address. And in any case, we don't know if it's him for sure. I could be wrong, you know."

"Yeah, like that's ever happened." Liam shook his head but made the call to dispatch. "It's Detective Wells. I need an address on a Bucca—goes by Finn. Works at The Rotting Corpse."

"Okay, checking that for you," said a female voice over the static.

Liam dropped the radio and shook his head. "Geez, Dionne, I thought you had some sense."

"Roger that, Detective Wells," the crackly voice continued. "We have an address on Race Street. Subject has a history of violence; his arrest record is as long as your arm. Approach with caution."

As soon as she gave the full address, Liam hit the metal. It wasn't that far away; we'd be there in a couple of minutes.

Like the man said, I wasn't wrong that often. But as I sat back in my seat and buckled myself in, I prayed to Gaia this would be one of those times. Finn was a top informant. I didn't want to lose him.

---

I loved the sound of the bells as the Septa trolleys passed on the line, and the whistle of the cars as the Frankford El rolled overhead. But once the trains had passed, I felt that eerie silence you only feel when alone in the snow.

Here we were, a few miles north of The Rotting Corpse, standing outside of an old, run-down red brick warehouse. The windows were broken, and nature was slowly rotting the place from the inside out. The building looked dark, lit only by the glare of the snow and the streetlights overhead.

"I still can't believe you used a Bucca as your informant." Liam said, as we began walking around the perimeter. It was still bugging him, I could tell.

I'd hated giving up the name of my informant. Hated it. But what else could I do? Finn had just catapulted to the top of the murder suspect list, and no matter what he'd done for me in the past, I couldn't protect him if he turned out to be the killer. Nor would I want to.

"Give me a break," I sighed. "Just remember, you promised, if this lead turns false, you'll forget I ever told you about him."

"Let's worry about the job in hand first, and anything else second. And remember, no magic. Unless you're faced with imminent death, keep your wand down, Dionne, I mean it!"

"What about a light spell? It's night! It's dark!"

"Okay but that's it, that's all, you hear me? No tainted evidence. If we catch this guy, we catch him clean."

"Yeah, well, let's hope Finn read that rule book, too, or we'll be in trouble," I retorted. "If he is our man, the place might be booby trapped, so watch your back."

I looked up at the tall walls overhead, wishing I could cast a spell or use a charm to detect life inside it. It sure as heck didn't look inhabited. "Are you sure this is the right place? I was expecting a studio flat or something. I know he has lady friends over. I can't imagine him bringing anyone back here."

"This is where they told me to go. I mean, if he has some unofficial digs he shacks up in, then we're out of luck, but this is his address and it's all they gave me."

I couldn't argue. I hadn't even been surprised when the address checked out with the top one on my list of suppliers. But even Finn needed to sleep, and this just didn't look nice and cozy, by any stretch of the imagination.

We were at the main entrance, a large set of black double doors that looked sturdy enough. Liam gave one a hard pull, it rattled, but didn't give. Neither of us were surprised.

"You wanna try round the back?" I suggested.

"Sure, why not?"

The ground was a little rougher off the main path. There was a beat-up Ford Transit parked to the side of the building, but no other cars were in the lot. I took a peek inside the windows. The passenger seat was a mess of trash and empty Chinese cartons, but it didn't look like it had been on the road in a while.

There was also a boat, set up on stands and winterized for the season. A tarp was tied tightly over the top to keep out the sleet and snow. There were no footprints around it, and everything seemed quiet, so I rejoined Liam, who was checking the fire exit on the side of the building. This was also locked.

"Striking out, huh?" I said.

"Looks that way, don't it."

The warehouse backed up to the Delaware and had direct river access. I wondered what it had been in its glory days, and how long it had been left in this derelict, lonely state. If nothing else, it seemed a total waste of good real estate.

The Delaware was calm tonight; there were hardly any boats on the water and those that were, were some way off from the banks. Without the benefit of the streetlights, it was really dark out the back, and Liam pulled a flashlight from his belt to light our way. I pointed my wand ahead of me. "Lux!" A bright spot of golden light sputtered into being above us, illuminating our surroundings. Liam frowned but said nothing.

There was a ramp leading directly from the warehouse to the dock, but no boats were tied to it. I didn't fancy walking along it, the snow and ice looked treacherous there and I had no desire to take a second dip in the water. Especially without a bubble to keep me afloat. But there was a large docking door at the back and since we'd come this far, we had to try it.

"Well, looky here," Liam said, as the door opened when he pulled it. "It seems we have a winner." He disappeared inside, and I scurried in after him, my light turning and following me inside, as if it had a will of its own.

The inside of the warehouse was a lot more organized than I'd been expecting. What I'd thought I'd see was a big, vacuous nothing. But part of the building had shelves, and there were iron steps, leading to an upper floor where there were probably offices at some point. But what struck me more than anything as I walked through the door was the overwhelming reek of vinegar.

While Liam explored the upper floor, I wandered over to the shelves which contained various boxes, which on closer examination proved to be all sorts of exotic candy, like gummy intestines, candied rat tails, and chocolate covered cockroaches, tailored especially to the goblin market. There was also row upon row of mason jars filled with picked eyeballs. My gut lurched as I realized where I was. My body became tense and cold, as if my DNA remembered this was where I'd been bubble wrapped and dumped into the Delaware.

"Liam!" I hissed, trying to keep my voice down since we had no clue what lurked in the shadows. "I believe I've been here before."

"And so ya have," said a high-pitched screech I knew only too well. The voice came from above me and I squinted as the warehouse lights buzzed on. My wand pulsed as my light slipped back into it. At the top of the steps stood Liam, his hands raised in the air, his face completely devoid of emotion. Behind him was the cause—Finn had a wand pointed directly at his back. I didn't even know Finn could do anything but charm earth magic, and I certainly hadn't known he had a wand.

My hand tightened on my own as he nudged Liam down the first steps.

"What are you doing, Finn?" I asked. "We already know what happened. Don't make things any worse than they need to be."

Finn laughed a high, eardrum-splitting laugh that chilled me to the bone. "Oh, you knows what's going on, do ya? That'll be a first, Ms. Cruz."

Finn descended the steps one at a time, being very careful, pushing Liam ahead. At the bottom he said, "I'll be needing that wand of yours now. Drop it to the floor and kick it over, there's a good dear."

I hesitated, and seeing this, Finn flicked his wand, there was a rapid swish and Liam yelped as if he'd been lashed by a whip. He bent over double, wincing in agony.

"Come, come, Dionne, no more shenanigans. It seems your friend the policeman ain't no big fan of pain."

Liam glared at me, beseeching me with his eyes not to surrender my wand, but what else could I do? Who knew what Finn was capable of with that thing in his hands? Reluctantly, I did as I was told, and dropped my wand to the floor.

"And the gun. You think I'm an idiot?"

Sighing, I put my .38 down, too.

"Very good. Now kicks 'em both over, there's a dear."

I turned my foot to the side and nudged the wand in his direction. It rolled to a halt just a few feet away. Finn bent down and fumbled to pick it up, carefully watching myself and Liam, who he knew was looking for his chance to fight back. I kicked my gun, too, but it rolled right past him and got caught in a stack of boxes, out of his reach. Finn stood up straight and slipped the wand into his ill-fitting trousers.

"That's better," Finn said. "So, tell me, 'cause I'm curious I am, how'd ya figure it out?"

"Cranky," I said. "I'd almost forgotten you had a sister. Your friend reminded me."

"Ha. My friend," Finn said, spitting on the concrete floor. "I got no friends, and if I did, Cranky sure wouldn't be one. That dirty little peeping goblin. Always watching her, he was. Wouldn't surprise me at all if he'd done the deed himself and spared Redcap the trouble."

"Done what?" I asked, anxiously keeping him talking while I looked for a chance to take him down.

"Kill her. What you think? Kill my sister. Maybe he didn't do the killing but Cranky would'a been the one to get rid of the body. He did all the dirty goblin's work, he did. Scumbag." He spat again.

"You know, you could be right, the way Cranky was behaving, I could smell the guilt on him." I said, trying to appease him. "You know what I couldn't work out? How you got the poison into Redcap's body? The autopsy revealed no puncture wounds from darts and Redcap's medicine bottles all came back clear. How did you do it?"

A wry smile twisted Finn's face, as he mentally congratulated himself. "I suppose I can tell you that. You'll both be dead in a minute anyway, ha, ha. Killing that low-down goblin pig was easy. Stupid goblin and his dirty ways. When I learned he wanted to play Lick the Frog, I laughed. I just 'ad to wait for the right moment."

Liam rolled his eyes, catching on just as I was. "But how? Those frogs are lethal. How did you get it to him?"

"Very carefully, with gloves. Of course, I 'ad to mess with it at first. The box it came it was covered with safety warnings, so I 'ad to switch it into something less obvious, I did. But I managed. And then I watched for my chance all morning. Luck was with me—things were going nuts, thanks to your shenanigans earlier on. It was you who gave me the chance I'd been looking for, bless ya."

I half expected him to twirl his mustache, if he'd had one. "I don't understand."

"I needed that creeper Cranky out of the way, didn't I? I could hardly give him a fake message, that'd be too risky, and he'd likely remember it later, spiteful pig, and would blag me to the police. I'd thought of doing him as well, kind of a two-fer, but I hadn't planned for that, so didn't dare risk it."

"So, what was the plan?"

"Even goblins have ta take a leak. So, I waited."

Liam, who had been slowly edging back to Finn, turned to make a swing at him, but the Bucca was too quick, and Liam got another wand lashing for his trouble. This time he dropped to his knees. His body was trembling with shock and his hands had curled into claws. This time it had been far more severe. He might not recover from a third lashing.

"Now, now, don't be rude, let me finish," Finn said, "As soon as Emily gave Redcap his meds and swannied off, I showed him the frog, he was all over it, licking it like it was made of candy. Next thing you know his eyes are bulging and he's choking, he's looking at me, he knows I switched boxes, this isn't goblin candy. Hah, no kidding. I leaned in close, and I told him, this is for Fingal, you son of a goblin dog, this is for what you did to my little sis. And then I watched him die. Five agonizing minutes. Gotta say I enjoyed every second of them. Getting rid of the body, no problemo, I conjured a bubble and dumped him in da Delaware, *splish splash*. Don't go shedding no tears for that rat bastard, he got what he deserved, and then some."

"And Cranky? When do you plan to take him out?" I asked.

"I saw ya leaving Cranky's apartment, I was right there in the shadows, ya walked right past me. You don't gotta worry about Cranky no more, no sir. He got what was coming to him, too."

Jesus, I could have stopped him there if I'd known. I'd been so pleased with myself for extracting information from Cranky, I hadn't even sensed Finn's lurking presence. "What I don't understand, is why go to all this trouble? You worked in the kitchen. If Emily kept Redcap's medicine there, why not just dose the bottle? Wouldn't that have been easier?"

"Easier? Sure, I guess. But Finn wasn't after easy, no. Imma want poetic. He killed her because of them silly games, and I wanted him dead the same way. So, cue frog. Cue river. Game over."

And so it was. And we were both going to die. It was just a question of when and how.

---

Finn raised his wand and aimed it directly at Liam. His irises turned jet black, with a malicious squint to them, and my heart leapt into my throat. No! Not like this!

"Your plan was genius!" I said, my brain scrambling to think of anything to stop him. Finn's wand arm paused mid-air. "But there's one last piece of this crazy jigsaw puzzle I couldn't solve; you were just too clever for me."

Finn paused, and for a second I thought he might still strike, but then he lowered his wand and stared at me, his ego getting the better of him. "And what might that be?"

"Well—me? I understand you wanting to drop Redcap in the river—but why me? You could have cut my throat while I was unconscious in my apartment lobby. Why go to all that trouble?"

Finn pulled his wand close to his chest and squeezed it, like he was remembering some delicious thought. "Ah, well now, that was a favor."

I wasn't expecting that. Someone else wanted me dead? Or maybe not dead? Maybe just shaken up? I was confused. "Who?"

Finn tapped the side of his nose and beamed. "Poor witchy-goblin girl thinks she knows everything, but she don't. I had to do it that way, so they knows it was me what did it. Bubble Magic is my trademark."

"Dammit, Finn, make sense!" I had no idea what he was talking about.

"You'll see, just you wait. I'm sure they'll fills you in on the other side. Hehe, sooner rather than later, I reckon."

"No Finn, come on, you can't leave it like that! We've been friends, haven't we? I never treated you bad."

"Buccas don't have no friends! Say goodbye, policeman! *Sic faciet avolare!*"

This time when Finn raised his arm, I was ready. As the bubble began to form out of the tip of his wand, I concentrated on the tips of my fingers and sent all the energy I could muster in a great whoosh!

*"Et accersi turbinis vasti!"*

The deadly bubble turned back on Finn, trapping him like a huge pink bubble gum balloon. His wand was lost in the swirling tornado I'd just summoned, giving him a taste of his own medicine. He fought against the slippery inside of his own bubble, arms and limbs thrashing everywhere in his panic but unable to find a hold. And up he went, caught in the power of the violent wind I had summoned. Even Liam, who was taller and surer of foot, struggled to stand his ground in the ensuing madness. I felt something akin to a river running through my fingertips, as my magic weaved a fury all around us, with myself, Finn and Liam caught in the eye!

All around us, boxes were flying, glass jars were smashing, and random eyeballs and intestines were spinning madly in the air.

None of us were immune to the forces I'd unleashed. They plucked at us and lifted us bodily off the floor. Up, up we climbed, and a new terror caught me. I could use magic to break my fall, —I hoped!—as for Finn—who cared?—but Liam was human, and if my energy flow ended suddenly, he could fall and be injured, or perhaps even die. What if I couldn't sustain it? The result would be the same. And all the while, Liam twisted up and up, his arms and legs flailing as he sought to find save himself, but there was nothing for him to grab onto.

I closed my eyes, focusing on the maelstrom that originated in me. I didn't dare kill it, I had to soothe it, to control it, and bring us down gently. I could see the torrent, even with my eyes closed. It was there in my head, a violent madness that somehow I'd tapped into. Who knew I could command such power, and so quickly? I cursed Patsy for not giving me a user manual.

The tornado roared, and I lowered my hands, whispering to it, calming it, as if the very winds were alive. The chaos was wild, but I had to control it, to make it obey me, to bring it to heel.

The howling grew less violent, and I felt myself sinking. Opening my eyes, I could see we were still spinning about the room, but the madness was abating, and slowly, but surely, we were descending to the floor.

The second Liam's foot safely touched the ground, I focused on my gun, which was spinning up in the air along with everything else. With a final jolt of magic through my hands, I flung the gun toward Finn. It broke through his bubble and bounced off his oddly shaped head. The bucca hit the ground like a sack of potatoes, out cold. *Wow!* I knew the gun would come in handy for something!

Down on one knee, I put my hand to the scar on my chest, where I felt my heart pounding.

"This is no time to get all romantic," Liam said. He was standing over me, a wide grin on his stupid face. I realized it must look as if I was proposing to him. Oh, such wit. He offered me his hand; I took it, and he lifted me up easily.

"Maybe I should have hit you with the gun first," I retorted. I glanced over at Finn. Blood matted the straggly hairs on the back of his lumpy head. "Is he dead?" I asked. How the heck would I explain this to Captain York?

Liam nudged him with the toe of his shoe, and Finn groaned. "No such luck."

"Quick, don't mess about, get your cuffs on him before he wakes up and thinks of some other way to ruin my day."

Liam nodded and did just as I asked. Finn groaned as Liam pulled his short arms back none too gently, and I was surprised Liam didn't kick him in the ribs. I know *I* would have. Hey, maybe that was a good reason for me not to be a cop.

"I didn't know you could do that!" Liam said, wiping a bloody scratch on his forehead.

"Neither did I," I confessed as I straightened up. It was still blowing my mind that I could. "Remind me to thank Patsy when I get home."

"Huh?"

"Never mind." I crossed the floor to where Finn was just regaining consciousness and whipped my wand out of his trousers. "I'll have that, if you don't mind, thank you very much!"

"What, hey, who's that?" Finn said in a blurry daze. His eyes had returned to their normal hue but looked glassy and confused. I wondered if I'd given him a concussion.

Hmm, he sounded out of it. I looked around. There had to be a first aid kit, someplace in amongst all this mess. *"Veni ad me primo auxilium buxum!"*

A grubby looking kit quavered under a rubble of nastiness, then flew through the air into my hand. I opened it and pulled out some antibiotic cream and a bandage, then handed them to Liam. "Here, you'd better. I ought to keep an eye on him in case he tries something stupid. Again. And I guess we should call an ambulance."

Finn had managed to sit up and was pretty docile as Liam set about bandaging his head.

"How's your back?" I asked.

Liam glanced over his shoulder and down, as if he could see it. "Hurts like hell, but I'll get over it." He tugged a little more than he needed to and the bucca winced.

"Ow, that hurts!"

"No kidding," Liam said. "Sit still or it'll hurt more."

Finn grumbled but remained compliant. When he was done, Liam walked over to the door to get a better signal before calling the ambulance. On the way, he picked up Finn's wand. He examined it for a moment, then snapped it in two and threw it into the river. A spark of purple light flared, then vanished.

I knelt down before Finn and studied him intently. "So, are you gonna tell me?" I asked.

Finn smiled, a cold, mirthless smile. "No, I ain't. That be more than the Finn's life's worth." He swished his head from side to side in a sing-song way. "You'll find out, soon enough! Ow!" Finn's eyes rolled and he turned a little green, I guessed he wasn't ready to move his head quite so freely just yet.

I racked my brains, trying to imagine who would want me dead? Someone from my police days, perhaps? A client? But no matter how hard I tried, no name came to mind.

"Poor, poor Dionne," snarled Finn, clearly recovering. "You'll have to watch ya back now won'tcha witch. Haha!"

I stood up, and feeling a little sick myself, wandered over to the door to be with Liam and to get some air. I was shaking, but this time it had nothing to do with magic. It seemed I was a marked witch, but I didn't know who, and I didn't know why, and that uncertainty was terrifying.

"I'm sorry for using magic, after swearing not to."

Liam laughed, but I heard the tremor in his voice. "Just as well you did. I'd be dead, and so would you. You saved us both. Any judge will take that into account."

"Glad you see it that way. I'd have been really annoyed if you popped your clogs. I mean really annoyed." I glanced back over my shoulder at Finn, who hadn't moved. "Can we wrap his legs in chains and drop him in the river?"

"Captain might not like that."

"I suppose."

"You really are a witch, aren't you? Not just, you know, light spells, and stuff. What you just did back there. You didn't even use your wand. When you put it down and kicked it over to him, I thought we were finished. But you, you just... *pow!* Like something from the X-Men."

I liked being compared to a superhero like Storm. Who wouldn't? I said, "Sorry if I scared you. I think I scared myself."

"So, what now? Are we done?" Liam scrunched his nose as he pulled off a gummy intestine sticking to the arm of his coat.

"As far as Redcap's murder is concerned, yes. Anything else, that's up to you."

He looked out across the river, mulling this over. "What did you have in mind?"

"Maybe dinner sometime, if you'd like to. Anywhere except The Rotting Corpse."

"I'll take note of that. Give me a couple of days to think about it, by which I mean recover from the eldritch terror I just went through. That okay?"

I chuckled. I liked it when he smiled, and he was smiling now. "Sure, take your time."

## Chapter Twenty-Six
# AFTERMATH

WHEN I WALKED INTO MY APARTMENT, WITH LIAM A STEP BEHIND ME, Derek was sitting in the kitchen, a dirty plate with a half uneaten sausage coated in ketchup sitting in front of him. He was talking to Mom with a fresh cup of coffee in one hand and my copy of *Is It Magic, Or Just Hormones?* in the other. Wow, he was really scraping the dregs from my bookshelf.

Harrison, as ever, was camped out in front of the T.V. Patsy sat beside him, her feet tucked under her, her hair tied up in a single ponytail, and dressed in her favorite cheerleader garb. She was rubbing Scratchpoop, who was currently laid out between them in a most undignified manner, as she nattered away about the Jinn Revolution of 1776 and how it ultimately resulted in the defeat of the British. Harrison shifted about uncomfortably, clearly trying to ignore her, but she wouldn't take the hint.

"Dee-Dee!" Mom gasped as I closed the door. "Why didn't you call to tell me you were coming? I'd have fixed you some dinner, there's still plenty of sausages. Look at you two, you both look like death warmed up. Let me make you some coffee at least."

"Thanks, Mom." I slouched down next to Derek, exhausted and ready for little more than a hot shower and a warm bed.

"Actually, I'd better get going," said Liam. "I have stuff to do down at the station. I just wanted to see Dionne safely home. It's been a long day."

"It can wait five minutes, can't it?" Mom said. She looked over both of us, no doubt taking in our unkempt appearance. "They can't expect you to work like this without a little something to keep you going."

Patsy strolled barefoot into the kitchen, carrying two empty coffee cups which she deposited in the sink. When she turned around, she had one hand on her hip, and a saucy, knowing look on her face as she waited for news. I couldn't help but notice she had extremely long, toned legs.

Apparently neither could Liam. The exhaustion vanished from his face, and he perched at the end of the counter, apparently changing his mind. "Okay, Mrs. Cruz, I'll stay for one." I bit my lip and fought against saying something catty.

"We have news," I said instead, loud enough to stir even Harrison from the sofa. "Gather round people, you'll wanna hear this."

Scratchpoop was the last to join us. He jumped up on the counter, taking center stage, his tail high as he proudly paraded his bum. I let it go this time. He sniffed at Derek's unfinished sausage, then set about eating it, ketchup and all.

"We caught the killer! You guys are off the hook!"

Their relief exploded more powerfully than a spell bomb in a magic store.

"Oh, by Gaia, you mean I can finally get back to my store and start fixing everything?" Derek's eyes were bright with delight, and he looked more like his usual self again. "I have to say, I can't wait to sleep in my own bed! I'm gonna call my interior designer as soon as I get home. He's a real wizard and works absolute magic!"

"You surely can. It's all over," Liam said. "I told my captain you were off on a mini break and had no idea anyone was looking for you."

"Some mini break!" But Derek laughed and took a deep swig of his coffee.

Harrison's joy wasn't so pronounced. We exchanged glances. We both knew words needed to be spoken, and trust rebuilt, or what future was there for our partnership? But perhaps not today. I smiled and winked at him, and relieved, he allowed himself a faint smile.

"So, who was it?" Harrison asked. "Anyone we know?"

"A bucca called Finn," Liam said. "He was a cook in the kitchen. He believed Redcap killed his sister, so he killed Redcap out of revenge."

"Oh, and thanks for the .38," I said to Harrison, "it came in real handy."

I didn't elaborate. He raised his eyebrows but said nothing. I tried not to laugh.

"You know, in the beginning, part of me wondered if maybe you and Derek staged the whole bomb and abduction thing yourselves."

Harrison looked puzzled. "Why would we do that?"

"Insurance fraud?" I suggested. "I thought maybe the two of you planned to swan off together to Acapulco or something to live the good life."

"You really think I would do something like that?"

I smiled and left him dangling.

"Wow. Well, that's a relief," Mom said. "But I don't know who to feel sorry for the most. It sounds like an ugly business."

"It most certainly was," I agreed. "But Finn will go to jail. You know, I might have felt sorry for him if he hadn't attacked me as well. I mean, he was avenging his sister after all."

"Yeah, well, the courts will take that into consideration when sentencing him," Liam said.

"Yes, I suppose you're right." At least I hoped he was. The mob had long arms and were unforgiving. I just couldn't think about that. Finn had made his choices. It was for him to live with them.

I took a deep breath, and let it out, relieved this was finally all over. "If you don't mind, me and Scratchpoop would like our apartment back! You can all go home!"

"You got it!" Derek said, sliding from his seat. "I'll just need a moment to gather my things then I'm outta here."

"Same," Harrison said. "I'll call us both an Uber."

"No, don't do that," Liam said, as Mom slipped a hot mug of coffee into his hands. "Once I've downed this, I'll drop you both off."

Harrison lowered his phone. "You don't mind?"

"Nah, as long as you don't mind riding in a cop car. Wouldn't want to ruin your street rep."

"Thanks."

"You want me to go too, Dee-Dee?" Mom asked, a little down in the mouth.

"No Mom, love," I said. "Not you. I've hardly seen you. And you've been a total lifesaver, I don't know how I'd have got through all this without you. You need to stay for a few more days so I can take you out and spoil you for a bit. It's the least I can do, really. You deserve it."

Mom's smile went practically supernova. She walked around the counter to give me a big squeeze, then carried on cleaning up their dinner things.

While the two men gathered up their dirty underwear and socks, Patsy slipped into the seat opposite me.

"Well, how did you feel, not using your wand?" Of course, she would know about it, she was a jinn, made of magic.

"Amazing," I confessed. "But scary. I didn't feel in control. I hate not being in control."

Patsy beamed. "I knew you had it in your heart, Dionne of Philadelphia. But worry not. Control can be learned. I can teach you. Did I not promise that I would?"

"Yeah, what can you teach me?" Liam asked, his eyes all bright with expectation.

"Yes, well, maybe not tonight," I said, shutting him down before he started, while losing myself for a moment in Mom's excellent coffee. I wondered why mine never tasted quite so good. "I've had just about all the magic I can take for one day, thank you both very much."

I was sure Liam was about to say something cute when his phone rang. He looked at it, then stood up. "I have to take this."

"I must say, this has been quite an adventure," Mom said. "Things haven't been this exciting since your father and I were together. I'm so glad I came!"

I glared at Mom over my coffee mug. She sure as heck was off her rocker.

It was a bad habit, I know, but I couldn't help listening in on Liam's conversation. Of course, I could only hear half of it, but what I did catch didn't bode well.

"When—How many? —What, dead? Yes Sir, first thing tomorrow. Thanks for letting me know."

When he rejoined us, I looked up at him expectantly. "What was all that about?"

Liam sat down and took another swig of his coffee while he gathered his thoughts. "You're not going to believe this."

I held my breath, thinking the worst. "Please don't tell me Finn somehow escaped?"

Liam shook his head. "No, nothing like that. He's locked up in a Magic Box, ain't no sucker ever breaking out of those bad boys. But it's just as bad. There's been a huge altercation up in Allentown. Riots are breaking out all over the place. Missy Grendell's place got hit tonight. The details are still sketchy, but a number of fatalities were reported. It's pretty ugly. Somebody did a number on Missy and her bodyguards —it's pretty bad by all accounts. The Grendell Clan is in complete disarray, apparently, it's all over the news."

I glanced over to my T.V. which was still set to the Hallmark Channel. Figures.

"And so it begins," I said. "It was only a matter of time before the goblin factions started fighting for power. This is really bad." Gangsters or not, goblins were dying; they were my people and I hated it. "Who do you think ordered the hit? Steely?"

"Maybe?" Liam said. "She certainly pressed all his buttons at that funeral."

"And Jordan's. To be fair it could easily have been either of them."

"I don't think Jordan has the muscle yet," Liam reasoned. "He's still wearing training wheels."

"Or maybe this was his way of showing the underworld he means business. Shock and awe and all that."

Liam nodded, then drained his mug. "Yeah, could be. Anyway, I'm all in." He glanced back to Harrison and Derek who both carried backpacks full of their dirty laundry. "You both ready? I'm outta here."

"Totally."

Harrison and Derek both approached Mom and gave her one hell of a hug. I suspected she wanted them out of here as much as I did, but you'd never know it from looking at her.

"Thanks for everything, Mrs. Cruz," Derek said. "You make the best spaghetti in Philly. You're gonna have to give me the recipe."

"Oh tosh," Mom said, punching him lightly in the chest, but happy.

"You're an angel," Harrison chimed in. "It'll be weird making my own coffee again."

Mom laughed. "Somehow I think you'll manage."

After they kissed Patsy and me, the two men stood waiting for Liam by the door.

Last, but not least, Liam leaned in and kissed me on the cheek. He lingered for just a moment, at least long enough for me to take in his scent, which right now was an odd but pleasant mix of male sweat, snow, faded aftershave and Mom's coffee. "I'll call you, okay?"

"You betcha," I said, hoping he would. "Get some sleep."

And then they all left, leaving me, Mom, and Patsy in the kind of shocked silence that only a special kind of magic could dispel.

"He *likes* you," Patsy said.

"More coffee?" Mom said. And my heart began to beat again.

## Chapter Twenty-Seven
## DARK AND STORMY

The unseasonably warm sun soon melted off the last of the snow. I listened to the musical tinkle as water ran down the streets to the drains, to be forever lost in the secret rivers that perpetually raged beneath our feet.

The sky was beautifully blue, and a calmness fell over the Delaware, which now looked so innocent, not betraying even a hint of the terrors it had recently inflicted on some.

At The Rotting Corpse it was business as usual. Inside the pub there were no signs of last night's wild party. Tables had been straightened, chairs uprighted, bars cleaned, and floors meticulously vacuumed. The only difference I noticed as I walked through the doors were the numbers of serious looking werewolves hanging about. They were big guys in Italian suits with shaggy wolf heads and huge hairy paws with razor claws. And all the regular goblin soldiers were with them. Roll call, maybe? Ramped up security after last night's bloodbath? More than likely. They gave me the goddamn creeps. My scar practically throbbed, as if it remembered the fateful night.

Jordan was behind the bar, checking the takings at the register when I walked in. He glanced up as I approached yet didn't look surprised to see me there. I sat down on a bar stool in front of him and he slammed the cash door shut.

"What'll it be?" he asked, as if I were a regular customer. "A cup of murder? A hit of abduction? What's your poison today, detective?"

"Ha ha," I laughed, sarcastically. "Demoted to barman, are we? In that case I'll take a Dark and Stormy. Lots of ice. Heavy on the lime."

"I didn't think you were a drinker?" he remarked.

"I'm not. Today's special."

"What? Your birthday?"

"Ha, ha, you're a hoot," I said flatly.

While Jordan set about fixing my drink, I looked around. There was no sign of Emily, but it was early yet.

Jordan dropped a beer mat and napkin in front of me and placed my cocktail on top. I offered him a credit card.

"This one's on the house," he said.

"Thanks," I said. "It's quiet today. Where's my friend Emily?"

A smile tugged at the corner of his mouth. "I gave her a couple of days off."

"What, resting her bitch face?"

"No. She's kinda beat up over Redcap. I told you; they had a thing. Anyway, she'll be back soon enough. I promoted her to my old job, as manager. She's very good at what she does, you know. If you gave her a chance you might like her."

I found that hard to imagine. "Why should I? She doesn't think very much of me."

His smile broadened. "Nothing to do with you suspecting her of murder, I'm sure. Give her time. You'll like her, you'll see."

"Maybe," I said, not wanting to sound like a twit but suspecting it wasn't likely. She'd been riding my back since I'd met her. "I'll keep an open mind." *If she does.*

I took a sip of my Dark and Stormy, which he'd made just right.

"Hey, this is good," I said, tipping my glass toward him so that the ice cubes jingled.

"Yeah, well I used to be a bartender once. Which is a good thing, since we're down a few bodies and I won't have time to hire anyone until Emily gets back. Even Cranky, who's worked here for over twenty years, didn't show up for work this morning. It's been madness."

"Umm, about that."

"What?"

I took another sip from my drink. This was what I'd come to tell him, but that didn't make it any pleasanter.

"I don't think Cranky'll be turning up for work anytime soon."

"Huh?"

"We arrested Finn last night after he confessed to Redcap's murder. He also claims to have murdered your tap-man Cranky, but I don't think that kill's confirmed yet. I suspect they'll pull his body out of the Delaware pretty soon, that would be my guess, anyway. Finn knows bubble magic. That's how he got Redcap from his office into the river after he poisoned him. It had to do with Finn's sister. Finn believed Redcap murdered her. He wanted revenge."

The smile vanished from Jordan's face, and he leaned closer to me over the bar.

"Finn? Killed Redcap? Are you serious?"

"Totally on the up and up, I swear it. You think I'd joke about something like this? It's why I'm here. I had to let you know."

Jordan took a step back as he digested this. I totally understood his shock, this had come totally out of left field for me, too. I looked away, letting him have a moment of privacy to deal with his thoughts.

"On the upside, it does mean the heat's off you and Emily, if you're looking for a silver lining."

"Thanks for telling me," He said.

I expected more, but whatever thoughts were racing through that handsome head, he clearly wanted to keep them to himself.

He walked across the bar to see to one of his other customers. His handsome smile was fixed, and though he'd returned to his usual charming self, I knew his thoughts had to be racing. Capo di tutti goblins? Yeah. I could see that now. The half-goblin kept his feelings buried deep in some impenetrable fortress.

Maybe the extra muscle at the restaurant wasn't so much ramped up security after all, but a show of strength? Mess with me at your peril? After all, neither Steely or Missy had threatened Jordan. Maybe Jordan had hired them to smack down his rivals, and maybe they had been responsible for last night's Allentown massacre. Who knew?

I looked around, wondering if all this muscle was going to be a new thing at the pub.

"So, what's with all the new faces?" I asked when Jordan returned. "Werewolf sale down at Macy's? Buy one, get one free?"

Jordan laughed. "Nah, bake sale at Dunkin' Donuts. They can't resist the munchkins." I laughed, even though he hadn't really answered my question.

Half of my drink still remained but I'd had enough. I pushed it across the bar, signaling I was done.

"Thank you for the drink," I said.

"You're welcome. And now we're all chums again, I'm going to buy you dinner. Let's say Friday, at eight?"

For a second Liam's face flashed through my thoughts. Still, Liam was a friend, I wouldn't exactly call what we'd just half-arranged a date. It was more of a thank you thing. And Jordan was, well, time would determine what Jordan was.

"Sure," I agreed, silencing my inner feminist because I liked his macho way of proposing it. "I'll meet you here?"

"No. I'll pick you up at your place. Eight o'clock, sharp. Wear something girly."

A dart of something pleasant shot through me. Things were working out just as I'd hoped they would. "It's a date," I said, almost blushing.

I slid off the bar stool and was about to leave when Jordan came round from behind the counter to walk me out. I liked this. I liked this a lot.

We had just turned when one of the werewolf guards got up from his table. He looked oddly familiar, and even as I thought this, the scar over my heart began to tingle and the hairs on my arms stood on end. My breath caught in my throat when he stepped forward, blocking my way.

The werewolf held out his hairy paw, and with a raspy voice and fiery red eyes he said, "Hello, Miss Cruz. How nice to see you, again."

---

Thank you for reading! Did you enjoy? Please add your review because nothing helps an author more and encourages readers to take a chance on a book than a review.

And don't miss more in the *Dark Encounters* series coming soon, and find from Adrienne Blake with PRIDE AND PARANORMAL available now. Turn the page for a sneak peek!

You can also sign up for the City Owl Press newsletter to receive notice of all book releases!

# SNEAK PEEK OF PRIDE AND PREJUDICE

The parking space was too tiny. There was no way my poor little Beetle was going to squeeze into the one solitary spot in front of the pub, but this was an emergency and there was no other spot in sight. My best friend, Charlotte Lucas, never went out drinking in the middle of the week. She was far too busy with her work. So I was more than surprised when I got the call asking me to meet her at The Cauldron.

My family lived in a quiet little valley in Misty Cedars, Pennsylvania, surrounded by mountains. It was the kind of out of the way place easily missed in a blink. I glanced furtively up and down the street. No one was watching, so I pulled out my wand.

"*Minorem ad quietiora*," I said, pointing at the two cars flanking either side of the parking space.

A shot of green light pulsed from the tip of it, circling both. They wobbled, just a little, like they'd been hit by a strong gust of wind, but in less than five seconds, they were suddenly each about a half foot shorter, opening up the space. I backed into the now wider spot, and after turning off the engine, I wound down the window and sat perfectly still. A parking violation was hardly a major offense, but if a Hag appeared out of the shadows, they could still cart me off to Bitterhold for the night. Unnecessary magic in a public area was an arrestable offense. How would I ever explain that one to Mom and Dad?

Climbing out of the car, I glanced around me. Sensing all was clear, I hurried inside.

Charlotte was sitting at a high table, checking her phone when I saw her. The Flaming Cauldron was a dark basement drinking hole, with slate flooring and a magically illuminated bar that always reminded me of the aurora borealis. The magic was mostly cosmetic—there wasn't any obvious source of electricity, but there was just enough light to see and be seen.

A young warlock worked the bar—there were usually two on duty. The other was a vamp. I had no clue where she was tonight.

"Hey, Benny. No Sue tonight?"

Benny was a good-looking warlock who had his life history tattooed all over his body. More than once he'd asked me to check out some of the more personal tats, and with a show of feigned reluctance, I'd always managed to turn him down.

"Hey, Iz. Nah, she's not here. Anemia. Again." He worked while he talked and was busy stashing dirty glasses into a dishwasher under the bar. "Luckily, we're not too busy. What can I get you, babes?"

We'd known each other long enough I wasn't offended by the *babes*. "I'll take an Angry Orchard," I said. "And whatever Charlotte ordered."

"I'll bring it over," he said.

I turned and strolled past the handful of tables currently occupied by a group of young werewolves to join Charlotte. A small light illuminated the center of our table, resembling a white orchid. The small flower was suspended in the air, emitting a warm, incandescent light that became dimmer and brighter as was needed.

"You found a spot then?" Charlotte took a sip of her drink and looked over my shoulder toward the entrance. "I had to park halfway up the street."

"I, um, improvised."

Charlotte's eyes opened wide in disbelief. "You didn't. You know you're lucky you didn't get caught. This place has been crawling with Hags lately. If they catch you using ley line magic in broad daylight where anyone can see it…"

I slid into the seat beside her. "Don't worry, I was careful. I checked everywhere at least a dozen times before I used my wand. I promise, no one saw me."

"For someone who works in the legal profession, you sure like to live dangerously."

The bar went silent, and Charlotte, who had a better view of the place from her seat, shot me a pointed look. Curious, I turned to see two Hags making their way over to the bar. Years of unfiltered ley line magic had taken its toll on their skin, which was leathery and covered in warts. Wisps of hair protruded from the top of their heads and out of their ears. Their features drooped so pitifully it was hard to tell their sex. They were bereft of any kind of shape, and only their height hinted at what they once might have been. My heart stopped. Had they been watching after all? Had they come for me?

In a shadowy corner of the bar, a hooded figure sat perfectly still, hunched over a half-full beer glass. Whoever it was, they were the only person not following the Hags as they made their way toward Benny. When the Hags were just a few feet away, the individual jumped from its barstool and sprang up on the counter, running along the length of it. Glasses smashed, and plates of food went flying as they made for the emergency exit on the other side of the bar. A bolt of white light flashed overhead; its tip wrapped around the neck of the escapee, who went down with a violent crash. Their hood down, Charlotte and I stared aghast as a female goblin writhed against her restraints but to no use. The more she fought, the tighter the restraints held her.

When the Hags reached her, with a click of their gnarled fingers, the goblin rose from the ground, hovering in midair, her hands still grappling with the rope. The first Hag turned to leave, and as she left, the goblin floated through the air behind her. The second surveyed the bar area, and with a similar click of their hand, chairs were uprighted and broken glasses mended, until everything was put back to how it had been before. The Hag bowed to Benny and then followed her companion and captive to the exit. The door closed behind them, and only then did anyone dare breathe. Everyone began chattering at once, and order was restored.

"You know, that could have been you." Charlotte picked up her glass and stared at it thoughtfully.

I buried my private fears and laughed. "Oh, come on, they'd hardly do that for a parking violation."

Charlotte shook her head. "You never know. And in any case, have you looked closely at those Hags? They weren't born like that—unfiltered magic did that to them. It'll happen to you, too, if you're not careful."

I laughed out loud. "Oh, Charlotte, really. You know I do mostly earth magic. The plants pay the price, not me. In any case, I hardly ever use the ley lines. They're strictly for emergency use only."

"Like getting a parking place? Look, just be careful. You don't want to get old before your time."

"What did she do, the goblin?" I asked, wanting to deflect the subject from me.

"No clue. Probably dealing in illegal love potions. There's been a lot of it about, I heard, and the Hags are clamping down."

I nodded. "That would do it."

Charlotte shook her head indulgently, reminding me of Mom. "Did you eat already?"

I was glad of the change of subject. I'd had enough talk of Hags for one night. "Yes, you?"

"I had a little something before I left." She looked me up and down appraisingly. "You know, I love what you did to your hair. Did you braid it yourself?"

I automatically reached for the intricate braids I'd conjured the night before, and I ran my fingers over them, checking to make sure everything was just as it should be and that the magic still held. Four longer braids fell forward over my shoulders down to my boobs and I checked the ends. I considered it was probably not a good idea to mention I'd used ley line magic rather than fussing with them myself. My sensible friend would have had a fit. "Um, yes, yes, I did. You like it?"

"I do," Charlotte said. "You're so lucky. You have perfect bone structure. You look good no matter how you wear your hair. And I wish I could wear mascara too."

"I don't see why you can't," I said.

"My mom says it makes me look like a fierce raccoon."

We both laughed at the familiar joke. It was true, though. Charlotte and I couldn't look more different. I had an athletic build, with dark-auburn hair and clear skin my sisters would die for. Not that I was the best at taking care of it, because I liked to goth it up—with purple lipstick and heavy on the kohl around the eyes. My magically-knitted leotard-style dress had a V-neck, exposing just enough boobage to tease, with long leaves of black forming the skirt, which stopped just above my knees. I hated shoes, preferring to run wild without them at home, but here I wore a pair of open-toed sandals, showing off my black nail polish and ankle tattoo of a hummingbird. Half the time, people took me for a vamp. Easy mistake.

In contrast, Charlotte was slim, but her figure was otherwise unremarkable. Today she wore a simple, off-the-shelf dress adorned with an equally neutral scarf, high heels, and a matching purse. Her blond hair was cut into a short bob, and her pale face was devoid of any makeup. It bugged her to no end, but the fact was she had sensitive skin and could only get away with a few products. We'd tried a few spells to ease her condition, but so far, no luck.

Benny arrived at our table with our drinks in hand. "Do you want to run a tab?"

"Sure."

Benny grinned at the wink I gave him and shot me one of his own before returning to the bar.

"So what's the big to-do?" I asked Charlotte once the cute warlock left.

"You'll never guess who I had dinner with last night."

"Who?"

"Charlie Van Buren!" Charlotte seemed so excited I thought she might launch from her seat.

"The matchmaking guy?"

"Yes, him. It looks like Dark Coven is let at last. My dad arranged the lease, and we had him over for dinner last night. Hell, Iz, he's so gorgeous —much better than in the magazines, and he has such nice eyes. Not to mention, he's single. He was telling us all about it, all about Wendy and the big breakup." Charlotte shuddered and covered her eyes for a moment, embarrassed. "God, you know I think I drooled all the way from Mom's appetizer right through to dessert. He probably thinks I'm a total idiot."

I laughed. "I somehow doubt that."

Charlotte grinned. "But it's true. Anyway, I managed to sneak a picture of him on my phone while he was talking to Dad in the kitchen. Wanna see him?" She picked up her cell and began swiping.

"Not especially."

Truth was, I was dying to see him, but I wasn't going to tell her that. Charlie Van Buren was all anyone talked about these days: the self-made warlock who'd made a fortune with his supernatural dating app, Magical Moments. I hadn't tried it myself, though if my mother was to be believed, it would solve all my man troubles. Apparently, it never failed—users got a love match every time.

"Yeah, I believe you." Charlotte smiled at me sideways, knowing me better. Of course I was as curious as everyone else about the new tenant of Dark Coven. "Ah, here he is." She turned her phone to me. "What do you think?"

Hmm. Charlie Van Buren was certainly hot. I could see why everyone was swooning. He had sandy-brown hair with just enough natural wave to be appealing but not overly fussy. And he was tall. Charlotte's kitchen had a high ceiling, and he was way up there in mortal danger from the pendant lighting.

"Nice," I said. "So he's only leasing Dark Coven—he didn't want to buy it?"

"It's up in the air, I think," Charlotte explained. "I think he just wanted something easy while he sorted things out with his ex."

"Lucky for the neighborhood."

Charlotte's eyes glazed over as she stared off into space. Who could blame her? The population of warlocks in Misty Cedars had thinned out over time. The east side was too suburban for most young warlocks, and since most of us were third-generation or less, we had little money. And the Hags prohibited conjuring any—unless you fancied a solitary cell in Bitterhold. It was the price we paid for sharing an economy with nonmagical beings, who my generation affectionately referred to as numpies.

"You're lucky. At least your dad is in a position to meet new people as they come and go. Once in a blue moon, Dad invites someone over from his university, but they're mostly old farts he knew when he worked there. All book nerds and bibliophiles. He definitely doesn't know anyone as hot as this Charlie guy."

I amused myself by running my hand around the orchid light, checking the redness of my fingers as the light illuminated my skin.

"Oh my God!" Charlotte's sudden outburst almost made me spit out my cider.

"Christ, what is it?" I followed her horrified gaze over to the door, thinking maybe the Hags had come back for me after all.

A group of young people had just entered the bar and were looking around, checking the place out. I recognized Charlie Van Buren at once but had no clue about the other four people with him. One thing I knew for certain: they were all magical. Their pulsating auras said witches and warlocks as clearly as if it were stamped on their foreheads.

Charlie's ready smile and eager expression made it clear he was out to have a good time, although I couldn't say as much for his four companions. Charlie traveled with two men and two women, all looked around his general age, and all were dressed impeccably well. They looked a little ostentatious in this spit-and-sawdust basement bar, and from the sneers on their faces, they knew it.

One in particular caught my eye. Charlie was tall, but his companion was even taller, and I would have been totally into him if it weren't for the permanent scowl glued to his face. Still, that wouldn't matter one bit if he were nice, because the wizard was hot—like smoldering hot. My keen gaze feasted on his broad shoulders, tanned complexion, and strong but manicured hands. I hoped to Gaia that scowl was only temporary.

Charlie headed straight for the bar as his friends surveyed the place.

"I heard this place was supposed to be happening," said the more sophisticated of the two women.

"Clearly we were misinformed," the tallest man said. He had a deep, commanding voice that made my skin tingle in the best possible way. I could hear him from our table in the corner and watched as he surveyed the place, like a lord overseeing his minions.

One of the werewolves walked by. The taller woman pulled the shorter one close and stuck her nose in the air, as if some nasty smell had irritated her. I always liked the musky werewolf aroma myself, but this lady had issues, and from the stiff gait of the others, I figured none of them liked the place. Not my type of crowd at all.

"We could go back to Charlie's place," the shortest man suggested. "At least there's free liquor there."

At that moment, the taller woman managed to catch my eye. I smiled, seeing no reason not to, but my smile was not returned.

"Too late now," said the taller man with the scowl. "Charlie already ordered the drinks. We're going to have to stay for one at least." It was his turn to stare directly at me. "You're going to have to put up with the local riffraff for one round."

I could feel the color rise within me. Riffraff indeed. "Anyone would think their poop didn't stink."

Charlotte laughed. "Or if it does, it smells of roses."

I snorted into my drink.

"This place does somewhat remind me of one of my late father's stables," the shorter woman said.

"Yes, or the pigsty. I'm definitely getting eau de swine." The other girl giggled.

"You're not wrong. The resemblance is remarkable." As he said this, the tall man glanced directly at me. I would have said something smart to Charlotte; however, I was so taken aback that for the moment I was struck dumb.

"Did he just say that? Did he just call us *pigs?*" Charlotte leaned into me, and her acknowledgement brought me to my senses.

"Just me, I think. Or maybe not. They're probably think they're being amusing. Stupid asses. Thank Gaia we don't have to talk to *them*."

Resigned to their fate, the group at the door moved over to the bar as Charlie handed back their drinks. They talked among themselves for a while but were now too far away for me to catch what they were saying.

Charlie glanced over at our table. Seeing Charlotte, he grinned warmly.

"Shit," I said in horror. "They're heading this way."

Charlotte kicked me under the table as, indeed, the group of five moved in our direction. Charlie was the first to arrive on the scene.

"Well, hello!" he said, his tone friendly as he leaned in to hug my friend. "I didn't realize you would be here tonight, or I'd have invited you along. This is a great place. I'm so glad you recommended it last night."

Charlotte's grin betrayed her delight. "I'm glad you found it. I honestly didn't think you'd be coming so soon."

"Ah, well," Charlie continued, "I have the urban family with me, checking out my new digs. I had to take them out somewhere, or they'd be driving me up the wall. They'd all just hang around and do nothing, given the chance."

Charlie and Charlotte chuckled, but I could clearly see his friends weren't impressed. Judging by their faces, one would think they'd all just trod in pig shit. I thought that kind of fitting under the circumstances. I fixed my gaze on Charlotte and tried to pretend the others weren't there.

"Everyone," Charlie said, "this is my new friend, Charlotte. Her dad is Bill Lucas, the man who runs the local real estate office and who fixed me up with Dark Coven."

His companions all nodded at once.

"Nice to meet you all," Charlotte said. "This is my friend, Izzy. Izzy Bennet."

I managed a polite enough smile, although I didn't feel it. I was surprised Charlotte could be so nonchalant under the circumstances, but then I supposed they hadn't just called *her* a pig. Satisfied, Charlie continued, "These are my sisters, Caroline and Louisa, Louisa's husband, old Hursty, and my best friend in the world, Fitz Darcy."

"Fitz? Is that German?" I asked with more politeness than I felt.

"I was born in Maine, but my mother was Pennsylvania Dutch," he replied in a clipped tone.

I spotted an intricately carved silver skull ring on his finger, which looked expensive, curious about its meaning. I also had a funny feeling I'd seen one like it before, but right now I just couldn't remember where.

"Have you lived here long?" Fitz asked.

"My whole life."

"I see," he said. "And it's the best place to be, you think?"

"Yeah, why not?" I said. "In fact, we love it down here. The Cauldron's the best paranormal hangout in the county. They have the best bands, the best people, in fact, the best of everything in my opinion."

"I suppose it rather depends on what you're used to," Caroline said. "I guess it's, um, what would you call it, Louisa?"

Louisa was the shorter of the two women. She glanced around the bar, taking it all in. "It's very, err, rustic, maybe?"

"And happening," I continued. "It might not be the most sophisticated place in the world, but it has a great atmosphere when there's a bigger crowd, and the people you meet here are great."

"I'm sure they are," Caroline said. She'd finished her drink quickly and looked anxious for the others to do the same. Her friends were at least taking their time, and I smiled on the inside.

"Did Charlotte say your last name was Bennet?" Charlie asked. He rubbed his chin thoughtfully.

"Yes. Yes, it is. Why?"

"I believe I may have bumped into your dad earlier this evening."

"You did?" I stared at Charlie with more than my usual curiosity. "Are you sure it was my dad?"

"Yes, I think so. He's a retired professor, no?"

"Why, yes, he is. How did you meet him?"

"I saw him at the bank, just as it was closing. We have the same financial advisor, and he introduced us. Nice man, your father. He seems to know a lot."

I laughed despite myself. "I suppose he does, but then he was a literary professor at Yule."

"That's so cool," Charlie said. "I sort of ran into him at the bank. He mentioned he had five daughters—are they all as pretty as you?"

I couldn't help but laugh out loud at that, and when I was done, I noticed Fitz staring at me intently. I had no idea what the man was thinking and, quite frankly, cared even less. "Shit no, my sisters are much prettier. I'm the ugly one." I half expected some kind of reaction from Fitz, but he didn't respond at all.

"You're a witch, right?" Fitz asked. "Only…"

He was looking at my clothes. "Yeah, totally a witch. Not a vamp. I'm just into goth. I get that a lot."

"I see."

"We're all witches and warlocks, and proud of it," Caroline said, her tone sharp. "I never see the need to display anything other than what I am."

"So am I," I said. "It's just a fashion thing."

"And it suits you," Fitz said. "I meant no offense."

"None taken."

Under the table, Caroline pulled on Charlie's shirt.

"Um, well, I guess we'd better be off then," Charlie said. "Lots of places to go and visit before the night is done. I'm running down the list you gave me, Charlotte. Can I buy you both a drink before we head off?"

"Err, no, it's okay," I said, not wanting the others to think we were sponges.

"Thanks for the offer, though," Charlotte added. "Maybe some other time?"

I glanced at Charlotte, realizing she had the hots for him. She probably wanted to get him all on his own, so he'd have the chance to molest her with his magical dating app. Fair enough.

"Right then, well, I suppose I'll be seeing you all soon."

"Good-bye."

They deposited their half-full glasses on the table in front of them, and I sighed with relief as, at last, they made to leave.

Charlotte still looked starry-eyed, as if they'd done us a great favor by noticing us at all. But I couldn't share her good feelings, I was still too upset by that great brute of a man and the pig comment he'd made the second he'd walked in the door. I smiled to myself. Like he was anything to talk about. Twit.

I was quiet as they left the bar, organizing my thoughts and thinking about everything they'd just said to us, especially that Fitz. The second they were gone, I turned in my seat, and for the rest of the night, we did nothing but talk about the town's newest arrivals.

Charlotte, who was a darling, couldn't stop singing their praises, whereas I, part witch, and clearly part demon, couldn't stop laughing at their nonsense. On the upside, the two of us had nothing but praise for Charlie. He wasn't just smart, he was nice. But Charlotte and I had mixed views on his friends, and though she tried to persuade me to see the good in each of them, all I could think about was the snarky comments they'd made and was well on the road to disliking them.

---

Don't stop now. Keep reading with your copy of PRIDE AND PARANORMAL available now.

And find more from Adrienne Blake at authoradrienneblake.com

# INDEX OF MAGIC SPELLS

*Calida Aqua* - Heats water

*Veni ad me* - Come to me - summoning spell

*Comae excoquatur!* - Dry hair

*Vox amplificus!* - Louder voice

*Protegas me* - Protect me

*Finis praesidium!* - End protection

*Aliquid defuit.* - Find what's missing

*Tersus sursum!* - Clean up

*Macula et abierunt!* - Spot-be-gone

*Inexpugnabilem!* - Impenetrable

*Exarmaueris!* - Disarm spell

*Ostende arcanum tuum!* - Show your secret

*Lux!* - Light

*Aliquid defuit!* - Make it fly

*Submitte defensiones!* - Lower your defenses

*Esse amicus meus!* - Be my friend

---

# DIONNE'S MAGICAL BLUEBERRY MUFFIN RECIPE

**INGREDIENTS**

½ cup softened butter (1 stick)
1 ¼ cups sugar (you can reduce this by half a cup if you want to)
2 large eggs
1 teaspoon vanilla extract
2 cups all-purpose flour
1 teaspoon cinnamon (optional)
½ teaspoon salt
2 teaspoons baking powder
½ cup whole milk
2 cups blueberries, washed and drained
I tablespoon grated lemon
3 teaspoons sugar

**PREPARATION**

Preheat the oven to 375.

Cream the butter and 1 1/4 cups sugar until light and fluffy.

Add the eggs, one at a time, beating well between each. Add vanilla.

Sift together the flour, salt and baking powder, and add to the batter, alternating with the milk.

Add the cinnamon.

Crush 1/2 cup blueberries with a fork, and mix into the batter.

Fold in the remaining whole berries and lemon zest.

Line a 12 cup standard muffin tin with cupcake liners, spray the cups with a little oil, and fill with batter.

Sprinkle the 3 teaspoons sugar over the muffins, and bake at 375 degrees for about 30-35 minutes.

Remove muffins from tin and cool for another 30 minutes.
Store, uncovered, as these are very moist.

Magic!

**Dionne's Magical Tip!**
Toss the whole berries in flour before folding them in. This will keep them from sinking to the base of the muffin.

**Don't miss book two of the *Dark Encounters* series coming soon and find from Adrienne Blake with PRIDE AND PARANORMAL available now.**

---

**What do love potions and banshee karaoke have to do with one of the greatest enemies-to-lovers tales of all time?**

Izzy may be the only responsible witch in her poor family of misfits, and as such, she has duties to uphold. Only a hot, mysterious, and infuriating warlock is determined to get in the way.

When the rich and handsome Darcy Fitz blows into town, sparks fly.

The wrong kind...

He has earned her ire as much as her eye with his constant harsh words and acts, but what will happen when a bit of magic goes awry, and Izzy needs the help of this powerful man she claims to hate?

Will Izzy's pride get in the way of saving her family's welfare and reputation? Find out in this witty, funny, fantasy retelling of Pride & Prejudice.

---

Please sign up for the City Owl Press newsletter for chances to win special subscriber-only contests and giveaways as well as receiving information on upcoming releases and special excerpts.

All reviews are **welcome** and **appreciated**. Please consider leaving one on your favorite social media and book buying sites.

Escape Your World. Get Lost in Ours! City Owl Press at www.cityowlpress.com.

# ACKNOWLEDGMENTS

"No man is an island," and no author writes a book without the support and guidance of others. I'd like to thank everyone I've met on this journey, especially for their and suggestions feedback. All you guys from Absolutewrite—Salute!

More specifically, I'd like to thank my editor, TT. Thank you for seeing the potential in this book and as always, for your diligence and care when editing it. Last, but not least, I'd like to say a special thank you to City Owl, for promoting my stories. You rock.

# ABOUT THE AUTHOR

ADRIENNE BLAKE is a *USA Today* bestselling author of paranormal mystery and urban fantasy. She is also an Amazon Top 100 bestselling author. Her stories blend plot, humor, and darkness, all in one sizzling cauldron. Born in the UK and writing in the US, she and her partner are managed by three ruthless cats.

authoradrienneblake.com

# ABOUT THE PUBLISHER

City Owl Press is a cutting edge indie publishing company, bringing the world of romance and speculative fiction to discerning readers.

Escape Your World. Get Lost in Ours!

www.cityowlpress.com

- facebook.com/CityOwlPress
- twitter.com/cityowlpress
- instagram.com/cityowlbooks
- pinterest.com/cityowlpress
- tiktok.com/@cityowlpress

www.ingramcontent.com/pod-product-compliance
Ingram Content Group UK Ltd.
Pitfield, Milton Keynes, MK11 3LW, UK
UKHW041918140426
5217IPUK00013B/213

9 781648 983115